A Measle Stubbs Adventure

The Monster of Mucus!

A MEASLE STUBBS
ADVENTURE

The MONSTER of MUCUS!

IAN OGILVY

Illustrated by Chris Mould

4

OXFORD
UNIVERSITY PRESS

FOR BARNABY AND MATILDA—AS ALWAYS

OXFORD
UNIVERSITY PRESS

Great Clarendon Street, Oxford OX2 6DP

Oxford University Press is a department of the University of Oxford.
It furthers the University's objective of excellence in research, scholarship,
and education by publishing worldwide in

Oxford   New York

Auckland   Cape Town   Dar es Salaam   Hong Kong   Karachi
Kuala Lumpur   Madrid   Melbourne   Mexico City   Nairobi
New Delhi   Shanghai   Taipei   Toronto

With offices in

Argentina   Austria   Brazil   Chile   Czech Republic   France   Greece
Guatemala   Hungary   Italy   Japan   Poland   Portugal   Singapore
South Korea   Switzerland   Thailand   Turkey   Ukraine   Vietnam

Oxford is a registered trade mark of Oxford University Press
in the UK and in certain other countries

Text copyright © Ian Ogilvy 2006
Illustrations copyright © Chris Mould 2006

The moral rights of the author have been asserted

Database right Oxford University Press (maker)

First published 2006 as *Measle and the Slitherghoul*
First published in this edition 2011

British Library Cataloguing in Publication Data

Data available

ISBN: 978-0-19-272973-6

1 3 5 7 9 10 8 6 4 2

Printed in Great Britain

Paper used in the production of this book is a natural,
recyclable product made from wood grown in sustainable forests.
The manufacturing process conforms to the environmental
regulations of the country of origin.

CONTENTS

SHEEPSHANK

It all started with a sneeze.

A very, very long time ago—eight hundred years, to be precise—there lived a young wizard called Sheepshank. He only had the one name—'Sheepshank'—because at this time of history, that was the way wizards did things. Think of the most famous wizard that ever lived. Merlin. He wasn't *Duane* Merlin, or Merlin *Higginbottom*—he was just plain Merlin.

And so was young Sheepshank. Just plain Sheepshank.

Sheepshank was an apprentice wizard, which means he was still learning to be a real one. He was small and skinny and pale, with long stringy black hair, pale watery eyes, and a chin that was so small it didn't look as if he had one at all. Sheepshank's face made up for a lack of chin by having a really *enormous* nose. Sheepshank's nose looked like the big triangular sail that billows out at the front of a racing yacht. Sheepshank was teased about his nose a lot. But, apart from the teasing, the other apprentices pretty much ignored him, because Sheepshank wasn't a very likeable person.

One of the reasons for Sheepshank's unpopularity was his bitterness. He could never say anything nice about anything or anybody and all his remarks were tinged with sour sarcasm. There was not a trace of sweetness in Sheepshank—he was nothing but bitterness, through and through.

Another reason why his fellow students avoided him was because Sheepshank was brilliant—and he knew it. There's nothing worse than somebody who knows they're cleverer than everybody else, which was exactly what Sheepshank knew about himself. He was at the top of every class he attended. He was so brilliant that his teachers had started to say that there was nothing more they could teach him and—if ever Sheepshank wanted to start a class of his own—then they'd love to come and be his pupils. (Well, perhaps not *love*—the teachers didn't care for Sheepshank any more than the other apprentices did, but they couldn't help admiring his brilliant brain.)

The only trouble was, Sheepshank was just a little *too* brilliant. And a little too ambitious as well—with the extraordinary result that Sheepshank, at a very young age, had become a warlock. Nobody knew this. The idea of an apprentice wizard being a warlock was ridiculous —it could take years of expert wizardry before that happened. But Sheepshank was a phenomenon and had managed—through hard work, a lively imagination, and an obsessive yearning for power—to reach the rank of warlock while still a lowly student. He was careful to keep this a secret, of course. He grew his hair long to cover the telltale Gloomstains on his ears, and he kept himself to himself during classes and behaved like a hermit, staying in his cell, the rest of the time. So, for the moment, his secret was safe.

In those days, apprentice wizards lived in a series of deep, underground cells, beneath the building that would, eventually, become the headquarters of the Wizards' Guild. At this time, however, there was no large and imposing office-like structure above ground to mark the spot—just a plain stone house in a quiet corner of what was then a very small town.

The stone house just happened to be sitting directly above the greatest accumulation of natural mana the world had ever seen, which was why it was there in the first place. As everybody knows, mana fuels magic spells, so when a rich source is discovered, wizards are inclined to gather at that spot. The house itself was only there in order to hide the opening in the ground that led to the warren of corridors and rooms and cells deep beneath it—and it was here that young apprentice wizards like Sheepshank lived and studied and worked.

Sheepshank liked his cell. It was small and dark and quiet, and far away from most of the other apprentice cells.

Sheepshank didn't want anybody to know what he was doing, because he'd started experimenting with *combining* spells. Combining different spells was so *absolutely* against every rule in the apprentice wizard handbook, that nobody ever thought of doing it—except for Sheepshank.

Combining spells was dangerous, which was why it was forbidden. The only spells wizards were allowed to perform were 'clean' spells— spells that were pure and had only one function. Like the fire-lighting enchantment, *'Calorimus Nuncibut Carborflam!'*—which produced a small ball of intense heat, hot enough to light even the dampest of logs—or the rejecting spell, *'Regrasso Fulmina Expedita!'*—which sent objects flying away from you at high speed.

What Sheepshank was doing—secretly, of course—was seeing what happens when you put spells like that together. Sheepshank discovered a way of putting the fire-lighting enchantment together with the rejecting enchantment, with the result that he found he could shoot a ball of white-hot flame several hundred metres—a devastating weapon in the wrong hands. And Sheepshank's hands were definitely the wrong ones, because (though brilliant) he simply wasn't grown-up enough to handle such power.

There came a day when young Sheepshank decided to work on something really special. It involved trying out various word combinations in an attempt to create a brand-new enchantment. One of the spells he was working with was a very dangerous one indeed. It was reserved for the most senior wizards and Sheepshank had no business even *knowing* it, let alone playing with it. The spell was the Death Hex, and could be used only when a great wizard was in imminent danger of losing his life and needed it for self-defence.

Sheepshank was trying to see if the Death Hex could be *reversed*.

He was trying to see if it was possible to bring something dead back to life.

He'd killed a spider that morning and placed its small, curled-up body on a tin dish on the surface of his desk. Then he'd tried various combinations of words from the Death Hex, mixing them up with words from a number of fairly harmless spells all designed to make the recipients of the magic feel better—but Sheepshank was saying them all, first *forwards*, then *backwards*.

Sheepshank had been doing this for most of the morning and the spider hadn't even twitched.

Sheepshank sighed—then, feeling an itching sensation deep in his nostrils, he sniffed loudly. He wiped his enormous nose on the back of his sleeve.

Staring hard at the body of the dead spider, Sheepshank tried again.

'*Morticlo olcitrom! Pivaculus sulucavip! Dropsihop pohispord! Zorgasfat tafsagroz—*'

Suddenly, Sheepshank felt a sneeze coming—but he couldn't stop now! Not in the middle of such a complicated combination of magical words! He sniffed again and the tremendous need to sneeze subsided a little—

'*Baffabis sibaffab! Oominoligos sogilonimoo! Kromkrumquoo—*'

Oh, no! Here came the sneeze again! Sheepshank sniffed but the need to sneeze began to grow ... and grow ... and grow ...

'Ah—ah—ah—' said Sheepshank, without at all meaning to. And now he was *furious*.

The spell was ruined and he'd have to start all over again—once this wretched sneeze finally arrived, that is.

And then, at last, it did.

'Ah—ah—ah—*SCSCSCHHHHHCABLA-MOOOOO*!'

The sneeze was a huge, explosive one. Sheepshank didn't own a handkerchief—and didn't think to use his sleeve, either. So, when the enormous sneeze blasted from his nose, a nasty little glob of greenish-yellowish-brownish snot shot out of one nostril and landed with a plop on top of his desk, only a few centimetres away from the dish with the dead spider in it.

Sheepshank's eyes were running, which sometimes happens when you do a really big sneeze. He wiped his eyes with the backs of his hands and, in that moment of blindness, he missed seeing something very extraordinary indeed.

What Sheepshank missed was this: the slimy little lump of snot ... *moved*.

It seemed to slither a couple of centimetres closer to the body of the spider. Then, in the blink of an eye, it extended a little section of itself, forming what looked like a tiny tentacle of slime.

The tentacle reached out and touched the body of the spider—

Sheepshank blinked several times, trying to make the tears go away. Slowly, the mist cleared from his eyes and he turned back to the spider, determined to start the laborious process of spell-making all over again.

The spider wasn't there.

Sheepshank frowned irritably. Obviously, the force of his sneeze had blown the little body clean off his desk. Sheepshank knelt down on the hard stone floor and peered around but he couldn't see anything.

'Botherissimus!' muttered Sheepshank. 'Now must I seek out a second subject for my work! 'Tis a vexation, to be sure!' (*That's* how long ago this happened—when people talked like that.)

His knees were hurting a little, so Sheepshank reached up and put his hand on his desk, in order to pull himself upright again.

Sheepshank's thumb squelched against the glob of snot.

'Ugh!' He stood up and was about to wipe his thumb against his dirty robe, when something extremely horrible started to happen to him.

Sheepshank's cell was at the end of a short passage and the nearest room to his was a corridor and a half away—so his screams of terror weren't heard at first. But then they grew louder and more shrill and a fellow apprentice wizard, called Barstook, looked up from the manuscript that he and his friend Gantry were studying and listened intently.

'Hark,' said Barstook, putting one hand behind his ear and tapping the shoulder of Gantry with the other. 'Methinks I hear some commotion!'

''Tis that dolt Sheepshank,' said Gantry. 'Leave him be, Barstook—'tis an offence to be near him.'

'Nay, Gantry—he suffers! Hear his cries! Come, we must to his side!'

Barstook and Gantry ran from Barstook's cell and, together, the two young apprentices raced down the dark corridor towards the awful sounds of terror. When they reached the open door to Sheepshank's cell, both skidded to a stop and stared into the small room.

Their mouths gaped in horror.

Something seemed to be eating Sheepshank—eating him alive!

Already his whole right arm was engulfed in some sort of yellowish-greenish-brownish slimy jelly and now the jelly was moving steadily across his shoulder towards his open, screaming mouth—

Some instinct for self-preservation told Barstook and Gantry that there was nothing they could do. Neither apprentice had any intention of trying to get the revolting stuff off Sheepshank, because there was something about it that made them think that, perhaps, it was in some way *alive* and, if they touched it or even got too close, there was every likelihood that what was happening to Sheepshank would happen to them.

They watched with disgust and terror as the slime spread steadily over Sheepshank's skinny body. The stuff stank and both young wizards put their fingers to their noses. What was particularly ghastly was the fact that, once the foul-smelling slime had taken over any particular part of Sheepshank, then that part seemed to become the same shapeless substance as the slime itself.

And now the goo had reached Sheepshank's chin and, the moment it slid across his gaping mouth, the screaming stopped. Quickly the stuff spread over Sheepshank's head, and then it didn't look like a head at all, just a formless mass of moving jelly, which now moved downwards towards Sheepshank's legs and feet . . .

Sheepshank's knees buckled suddenly and the whole mass of slime—and what was left of his body—crumpled to the stone floor.

The sudden collapse of what, only a minute before, had been Apprentice Wizard Sheepshank, shook Barstook and Gantry from their paralysis. They both had the same sensible thought at precisely the same instant—

Together, they grabbed the heavy ironwood door and slammed it shut. Then Gantry, who was a little bigger and heavier than his friend, volunteered to stay and make sure that the door remained firmly shut. He leaned all his weight against it—and Barstook ran for help.

Inside the dark cell, the slime slid over Sheepshank's legs, then his ankles, and finally over his feet. Then it simply lay there, a shapeless mass of slimy jelly, not doing anything in particular. And that's what the crowd of senior wizards saw when they arrived in a breathless collection of billowing robes a few minutes later.

The most senior of the wizards, an old wizened fellow called Crabgrass, carefully eased the ironwood door open. He put his eye to the crack and peered into the room but it was too dark to see anything.

But there was a horrible smell filtering through the shadows.

'*Luminensis temporando volantulum,*' muttered Crabgrass, and a little ball of pale blue light appeared in the cell and hovered in the dark air. It showed Crabgrass what he needed to see—and obviously it showed the mound of slimy jelly something too, because the stuff quivered suddenly and then began to flow over the floor, moving steadily towards the open door . . .

Crabgrass slammed the door shut. From the voluminous folds of his purple robe he produced a large iron key. Crabgrass slotted the key into the keyhole and turned it. There was a grating sound as the lock slid home. Only then did Crabgrass take his shoulder away from the door. He turned and glared at Barstook.

'You say that our poor friend Sheepshank is now utterly within that foul entity?' he growled.

Barstook gulped and nodded.

'You and Gantry here witnessed the horrid occurrence?'

'Aye, sir.'

'And can you inform us in what manner this monstrosity came into being?'

'N-nay, sir. We cannot.'

Crabgrass turned and raised his bushy white eyebrows at the rest of the crowd of wizards.

'Can any person here enlighten us?' he rasped.

Almost as one, the collected wizards slowly shook their heads.

'Seal that door,' said Crabgrass. 'Post a guard. Let none come near. We shall study this manifestation at our leisure—and we shall, in time, understand it.'

They never did understand it.

They studied it—at a safe distance—for many, many years. They shot a thousand spells at it, to absolutely no effect. They shouted questions, they showed it pictures. They tried to burn it, then to freeze it. Nothing whatever happened. It ignored them, unless they got too close—then it would start to move towards them, which was why nobody ever opened the door of the cell by so much as a crack, unless they had a strong man by their side, ready at a moment's notice to slam the door shut again.

Nobody wanted to live anywhere near the

ghastly thing in Sheepshank's cell, so the apprentice wizards' rooms were vacated and the young scholars were moved to other quarters. Over time, the little rooms were turned into jail cells and the entire complex became known as the Detention Centre, where captured wrathmonks and other undesirables were held imprisoned.

They came and went, these other prisoners. Only the creature remained, forever locked in its sealed cell—and nobody ever discovered how, exactly, it had come into being. The fact was that the only person who understood even a fraction of what had happened was Sheepshank, and he was in no position to explain it to anybody.

The spell had worked, of course, but in a very peculiar way. Instead of bringing a dead spider back to life, it had actually created a very basic form of life and given it to the lump of snot that had shot from Sheepshank's nose. And the reason it had done this lay entirely in the sound that Sheepshank had made when he sneezed.

It was a sound that nobody else could make.

Everybody sneezes in a different way and nobody's sneeze sounds the same as another.

Which was why only *one* of these horrible creatures was ever produced.

Even if they had heard Sheepshank's sneeze in the first place (and nobody did) not even the greatest wizards in the world would ever be able to recreate *exactly* the sound that Sheepshank's enormous nose had made. And that meant that of all the wizards that had ever lived—and ever *would* live—only Sheepshank could have performed that extraordinary and dreadful spell.

Which, when you think about it, was a Very Good Thing.

SAM HAS AN ANNOUNCEMENT

It was early evening at Merlin Manor.

Sam Stubbs had just gone to his study to answer a telephone call. Measle and his mother Lee were sitting in the living room, watching television. Tinker, Measle's little black and white terrier, lay on the carpet between them, his head on his paws, fast asleep. Measle's sister Matilda was fast asleep, too, but being only ten months old, she was fast asleep in her cot upstairs.

Nanny Flannel was sitting in the living room as well, but she wasn't really watching the TV—for two reasons. First, she was busy knitting another woolly hat for Iggy Niggle. This one was purple and it was the tenth woolly hat that Nanny Flannel had knitted for the little wrathmonk. Because of the constant drizzle that fell on Iggy's head, woolly hats were inclined to fall apart after a while.

Iggy himself was outside the living room, staring in through one of the windows—and that was the other reason Nanny Flannel wasn't paying any attention to the television. She was keeping half an eye on Iggy, just in case he tried to sneak into the house when nobody was looking. It was one of the conditions that Nanny Flannel had made when Iggy had first come to live at Merlin Manor: 'No wet things in the house, thank you very much. I'm not going to be mopping up after you all the time.' So, Iggy stayed outside or, when he wanted to sleep, he crawled inside his little house. Iggy's house was really Tinker's dog kennel but Tinker had always refused to use it. In return for the small wrathmonk agreeing to stay outside, Nanny Flannel, who had become secretly quite fond of the pathetic creature, knitted him a succession of woolly hats and, every morning, cooked up a batch of two hundred homemade, strawberry-flavoured, non-magical red jelly beans, which were the only things that Iggy Niggle would eat.

So, when Sam Stubbs walked into the living room and announced, 'We're going to the South Pole,' only Lee and Measle really heard him. The words meant nothing to Tinker, and Nanny Flannel wasn't paying any attention. Standing outside, Iggy Niggle couldn't even hear the *television*, let alone something that Sam had said from the doorway of the living room. (Iggy didn't mind not hearing the television. He wasn't bright enough to understand what was going on and he really only liked watching the moving pictures anyway.)

'We're going *where*?' said Lee.

'South Pole,' said Sam. 'Day after tomorrow.'

'It seems rather an odd place to go for a holiday, Sam,' said Lee, mildly. 'Not very sunny at this time of the year, is it?'

'Not going on holiday,' said Sam.

'Oh. Then why are we going?'

'Conference,' said Sam.

Measle was listening to all this with interest. First of all, he'd never heard his dad speak in such short sentences. He stared hard at Sam and noticed that he was looking a little nervous. The other matter that was catching Measle's attention was the prospect of going to the South Pole.

'What sort of conference, Sam?' said Lee. She too had noticed Sam's nervousness and her tone of voice was gentle and unhurried.

'Wizards' Guild Conference,' muttered Sam, staring at his feet. 'International thing. Wizards from all over the world are going. And I've got to go too—I'm the Prime Magus.'

'Well, of course you have to go, Sam,' said Lee. 'But why do we?'

There was a short silence, then Sam sighed heavily and said, 'Can't do it without you. You know that, darling. I need you by my side.'

There was another short silence, while Lee thought about this. Measle thought about it, too, and it made sense to him. Of *course* Sam would need his wife with him—for such an important event as this, it would be vital that the Prime Magus of the Wizards' Guild was accompanied by his wife, the celebrated Manafount. There could easily be circumstances where her ability to replenish his mana would be more than just useful.

Measle's thoughts were interrupted by Lee. She frowned and said, 'When you say "we", Sam, do you mean just you and me—or the whole family?'

Sam shook his head. 'Just you—and Tilly, of course. There's a lot of interest in Tilly.'

'I'm not surprised,' said Lee.

Sam shrugged. 'Besides, we can't leave her behind—she's still too young to be separated from us for so long.'

'And Measle?'

'No,' said Sam, sadly. 'Afraid not. Only magicals allowed.'

Measle's heart sank—but only a little way. The idea of going to the South Pole had sounded really cool—but then again, it sounded really *cold* as well.

By this time, Nanny Flannel was paying attention. Her knitting needles were still and she was looking up at Sam with one eyebrow cocked.

'And exactly how *long* will you be gallivanting about in the Arctic, Sam Stubbs?' she said.

Sam looked even more uncomfortable than before.

'Not the Arctic, Nanny,' he said. 'The *Ant*arctic. About ten days. And we won't be gallivanting. I wish we were! No, we'll be attending endless boring lectures, sitting around discussing lots of boring things—and I'll probably have to make lots of boring speeches. It'll be really, really boring, I'm afraid.'

Lee laughed. 'You make it sound such fun, Sam. Tilly and I can hardly wait.' Then she smiled down at Measle. 'I think you're the lucky one, Measle darling. As far as I know, there's not a lot to do at the South Pole.' She turned to Sam and said, 'In fact, *why* the South Pole, Sam? Why not just have the conference at the Wizards' Guild building?'

Sam shrugged. 'It's got to be somewhere really remote,' he said. 'Somewhere there aren't any people at all. There's always a lot of magical stuff going on at these things and we don't want to draw attention.'

Lee nodded and then turned back to Measle. 'You'll be much better off staying here with Nanny and Iggy and Tinker, darling. And it's only for ten days. You don't mind, do you?'

'No,' said Measle. 'I don't mind.'

The truth was that he *did* mind a bit but, on the other hand, the conference did sound extremely boring and Lee was probably right—there might not be anything interesting to do at the South Pole. And there was *plenty* to do here at Merlin Manor. He and Iggy had a plan to dig a swimming pool in the back lawn, which was something that Sam would probably tell them not to do; but if Sam wasn't *there* . . .

Nanny Flannel sniffed loudly and then barked out a single word:

'Security?'

'Security, Nanny?' said Sam, looking a little blank.

'You know what I'm talking about, Sam Stubbs,' said Nanny Flannel, sternly. 'Things always seem to happen to Measle when you and Lee aren't around. Bad things, too. If you are both going to be gallivanting round the Arctic—'

Sam nodded and smiled and said, 'Yes, you're quite right, Nanny. Not about the Arctic—but you're right that we should get some protection for you all. I'll organize that.'

Measle opened his mouth to say that he didn't think they really needed protection, but Sam was already out of the door. A few minutes later, he came back. He looked, thought Measle, even more uncomfortable than before.

'Well . . . er . . .' he said, 'I rang Lord Octavo and he's setting something up. There'll be a couple of people from the Wizards' Guild here day and night.'

'Who are they sending, Sam?' asked Lee.

Sam threw a guilty look in Measle's direction and muttered, 'Er . . . Needle and Bland.'

For the second time that evening, Measle's heart sank like a stone. Mr Needle and Mr Bland! Those two horrible officials from the Wizards' Guild, who were so cold and business-like and who had never given any indication that they held the Stubbs family in anything other than deep contempt—those two horrible men, in their matching dark suits and their matching dark sunglasses, were going to come and live at Merlin Manor?

'But, Dad,' said Measle, raising his voice almost to a shriek, 'they're *awful*! And they hate us! Why do we have to have *them*?'

Sam shook his head. 'They *used* to be awful, Measle,' he said. 'But they're not awful any more. They don't hate us, either. You see, they're just intensely loyal to whoever is the Prime Magus—which, right now, is *me*. So at the moment they're our best friends—and, since they're both warlocks *and* fully trained security people as well, we really couldn't ask for better protection. I wouldn't have them here if I thought they meant us any harm.'

Measle looked across the room at Nanny Flannel, to see what sort of reaction she was having to this news. Nanny Flannel seemed more preoccupied with the dangers she imagined Sam and Lee and Matilda might have to face. She said, 'You're sure to be eaten by polar bears.'

'There aren't any polar bears at the South Pole, Nanny,' said Measle. 'They live at the North Pole.'

'Is that so?' said Nanny, in a haughty tone of voice. 'But the creatures can swim, can they not?'

'Yes, Nanny.'

'Well, then,' said Nanny Flannel, in a triumphant

tone, 'who's to say that a polar bear couldn't swim from the North Pole to the South Pole? Eh? Answer me that, Mister Clever-Clogs!'

Measle started a long explanation as to why a polar bear really couldn't swim all the way from the top of the world down to the bottom—and that the only creatures his parents were likely to meet at the South Pole were penguins. But Nanny clucked her tongue and announced that, as far as she was concerned, penguins were the most dangerous birds known to man and had often been observed pecking explorers to death. So Measle gave up and went outside to tell Iggy the news.

'You know what this means, Iggy?' said Measle. 'It means we can make a start on the swimming pool.'

'Coo—dat will be nice,' said Iggy, a little uncertainly. He wasn't sure what making a start on a swimming pool entailed—but if his best friend Mumps Stubbs wanted to do it, then that was just fine by him. He pulled a handful of red jelly beans out of his pocket and threw the whole lot into his mouth. He didn't offer Measle any. He never had, and he never would. He was, after all, still a wrathmonk.

THE THING IN THE DUNGEON CELL

The thing in the dungeon cell, deep below the Wizards' Guild building, was eight hundred years old.

It had seven mismatched eyes. The eyes belonged to four other creatures—a wizard, two rats, and a one-eyed mouse. The wizard had once been an apprentice called Sheepshank. The rats and the mouse had—unfortunately for them—been tossed into the thing's dungeon cell without anybody asking them if they wanted to be there. The creature's captors wanted to see precisely what became of living creatures when the thing in the cell got hold of them. The lesson had been useful for the Wizards' Guild, but unfortunately, the lesson had been learned so long ago that it had become lost in the mists of time. Now, nobody knew what, exactly, made the creature so horribly dangerous. It was simply assumed that mere contact with it was fatal.

This wasn't entirely true.

There were several strange facts about the thing in the dungeon cell and one of the strangest was its ability to keep *alive* any creature it had absorbed within its body. It was a strange sensation for its victims, being trapped inside that body of slimy jelly. It wasn't uncomfortable. They simply floated there, not getting ill or hungry or thirsty—and not getting a day older, either. For them, it was as if Time was standing still.

Since the creature had no eyes, nor ears, nor nose with which to experience the outside world, it used the senses of its victims to do so. It looked through their eyes and it made as much use of their brains as it could—which wasn't very much, since three of the creatures it had absorbed were a pair of rats and a one-eyed mouse.

Sheepshank was another matter, of course. Sheepshank had once had a brain—a brilliant brain. Unfortunately, Sheepshank's brain was also highly unstable and, within seconds of being absorbed, he had lost his mind—but not in the sense of going insane. What had happened to his brain was a bit like the difference between a busy office building during the day, with lots of workers bustling about and phones ringing and computers beeping and everything bright and on the go, and the same office at four o'clock in the morning, when everybody had gone home hours ago, and all the lights and computers are switched off. The whole space appears to be asleep. But there's always the possibility that somebody might come by and . . . turn on the lights again.

So, Sheepshank's brain had simply switched off. And that meant that he was useless as far as the creature was concerned.

The thing had a name. The name had been given to it by Crabgrass.

Slitherghoul.

The Slitherghoul had been content there in the darkness of its cell, because there was no particular reason why it shouldn't be. It was warm and comfortable. It didn't need food or water. It just lay there in one corner, a slimy mass of jelly, not doing anything at all.

But, recently, something had happened that had changed its attitude.

A month ago, the Slitherghoul's peaceful existence had been shattered. There had been noises outside the door of its cell—the sounds of humans being happy. (The humans were Sam, Lee, and Matilda, who were naturally overjoyed at being rescued by Measle at the end of the Mallockee adventure).

These were sounds that the thing had never heard before, so it stirred itself and began to take a little bit of notice.

There was something else outside the cell door, as well as the sounds of happiness, and it was this something else that woke a tiny spark deep inside the closed-down brain of Sheepshank. The spark was nothing more than the simplest form of instinct. This little spark of instinct felt the presence of something—and it was something Sheepshank had always wanted more than anything else in the entire world.

Power. Magical power.

The sudden flicker of activity inside Sheepshank's mind caught the attention of the Slitherghoul and, for a moment, it considered the world through what was left of the little wizard's brain. And because the spark of instinct it detected *wanted* something, then so did the Slitherghoul.

Whatever was beyond the door also possessed the ability to store and regenerate its power at will.

And now the Slitherghoul—because of Sheepshank's spark of instinct—wanted that power within itself. And it would do anything to possess it.

For the first time in centuries, the Slitherghoul started to move. It flowed across the stone floor of its cell, leaving behind a wide trail of sticky slime. When it got to the door, it pressed itself against it, using its whole body in search of an opening—any opening—through which it could pass. But the door was sealed, without even a hairline crack round its edges.

And now the sounds of the happy people were

fading as they moved away—and so was the power that the thing had sensed.

Sheepshank's spark was no use to it—*wanting* something was pointless if there was no way to *obtain* it. So, the Slitherghoul pushed aside the fierce feeling of longing and returned to the minds of the rats and the mouse.

Rats and mice have teeth that are designed for gnawing. They can scrape away at a flat surface for hours on end, and their teeth never stop growing, which allows them to chew their way through very hard materials.

The Slitherghoul's cell door was six inches thick and made of ironwood. Ironwood is very hard.

A rat's tooth is harder—and the Slitherghoul had plenty of rats' teeth at its disposal.

It took the Slitherghoul a month to gnaw a hole in the door.

Since nobody ever opened the door to its cell, the Slitherghoul could work in perfect safety, scraping away steadily, day and night, until it had removed all but a thin layer of ironwood on the outer surface. Then, one morning, it had finally broken through.

The Slitherghoul began to squeeze itself through the aperture. Being made entirely of jelly, this was easy for it. The rats and the mouse had bones—but the hole their teeth had gnawed was more than big enough to let them through. When it came time for Sheepshank's head to pass through the opening, it was a tight squeeze but, luckily for the Slitherghoul, not *too* tight. Within moments, the Slitherghoul was flowing stickily across the stone floor of the outer corridor.

At the end of the short passage, there was a heavy iron door. It was ajar. There was a yellow light spilling out through the narrow gap and the Slitherghoul moved towards it.

A junior apprentice wizard was in the office of the High Security Wing. He had replaced Officer Offal as the Detention Centre guard. Officer Offal had been convicted of his crimes against Measle and was now serving a very long sentence in the very same cell block where once he'd been in charge. The junior wizard was sitting in his swivel chair, his feet up on the steel desk, studying a manual on the various uses of powdered emeralds. His name was Corky Pretzel. Corky was twenty-two years old and he'd been given the job because, though he wasn't very bright, he did have enormous muscles in his arms and chest. Most of Corky's prisoners were wrathmonks—and it was felt by the authorities of the Wizards' Guild that if a wrathmonk should ever get out of his cell and try to escape, muscles rather than magic might be the best way to subdue him. All wrathmonk prisoners wore the iron wrathrings round their necks which stopped them doing any of their insanely dangerous magical spells. However, the wrathrings were no use against the effects of a wrathmonk's *breathing* spell, so muscles might, for once, prove more useful than magic.

At the moment, in the High Security Wing, there were only three prisoners and, unlike the wrathmonks, they were very quiet. One of them never made any sound at all. This suited Corky, because he needed absolute quiet when he wanted to read. Corky was trying to pass his elementary wizard exam. He'd been trying to pass it for the last three years.

The first thing that made Corky think that he might be in some sort of danger was the smell. It was a dreadful, disgusting, revolting stink that seemed to be coming from beyond the office door. It was so strong that it made him choke. The smell was appalling, because it was a *mixture* of some of the nastiest stenches imaginable. Part was the sharp smell when somebody is sick on the carpet; part was the foul odour of Brussels sprouts that have been boiled for six hours; part was the stink that comes from a mouse that's been dead for a week; part was the sort of smell you get from the breath of a person who hasn't brushed their teeth in a year; and parts were the sorts of horrible smells you can't really write about in a book. There was something else mixed in with it too, a strong smell of something chemical, like ammonia mixed with bleach mixed with chlorine—and it was this last ingredient that was making Corky choke and cough.

Corky put his hand over his nose and got up from the swivel chair. Cautiously, he went over to the office door and peered round the edge.

There, in the corridor, between the two pairs of identical cells, was something that hadn't been there before and, as far as Corky was concerned, had no business being there now. It was a mass of shiny, brownish-yellowish-greenish substance, about the size of a coffee table. It was quivering slightly, like jelly on a plate—and it was moving slowly towards him.

The stink of the thing was even stronger out here and Corky coughed—

And, instantly, the brown mass moved.

A section of it extended, like a long brown finger—*no, more like a tentacle*, thought Corky. The next thing Corky thought was: *perhaps I ought to move back a bit?* But it was already too late. The tip of the tentacle touched Corky's leg—

Immediately—and so fast that Corky never really saw it happen—the tentacle wrapped itself round Corky's ankle. Then it gave a powerful jerk that yanked him off his feet. Corky fell heavily to the floor, banging the back of his head on the stone. Half conscious, he felt himself being dragged across the rough surface. Then something damp and slimy and horribly smelly wrapped itself over his face—and, a moment later, Corky stopped being Corky and became just part of the Slitherghoul instead.

Corky Pretzel had been a big fellow—and the Slitherghoul swelled. Now, it was the size of a small dining table.

And now, it had Corky Pretzel's brain. For the first time, it had access to a mind that could think a lot further than where its next meal was going to come from. As human brains went, Corky's wasn't all that impressive, but compared to the thinking capacities of a comatose wizard, two rats, and a one-eyed mouse, it was close to genius level. It opened up a whole world to the Slitherghoul. There was so much information in there that the Slitherghoul was forced to push away anything that didn't deal directly with its immediate surroundings.

So. First things first—
It learned where it was.
It discovered what was nearby.
It decided what to do next.

Toby Jugg was dozing in his cell, when he was woken by the electronic *clonk!* of his door unlocking. Half awake, Toby sat up on his bunk and peered blearily out into the passage. He heard shuffling footsteps.

Officer Offal poked his jowly red face round the cell door. He was wearing a set of clothes identical to Toby's—a plain white jumpsuit and a pair of white canvas shoes. The only difference in their prison uniforms was the dull silver wrathring that encircled Toby Jugg's neck. Officer Offal had no need of a wrathring, he had no more magical abilities than a stone, but Toby Jugg was a very powerful warlock indeed and the Wizards' Guild took no chances with such a dangerous prisoner. They had slapped a wrathring round his neck the moment he'd been convicted of his crimes, which meant Toby Jugg now had no more magical ability than Officer Offal.

'Mr Jugg, sir?' whispered Officer Offal, a puzzled frown creasing his pink forehead. 'Any idea what's going on, sir? My cell door just opened and so did yours—'

'So it would appear, Offal,' said Toby. He got up and joined the beefy ex-guard out in the passage. Together, they strained their eyes in the gloom, looking towards the door that led out to the office beyond.

'I—I think that's open too, sir,' muttered Officer Offal into Toby's ear.

'Hmm. Let's take a look. Quietly now.'

Toby and Officer Offal tiptoed down the short passage towards the door. A little yellow light spilled out through the crack—and so did a disgusting, dreadful smell. Both men put their hands over their noses.

'What's that stink, sir?' whispered Offal.

Toby didn't answer. Instead, he slowed his pace a fraction, allowing Offal to take the lead. When the big man seemed to hesitate, Toby put a reassuring hand against the small of Offal's back.

'I'm right behind you,' he muttered.

Cautiously, Offal crept to the door and peered round it.

The room was empty.

'Corky's not here, sir,' hissed Offal over his shoulder. He felt Toby's hand pushing him gently, so he stepped into the office. Toby was right behind him.

33

Then, without warning, the Slitherghoul flowed out from under the steel desk, rearing its whole shapeless mass high in the air. Before either of them could do anything—other than Officer Offal letting out a short, high-pitched squeal of terror—the Slitherghoul was upon them.

Now the Slitherghoul was even bigger. It had six working human eyes—and human eyes are much better than rodent eyes. It also had three functioning human brains, and, while two of them were limited, one of those brains was in superb condition. The Slitherghoul shoved the two inferior minds to one side. If needs be, it could use them later, but right now it concentrated its efforts on making full use of the brain of Toby Jugg.

The sound of all the cell doors opening in the Wrathmonk Block of the Detention Centre took its occupants by surprise. Measle's old enemy, Griswold Gristle, was the first to pop his round, white head out of his cell and look up and down the corridor. Gradually, other wrathmonks also thrust their heads out into the passage, their fishy eyes swivelling suspiciously. All of them wore wrathrings round their necks.

'A little early for our exercise hour, is it not?' said Griswold, in his oily voice, to nobody in particular.

Buford Cudgel's giant form emerged from his cell. 'Not due for another forty minutes,' he rumbled, clenching and unclenching his banana-sized fingers.

'A bit peculiar, if you asssk me,' said Frognell Flabbit, scratching irritably at his red and lumpy face. The boil spell that had been breathed on him by Judge Cedric Hardscrabble was still operating, although its effects were slowly diminishing. The only comfort that Flabbit could take from this was the fact that *his* breathing spell he'd performed on Judge Cedric was also still working, because here was Judge Cedric tottering out of his cell and both the old wrathmonk's hands were—as always—pressed to his aching teeth.

'Are we to be released, Griswold?' asked Judge Cedric, in his quavery voice. 'Are we to be released at long lassst, dear friend?'

'I would hardly think ssso, Cedric,' snapped Griswold. He glared irritably at the small mob of wrathmonks, who were now milling aimlessly about in the corridor. He gestured at them with a contemptuous flick of his wrist.

'Look at them, Cedric! Do you ssseriously imagine that the authorities would release all of usss? At once?'

'Perhapsss we have been given time off for good behaviour, Griswold?'

Griswold snorted scornfully through his little snub nose. He started to say something—but he stopped when he saw the heavy iron door at the far end of the corridor click open. It didn't open very far but it was enough to tell Griswold that something very odd was happening, because this door led out to the guard's office and it was never, *ever* open at the same time that the doors to the wrathmonks' cells were open.

Griswold, who always assumed that he would be listened to, hissed, 'Sssshhhhh!' as loudly as he could. Frognell Flabbit, Buford Cudgel, and Judge Cedric all turned towards him respectfully, because he had always led them and probably always would; but the rest of the wrathmonks took no notice of him and went on with their milling and chatting.

Then, slowly, one by one they fell silent because, centimetre by centimetre, the office door was opening wider and wider.

Those closest to the door obviously saw something unpleasant emerging from the office, because they started to retreat, edging their way backwards up the corridor to where Gristle, Cudgel, Flabbit, and Judge Cedric were huddled together. Their mass of bodies hid whatever was coming through the door from Griswold—he was very small—so he tapped Buford Cudgel on the arm and squeaked, 'What do you sssee, Missster Cudgel?'

'I dunno,' said Buford, uncertainly. 'It's sssome sssort of brown blob.'

'Brown blob?' said Griswold, standing on tiptoes and trying to peer over the mob. 'What sssort of—'

And that was as far as he got, because the

wrathmonks at the front of the crowd started to scream—and then the wrathmonks in the middle of the mob started to scream—and then the wrathmonks at the back of the mob (the ones closest to Griswold and Flabbit and Cudgel and Judge Cedric) started to scream as well—and there was a general stumbling retreat by the crowd back down the passage, which forced the four wrathmonks to press themselves against the rear wall of the corridor.

And Griswold saw, for the first time, what Buford Cudgel had described as a brown blob. The mass of jelly had reared itself up, its quivering top almost touching the ceiling—

It looks like a huge wave, thought Griswold, *a huge wave that's going to come crashing down on us all—*

And then the Slitherghoul did exactly that—it crashed down on the collected wrathmonks and, quite suddenly, there was no more screaming.

Just a soft, squelching sound as the Slitherghoul—now a *lot* bigger than before—slimed its way back down the corridor towards the open office door.

THE DIG

Mr Needle and Mr Bland arrived at Merlin Manor about an hour before Sam and Lee and Matilda left for the South Pole.

Measle let them in—and he was instantly struck by a marked difference in their behaviour. In the past, the two officials from the Wizards' Guild had been cold to the point of rudeness. Neither man had made any attempt to hide his disdain for the Stubbs family and, when Measle had needed their help, they had been thoroughly *un*helpful as well. So, when Measle opened the heavy front door of Merlin Manor and thin, dark Mr Needle smiled and bowed and said, 'Good morning, Master Measle, I hope you're quite well?' and stout blond Mr Bland had followed by smiling and bowing and saying,

'And may I add what a pleasure it is to see you again, Master Measle,'—Measle himself was about as surprised as it's possible to be.

He stepped aside and motioned for the two men to come in and Mr Needle and Mr Bland, both carrying small, identical suitcases, walked briskly into the house.

'Ah, there you are,' said Sam, coming out of his study. 'Welcome to Merlin Manor, gentlemen.'

Mr Needle and Mr Bland bowed and said, in unison, 'A pleasure to be here, Prime Magus. And, indeed, an honour, sir.'

Lee came and took the two men off to show them their bedrooms. As they walked away up the stairs, Sam turned and winked broadly at Measle.

'See what I mean, Measle?' he whispered. 'A pair of little baa-lambs now, aren't they?'

Measle wasn't sure that Mr Needle and Mr Bland quite qualified for that description, but he was certainly relieved that the two officials seemed to be a lot friendlier—and a lot more respectful— than they had ever been before.

An hour later, it was time for the departure. A big black car—the official vehicle for the exclusive use of the Prime Magus—purred up to the front door, its tyres crunching on the gravel. A smartly-dressed chauffeur jumped out and started to load the suitcases into the boot.

'Goodbye, darling,' said Lee, giving Measle a big hug. 'Look after everything, especially yourself.'

'Goodbye, Measle,' said Sam. Then he bent down and wrapped his strong arms around Measle and whispered in his ear, 'And, if you and Iggy are really determined to dig that swimming pool, just make sure it's a nice *big* one, OK?'

Measle grinned up at his dad. *I should've known that I couldn't get away with that!* he thought. *But, all the same, I wonder how he knew?*

The next moment, that question was answered. Iggy Niggle was standing by the black car, peering into one of the side mirrors and admiring his appearance. He was wearing his latest woollen hat. This one had orange and green stripes and a pink bobble on the top and Iggy thought he looked tremendously handsome in it. He looked away from the mirror, saw Measle and Sam together, and waved excitedly.

'I told Missster Ssstubbs dat we was goin' to dig de sssswimmin' pool *after* dey was gone, Mumps!' he yelled, happily. 'Dat way, dey won't know anyfing about it, will dey? And it will be all finished when dey come back, won't it?'

'I shall expect one at least twenty metres long,' said Sam, drily.

Lee was bringing Matilda down the steps. There was a delay while Matilda gave Measle lots of hugs and kisses, then another delay while she did the same to Iggy. Then Sam and Lee and Tilly all climbed into the back of the car and the chauffeur closed their door. He went round to the driver's side, climbed in and started the engine.

The car turned bright pink. Inside *and* out.

'Now, Tilly, stop it,' said Lee from the back seat, trying not to laugh.

'Sorry about that, Percy,' Sam called to the chauffeur. 'Don't worry—it'll wear off soon.'

Everybody shouted together, 'Goodbye!— Goodbye!—Be good!—Don't catch cold!—Keep warm!—Have a nice time!—See you in ten days!' and then the big pink car moved off down the driveway. Measle and Nanny Flannel and Iggy all waved until the car turned through the front gates and disappeared from sight.

Measle turned back to the house and saw, to his surprise, that Mr Needle and Mr Bland were standing, like a pair of sentries, on either side of the front door. Tinker was standing in front of them, eyeing the two men suspiciously and growling softly at the back of his throat. Tinker didn't care for Mr Needle or Mr Bland and being a dog, he hadn't noticed any change in their behaviour. They still smelt the same, and that to Tinker was all that mattered.

Measle went up the steps and approached the two men. 'Um . . . are you going to stand there the whole time?' he asked, politely.

'Oh no, Master Measle,' said Mr Bland.

'We were just seeing off the Prime Magus, Master Measle,' said Mr Needle. 'There's a way of doing these things, you see.'

Mr Bland nodded seriously and said, 'I expect you'd like to know our routine, Master Measle? Well, there'll always be one of us on duty, you see. Patrolling the grounds, keeping our eyes peeled, ready for anything.'

'Don't you worry, Master Measle,' said Mr Needle. 'Nothing bad is going to happen. Not with us around.'

Measle smiled politely and said, 'Thank you very much.' He wondered whether he ought to ask them to stop calling him 'Master' Measle—then he decided he quite liked it.

'Come on, Tink,' he said, bending down and patting the little dog on his fuzzy head. 'And leave Mr Needle and Mr Bland alone. They're our friends now.'

But, even as he walked away in search of Iggy,

Measle realized he didn't really believe that any more than Tinker did.

For the rest of that day, Measle and Iggy worked very hard.

First of all, Measle marked out a large rectangle on the back lawn, using a whole roll of silver duct tape.

'See, Iggy?' he said. 'That's how big the pool has got to be. Now all we have to do is dig it out.'

Iggy's fishy eyes grew even rounder than before. 'We is goin' to dig?' he whispered, in a tone of disbelief. 'But . . . but dat will make all de green ssstuff go away!'

It always amazed Measle how few words Iggy knew. 'You mean the grass, Iggy?' he said.

Iggy nodded. 'Dat's de ssstuff! De grass. Dere won't be any dere any more—jussst de brown ssstuff!'

'You mean the earth?'

'Dat's de ssstuff—de earf.'

'But there'll be water there instead, Iggy. And that'll look nice, won't it?'

Iggy—without really understanding what exactly they were doing—agreed that water would look very nice. So, without any further delay, he and Measle started to dig up the lawn.

It was a lot harder work than Measle had thought it would be. After half an hour they had managed to scrape away a patch of grass about three metres by three metres—and they were both hot and sweaty. For the first time, Measle felt a little envious of Iggy's tiny rain cloud, which scattered a fine mist of water down on Iggy's head, keeping the little wrathmonk just a bit cooler than Measle.

Tinker had joined in the digging when they first started, because he thought they might perhaps be burrowing for rabbits. But when no rabbits—nor even the *scent* of any rabbits—appeared, he'd quickly got bored with scratching away at the hard earth and had trotted off to a sunny corner of the lawn and gone to sleep.

'I don't like doin' dis,' announced Iggy, stopping his digging and leaning on his spade.

'Come on, Iggy,' said Measle, encouragingly. 'We can't stop now.'

'*I* can ssstop,' said Iggy, stubbornly. '*I* can ssstop whenever I want to.' He dropped his spade and began to wander off in the direction of the house.

Measle thought quickly. 'I'll give you some more jelly beans, Iggy!' he shouted and Iggy stopped in his tracks and turned round slowly.

'How many?' said Iggy, his eyes narrowing.

'If we finish clearing all the grass away today, I'll give you ten.'

'Wot colour?' said Iggy, slowly.

'Orange.'

Iggy thought about this for a moment and then nodded in satisfaction. He came back, picked up his spade and attacked the grass with renewed energy.

Measle joined him. He'd known all along that Iggy would do anything for more jelly beans. The two hundred red ones (which Nanny Flannel made fresh for Iggy each morning) were all that Iggy ate and, being a wrathmonk, he thrived on the dreadful diet. But Iggy craved even more sugar and was always on the lookout for ways to wangle an extra ration out of Nanny Flannel. Ever since he'd come to live at Merlin Manor, he'd had his eyes on the big jar of magical multicoloured jelly beans that stood on the sideboard in the dining room and, every now and then, Measle would slip him a handful of them. But never a green one. The green ones were Iggy's least favourite flavour and, if he ever bit down on a green jelly bean, Iggy would become invisible for thirty seconds, just as Measle would disappear from sight for half a minute if ever he swallowed a yellow one. It was lucky that Iggy never wanted to eat a green one, and it was equally lucky that Iggy's small brain had never made the connection between green jelly beans and half a minute of invisibility—because the last thing anybody needed was a small, damp, *undetectable* wrathmonk wandering about the place.

Just before Nanny Flannel came out to call Measle in for supper, they were finished with the first part of the project. It was growing dark now, but he and Iggy had finally managed to scrape away every last centimetre of grass from the marked-out area, exposing the earth beneath.

Iggy and Measle were exhausted, but Iggy had a big grin on his muddy face and he was dancing happily about on the bare earth, hopping from foot to foot like an excited stork. The pink bobble on his hat jiggled wildly, sending drops of water flying in all directions.

'I done it! I done it!' he shouted. 'I finished all de diggin'! All by myssself, I finished it!'

Measle couldn't help smiling to himself. Iggy always took the credit for something which had usually been done by somebody else. This time, Measle didn't mind—Iggy was a lot stronger than Measle and had, in fact, done at least half the work.

'Well done, Iggy!' he yelled.

'Can we put de water in now?' said Iggy.

I should have known he'd say that, thought Measle. Iggy was neither very bright, nor very patient.

'Not yet, Iggy. We've got to dig out all the earth, too.'

Iggy turned and stared beadily at Measle.

'We got to do *wot*?' said Iggy.

'Dig out all the earth. It's got to be deep, you see.'

'Why has it got to be deep, Mumps?'

'Because we can't swim in only a couple of centimetres of water, Iggy.'

Iggy wasn't entirely sure what 'swimming' entailed, but he began to get the feeling that—

whatever it meant—he wasn't going to like it very much. With water involved—and *deep* water at that—it sounded as if it meant getting wet and, if there's one thing wrathmonks hate, it's getting wet. What with their rain clouds hovering permanently overhead, they have quite enough wetness in their lives already.

'I don't want to dig no more, Mumps,' said Iggy, in a sulky voice.

'*Twenty* more jelly beans, Iggy?' said Measle, in a wheedling voice.

Iggy's hands were sore, and so was his back, and somehow he'd got a lot of mud on his nice new hat. The mud was mixing with the fine drops from his rain cloud and trickling in a little brown stream down his face. He felt tired and achy and rather cross, too.

'No,' he said, firmly.

'Forty?'

'No.'

'Will you do it for a hundred?'

'*No*. Not even for a *sssquillion*.' And, for the second time that day, Iggy threw down his spade and scuttled off towards the house.

Now what? thought Measle, staring gloomily down at the rectangle of bare earth. *I can't leave it like this—Dad'll murder me!*

And then Nanny Flannel's voice floated across the darkening lawn.

'Measle! Measle, dear! Time for supper!'

BREAKOUT!

The Wizards' Guild was in a state of panic.

Nobody discovered the disappearance of the prisoners from the Detention Centre for two days. Corky Pretzel hadn't reported anything to the authorities. He was highly trusted and there was no reason for anybody to check up on him, so nobody did. It was only when Corky's mother telephoned the Wizards' Guild to ask if anybody had seen her son recently that somebody thought to go down to the bowels of the Wizards' Guild building and see if anything was wrong.

When they did, pandemonium broke out.

Every single prisoner had escaped! All the wrathmonks in the wrathmonk block had disappeared into thin air, and so had both the special prisoners from the High Security Section! But how? The cell doors were wide open and the guard was missing, but the last door, which led out to the long staircase (which, in turn, led to various corridors and passages and, finally, to a set of lifts that arrived at street level and freedom), *that* door was still locked—and it had taken a powerful spell from one of the senior wizards to open it.

At first, nobody thought to look in the Slitherghoul's cell.

The door of the cell was still shut tight, so it was assumed that the Slitherghoul was inside. But a young apprentice wizard, who was a member of the search party, noticed a faint and disgusting smell that lingered in the air of the wrathmonks' cell block.

'What's that smell?' he asked, and one of the older wizards replied, 'That's the Slitherghoul, sonny. Smells horrible, doesn't it?'

'But . . . why can I smell it in *here*? This section only housed the wrathmonk prisoners, didn't it?'

'Merlin's Ghost! You're right!'

The search party returned to the High Security Wing—and it was the same young wizard who noticed the hole in the shadows at the bottom of the ironwood door.

So—not only had the entire prison population of the Detention Centre escaped, but the most mysterious and possibly the most dangerous creature the Wizards' Guild had ever had to handle had gone as well. The panic deepened. Nobody seemed to know what to do—

Then the sharp-eyed young wizard with the sensitive nose noticed something set in the floor of one of the toilets that adjoined the offices.

It was a manhole cover.

When they lifted the cover, they found dried slime round the edges of the hole.

The slime smelt bad. Very bad.

Only then did somebody think of calling Lord Octavo.

When the Slitherghoul's sticky mass had enveloped the entire mob of panic-stricken wrathmonks, its jelly body instantly enlarged to the size of a small lorry. Satisfied that it had caught every one of them, it squeezed its way out of the wrathmonks' corridor and into the office beyond. Once inside the room, it stopped and took stock of its situation. One by one, it discarded the minds of the wrathmonks it had liberated; they were all unstable and therefore almost useless to the creature, so the Slitherghoul examined the three that were still reasonably sane. One by one, it tested the minds of Toby Jugg, Officer Offal, and Corky Pretzel.

The Slitherghoul ended up using Toby Jugg's mind most of the time. It was Toby's brain which suggested that moving *upwards*, through the endless passages of the Guild building, was a bad idea. It was Toby's brain that made the Slitherghoul leave the final door of the Detention Centre firmly locked. It was Toby's brain that proposed that there might be *another* way out. But, while looking for an alternative route, it used the mind of Corky Pretzel. Corky knew every inch of those underground quarters. He knew about the manhole cover. He knew that under the manhole cover was a well and, at the bottom of this well, was a branch of the main sewer that lay beneath the Wizards' Guild building.

But, once Corky had told the Slitherghoul about the manhole cover, it was Toby's brain that put forward the idea of where to go next.

The huge thing slithered stickily out of the office and into the adjoining toilet. There, in the middle of the dirty tiled floor, was the heavy iron manhole cover. The Slitherghoul extended a section of itself, wrapped the jelly tentacle round the cover's handle and yanked it free. Then, without another thought from any of the minds inside it, the thing had slid over the lip of the gaping hole and, with a slopping, slurping sound, disappeared into the blackness beneath.

SOME
UNEXPECTED
HELP

Measle was fed up.

He'd been digging for three days and, for all his efforts, the projected swimming pool looked as if he'd hardly started it. All he'd managed to do was increase the depth of the dig by about ten centimetres, which was hardly scratching the surface of the job. At this rate, it would be at least a year before he could dive in! Already his hands were sore and his spine was so stiff he was having trouble straightening up.

Iggy hadn't come back to help. He hadn't even bothered to watch Measle at work. Instead he'd hung about at the kitchen door, hoping that Nanny Flannel might give him some more jelly beans. He was careful not to step over the threshold of the kitchen. He'd done that once and Nanny Flannel had whacked him over the head with a wet mop. Iggy was a little afraid of Nanny Flannel—but not so afraid that he wouldn't try a small lie on her.

'I been workin' ever ssso hard, Miss Fwannel,' he whined. 'For free whole days I been workin'! And I'm ever ssso 'ungry—'

Nanny Flannel was having none of it.

'You haven't been working at all, you lazy wet thing,' she said, peering crossly at Iggy through her glasses. 'You did a little on the first day and since then you've done nothing but clutter up my doorway. Now go away. If you're not going to help Measle, at least make yourself useful—go and breathe on the roses.'

Breathing on the roses in the gardens of Merlin Manor was Iggy's job. His wrathmonk breathing magic was a very weak spell—all it did was kill bugs. But that was useful on the Merlin Manor roses, particularly in the spring, when the aphids started sucking the sap from the stems.

'Go on now, Iggy!' said Nanny sharply. 'I won't tell you again!'

Iggy sighed mournfully and, muttering darkly about how cruel and sad his life was, he drifted off in the direction of the rose gardens. Nanny Flannel took his place in the doorway of the kitchen. She peered out across the expanse of lawn and watched the small figure of Measle in the distance, struggling with his heavy spade.

Poor little chap, she thought. *Well, good for him for trying. I wonder when he'll give it up?*

Measle was, in fact, at the point of giving up. The whole thing was obviously beyond him. Perhaps Iggy had been right to stop when he did—at least *he* didn't have sore hands, an aching back, and muddy feet.

'Hard at work I see, Master Measle.'

Measle turned round. Mr Needle and Mr Bland were standing there, at the edge of the rectangle of bare earth. Measle noticed that they were careful to keep their shiny black shoes away from the pile of mud that Measle had dumped by the side. Using the back of his hand, Measle wiped the sweat from his forehead. His hand was muddy and it left a brown streak across his face. He nodded politely.

'A major undertaking, Needle,' said Mr Bland, smiling faintly down at Measle.

'A *monumental* undertaking, Bland,' said Mr Needle. 'Perhaps a little *too* monumental, don't you think? For one so young, I mean.'

Mr Bland nodded. 'I'm rather inclined to agree with you, Needle. Master Measle could use some help.'

'Well, Tinker helped a little, when he thought we were digging for rabbits,' said Measle, leaning on his spade. 'And Iggy helped the whole of the first day but then he got bored and stopped.'

'Typical wrathmonk behaviour,' said Mr Needle.

'Typical,' said Mr Bland. 'What else could one expect?'

There was a short silence while Mr Bland and Mr Needle stood there, smiling faintly down at Measle.

It's no good, thought Measle, *I just don't like these two. So it won't matter if I tease them a bit—*

'*You* could help, if you like,' he said, smiling innocently up at the two men.

'Us?' said Mr Bland, slowly taking off his sunglasses.

'We?' said Mr Needle, doing the same thing. '*We* . . . help *you*?'

'Oh, thank you very much,' said Measle, opening his eyes very wide and grinning with pretend gratitude at the men. 'One of you could use Iggy's spade and there's a pickaxe in the potting shed.'

Mr Bland smiled uncertainly and then turned slowly and looked at Mr Needle. Almost as if he was a mirror image of Mr Bland, Mr Needle did exactly the same thing. For a couple of moments they stared at one another.

Mr Needle broke the silence. 'What if we—?' he said.

Mr Bland interrupted with, 'Possibly we could.'

'There's no particular reason why we couldn't.'

'None that I can think of.'

'I doubt it would do any harm.'

'It might even enhance our—'

'Our reputations, yes.'

'Which would be no bad—'

'Thing.'

Then both men fell silent for a couple of seconds before turning in unison to Measle.

'We would be delighted to help, Master Measle,' said Mr Bland.

'Delighted,' said Mr Needle. 'So—if you would kindly stand to one side, Master Measle?'

Measle stepped up from the bare earth and onto the grass next to the two men. He expected one of them to step down and pick up Iggy's spade, which was lying where Iggy had dropped it two days earlier, but neither man moved from his spot. Instead, Mr Bland said, 'A Restricted Excavatory Enchantment, I assume, Needle? Number three, do you think?'

Mr Needle inclined his head and said, 'The logical choice, Bland. It will be interesting to see how far we get with it. Shall I attempt it first?'

'Be my guest, Needle,' said Mr Bland.

Mr Needle narrowed his eyes and stared hard at the bare rectangle of earth in front of him. Then he said, in a loud, ringing voice, '*Humfuss quadrickle effodium limitudinus!*'

Measle had forgotten that the two men from the Wizards' Guild were minor warlocks. Two pale green beams of light shot from Mr Needle's eyes and sizzled through the air, striking a spot in the dead centre of the rectangle of bare earth. What happened next was very interesting.

A pair of gigantic, ghostly canine paws appeared

and started to dig in the centre of the rectangle. They were almost exactly like Tinker's white furry paws—only much, much bigger—and with no dog attached to them, either. They simply ended in a sort of wispy smoke, about where a dog's elbows are placed but they dug with all the enthusiasm that any dog shows when it thinks there's a rabbit down a hole. The earth started to shower upwards, landing neatly on top of the pile of soil that Measle had already dug out.

Tinker, asleep a few metres away, opened one eye at the sounds of frantic, doglike digging. When he saw what was happening, he pricked up both ears then he got up and trotted over to see what was going on. When he saw the disembodied paws, he flattened his ears and started to bark furiously at them.

'Shut up, Tink!' shouted Measle. 'It's all right!'

Tinker was used to strange things happening round the smelly kid but a pair of paws, smelling distinctly doggy and suddenly appearing out of nowhere, was a bit much to ignore. However, the tone of the smelly kid's voice was firm and reasonably reassuring, so Tinker turned and slunk back to his patch of warm grass, throwing suspicious looks over his shoulder.

Measle settled down to watch the process with growing delight. The magical paws dug very fast— far faster than he and Iggy could possibly manage, even with all the enthusiasm in the world—and, quite soon, there was a hole two metres deep. At that point, the paws popped out of the hole they had made and started another hole right next to it. In a few moments, this second hole was as deep as the first and the pile of earth at the side of the rectangle was growing fast.

After twenty minutes, about a quarter of the rectangle had been dug down to a depth of two metres and Measle began to hope that, perhaps, his swimming pool project was actually going to work.

Then, quite suddenly, there was a popping sound, like a cork coming out of a bottle, and the two giant paws faded into a thin grey smoke which blew away on a little gust of wind.

'Well *done*, Needle,' said Mr Bland. 'You're showing a definite improvement, particularly in spell-duration, aren't you?'

'Thank you, Bland,' said Mr Needle. 'I must say, I'm quite pleased with the result. But you'll do *much* better, I'm sure.'

'Oh, I'm sure I won't,' said Mr Bland. 'But I shall do my best, of course.'

Mr Bland directed his gaze at the centre of the rectangle and said, '*Humfuss quadrickle effodium limitudinus!*' A pair of pale blue beams darted from his eyes and sizzled to the centre of the rectangle—and Measle watched with delight as another pair of giant paws appeared and started to dig furiously. These paws were a little different from the ones that Mr Needle had produced:

Mr Bland's paws were chocolate brown in colour and perhaps just a little larger. However, they seemed to dig at the same speed as Mr Needle's—and, quite soon, another quarter of the rectangle had been dug out to two metres in depth.

But all too soon there was that popping sound again and the giant paws turned to smoke and then drifted away in the breeze.

'Oh, *excellent*, Bland!' said Mr Needle. 'I do believe you were almost up to my time!'

'You're too kind, Needle,' said Mr Bland, gazing down at his handiwork with a look of pride. Then he turned to Measle and said, 'Well, Master Measle, that's all we can do for today, I'm afraid.'

'We can continue tomorrow, of course,' said Mr Needle.

'When our mana has recharged,' said Mr Bland.

'Thanks so much,' said Measle. 'That's fantastic!' And he meant it. Fully half the rectangle was now two metres deep—and it looked good enough to be turned into the deep end of a splendid swimming pool.

All three stared proudly down at the neatly dug pit in front of them.

Then Nanny Flannel's voice came drifting across the lawn.

'Measle! Measle, dear! Lord Octavo's on the telephone! He wants to talk to you—urgently!'

TOO LITTLE, TOO LATE

The sewer beneath the Wizards' Guild building was a horrible place for anybody or anything, except for the rats that lived there—and for the Slitherghoul, of course.

The Slitherghoul, in its primitive way, rather liked the darkness and the slimy wetness of the ancient tunnels. The rodent parts of its brain even recognized certain sections and felt quite at home down there—and the wrathmonk and the warlock parts of its mind were simply glad to be out of the Detention Centre, even if freedom meant slithering around in the darkness of these endless tunnels.

The question was—where to go?

The question was answered very quickly.

It was obvious really. Enough of the thinking

parts of the Slitherghoul's collective brain wanted things that were to be found in one place, and one place only. The creature itself hungered blindly for the great untapped source of mana that Sheepshank's shuttered brain had detected outside the cell; Griswold Gristle, Judge Cedric Hardscrabble, Buford Cudgel, and Frognell Flabbit hungered for revenge; so did Officer Offal—he hated Measle for the way he'd tricked him into his imprisonment; and Toby Jugg (while also interested in taking a cruel revenge on the Stubbs boy) still had the same ambitions that had landed him in prison in the first place—to control a Mallockee and marry a Manafount.

All these desires were to be found in only one location.

Merlin Manor.

But—how to get there? The Slitherghoul explored its available minds again.

From Buford Cudgel, Frognell Flabbit, and Griswold Gristle it learned the location of Merlin Manor. But here, in the darkness of the sewers, it needed a direction to take.

More minds were explored and discarded.

Finally, in the limited brain of a ginger-haired young wrathmonk with grotesquely protruding ears the Slitherghoul found what it needed. The young wrathmonk's name was Mungo MacToad. Mungo MacToad had a strange hobby. He liked drains. Mungo knew a lot about drains and, in particular, how to move about in them. He knew these city sewers like the back of his dirty hand.

This knowledge gave the Slitherghoul a rough direction to take.

Then, switching back to the superior brain of Toby Jugg, the Slitherghoul set off.

And, now that it had somewhere to go, it moved quickly.

Ten metres above it, up on the surface, something strange was happening. A very large rain cloud, black and dense and swirling, moved steadily through the streets of the city. It didn't behave like an ordinary rain cloud at all. For a start, it was so compressed that it looked almost solid—and it hovered only a few feet from the surface of the road. But the oddest thing about this unnatural cloud was the fact that, unlike ordinary clouds, it didn't seem to be governed by the speed or the direction of the wind. Every now and again, it changed direction quite sharply, turning left round a corner at the side of a building, or veering right at a set of traffic lights—just as if it was *following* something.

Which, since it was composed of the tightly compressed individual rain clouds of about a dozen or so even *more* tightly compressed wrathmonks, it was.

That was three days ago. It had taken the Slitherghoul a day and a half to reach the end of the underground pipelines. The sewer down which it had travelled ended at a sewage works out in the country and it was here that the Slitherghoul emerged, late at night under the cover of darkness. Once again, it searched the collective minds inside itself for a new direction.

Toby Jugg supplied it.

When Toby was a young man, he'd enjoyed sailing. Toby knew how to navigate by checking the positions of the stars in the night sky. That night, the sky above the sewage works was particularly clear—apart from a single large black cloud that poured its drenching load down on the Slitherghoul.

Armed now with a new set of directions, the Slitherghoul set off across the fields. On its way, it met—and ran over—a large number of living creatures. Thousands of insects ended up inside the great jellified mass—grasshoppers and beetles and earwigs and flies and many other tiny bugs of every description. Several more mice, a couple of voles, and a sleeping weasel were caught in its sticky folds but, when it came across a herd of cows, the Slitherghoul steered a path round them. Something told it that a cow or two might impede its progress too much, so the Slitherghoul was careful to avoid such large creatures. It also took pains to bypass all human habitation and, when daylight came, it lay quiet and still in a ditch by the side of a cornfield, looking so much like a long deposit of brown mud that, even if somebody had passed close by during that whole day, it was unlikely that the person would have taken any notice of the thing at all.

Then, as night returned, the Slitherghoul slimed its way out of the ditch and started off again.

It shouldn't be too long now, whispered the brain of Griswold Gristle, and Buford Cudgel's mind agreed and so did Frognell Flabbit's. The reason for their conclusion was simple— the Slitherghoul had been oozing its way along the edge of a field and had just passed close by a crossing of two small lanes. There was a signpost there, with the words,'Dimwitch—2 miles' painted on it.

Griswold, Buford, and Frognell all knew from past experience that Merlin Manor was close to the village of Dimwitch. Judge Cedric Hardscrabble should have known as well but the poor old judge was too stupid to remember such things as directions, so he wasn't any help at all.

The Slitherghoul switched back to Toby's mind.

Go faster! it seemed to be whispering—and the Slitherghoul, sensing it was now near the end of its journey, began to glide quickly across a ploughed field, ignoring the ridges and the furrows in the earth beneath its huge, slimy body.

* * *

Measle took the telephone from Nanny Flannel's hand and put it to his ear.

'Hello?'

'Hello, young Measle,' said the familiar, gravelly old voice of Lord Octavo. 'How are things at Merlin Manor?'

'All right, thanks, Lord Octavo,' said Measle. Measle liked Lord Octavo a lot, and he was pretty sure that Lord Octavo liked him right back. The old wizard had been brilliantly helpful to the Stubbs family during the inquiry into the Dragodon adventure and, with Sam Stubbs down at the South Pole, he was now the most senior wizard around.

'Mr Needle and Mr Bland behaving themselves, are they?'

'Yes, they're being very nice. Very helpful, too.'

'Good. Now look, young fellow, you haven't seen anything unusual, have you?'

'What sort of unusual, Lord Octavo?'

'Oh, I don't know . . . people lurking about . . . strangers watching the place . . . odd noises. Anything like that been going on?'

'No. Why?'

'Well, something rather dreadful has happened, I'm afraid. All the prisoners in the Detention Centre seem to have disappeared.'

'*What?*' yelled Measle. 'But—but *how*? And—and *when*?'

'We don't know how. It happened at least three days ago and I'm sorry to say we've only just discovered it. But the point is, several of the escaped wrathmonks aren't exactly friendly towards the Stubbs family, are they? In fact, at least four of them have good reason to want to do you harm, Measle. And then there's Toby Jugg and that big prison guard—'

'*They've* escaped too?'

'I'm afraid so. And there's a creature called a Slitherghoul on the loose as well, but there's no particular reason why it should bother you, so I wouldn't worry about that. I am a bit concerned about those others, though. They know where you live, you see. Are you sure you haven't noticed anything suspicious?'

'Quite sure, Lord Octavo.'

'Good. Well, maybe they'll know better than to come anywhere near you. But if you hear or see anything even a little bit suspicious, I want you to call me immediately. Meanwhile, I'll try and get in touch with your parents; which won't be easy, I'm afraid. The South Pole doesn't have much in the way of a phone service and, what with the convention taking place deep inside a glacier, we haven't been able to make contact with anybody yet. But we'll keep trying. Now, I'd better have a word with Needle and Bland.'

Measle gave the telephone back to Nanny Flannel and went off in search of the two men. As he left the kitchen, he heard Nanny Flannel say, 'What's all this about, Lord Octavo?'

Mr Needle and Mr Bland took the call in Sam's study and, when they came out, their faces were serious.

'Well?' said Nanny Flannel, who had questioned Lord Octavo very closely while Measle was searching for them. What Lord Octavo had told her was making Nanny Flannel quite anxious.

'No cause for concern, Miss Flannel,' said Mr Needle. 'We shall be on special guard tonight.'

'Very special indeed,' said Mr Bland.

'Humph!' said Nanny Flannel, dismissively. 'And what, precisely, does that mean?'

'It means, Miss Flannel,' said Mr Bland, importantly, 'that one of us will be awake throughout the night and patrolling the house and grounds.'

'We shall take it in turns,' said Mr Needle.

'Humph!' said Nanny Flannel again. 'Well, that doesn't impress me at all—it's what you do already.' She shook her head firmly and said, 'No, there'll be no patrolling of the grounds, gentlemen. You can patrol *indoors*, if you must. I want all the doors and windows locked tight and I want everybody safe *inside* the house. Is that quite understood?'

Mr Needle and Mr Bland both opened their mouths to object but a second look at Nanny Flannel's determined face stopped them before they could speak. The two men nodded meekly and then set off round the house. They carefully checked every window and every door and Nanny

Flannel, Measle, and a curious Tinker followed them, watching their every move.

At last, when Nanny Flannel was satisfied that everything was safe and secure, she took them all into the kitchen, sat them down around the table, and dished out supper.

Supper was one of Nanny Flannel's specials—a wonderful steak-and-kidney pie, with mashed potatoes and peas and lots of rich brown gravy. Mr Needle and Mr Bland ate as if they hadn't had a proper meal in a week. Measle sat opposite them, with his back to the kitchen window, and he watched them out of the corner of his eye. In the soft light of the kitchen lamps, the Gloomstains on the tips of their ears were quite prominent, although they still weren't very dark, which meant that the warlock abilities of Mr Needle and Mr Bland were not yet fully developed. While he was thinking about this, it suddenly occurred to Measle that neither Mr Needle nor Mr Bland had, at this precise moment, any magical abilities at all! They'd used up all their mana digging out the swimming pool, which meant that, apart from their human abilities, they weren't going to be much use protecting him—at least, not for another twenty-four hours. Measle wondered briefly if either Mr Needle or Mr Bland had told Lord Octavo about this? Probably not—they wouldn't want to admit they'd used up their mana on something that had nothing to do with security.

It was at this moment that Mr Needle lifted his eyes from his plate and stared past Measle's right ear at the kitchen window behind him.

Mr Needle's face went white. He opened his mouth and screamed in sudden terror and Mr Bland jumped in his seat, looked up from his plate, and he too screamed in panic.

Measle's head whipped round.

There was something there! A horrible white thing, squashed against the glass of the window! The white thing had six pointed yellow teeth and a pair of mad, staring eyes—round eyes, like a dead fish—and some sort of disgusting pink ball seemed to be growing out of the top of its head.

Measle started to laugh. He turned back to see that both men had leaped to their feet, knocking over their chairs in the process. Now they were pressed tightly against the far wall and Mr Bland seemed to be moaning in terror.

'It's all right,' said Measle, trying to suppress his laughter. 'It's only Iggy. We forgot all about him. We usually leave the kitchen door open, you see, so that he can look inside.'

Mr Needle and Mr Bland relaxed visibly. They came forward rather sheepishly and picked up their fallen chairs and sat down on them, but neither man seemed to have much of an appetite left, because they left the rest of their food untouched.

'Can we let Iggy in, Nanny?' said Measle. 'Just for tonight? Just this once?'

'Well, all right,' said Nanny Flannel, reluctantly. 'But just this once, mind. And he's to keep his nasty wet head over a bucket—I'm not mopping up after a lazy little wrathmonk, thank you very much.'

Measle got up and went to the kitchen door and unlocked it. Then he poked his head out into the cool night air and called out, 'You can come inside, Iggy.'

Iggy took his face away from the window and came, a little cautiously, to the open kitchen door.

'I can come inssside, Mumps?'

'Yes, Iggy. Just for tonight, though.'

'Is she goin' to hit me wiv de mop again?' asked Iggy, peering anxiously over Measle's shoulder.

'No, Iggy,' said Measle. 'But you've got to sit with your head over a bucket, otherwise she might.'

'Okey-dokey,' said Iggy, nervously. Keeping a watchful eye on Nanny Flannel, he scuttled into the kitchen sideways, like a crab. Nanny Flannel set a big tin bucket down in one corner of the kitchen. She put it down with a definite CLANG! and Iggy jumped. Then Nanny Flannel fetched a spare kitchen chair and banged it down next to the bucket.

'There,' she said, pointing sternly at the chair and Iggy ducked his head, trotted obediently over, and sat down on it. Then he leaned over, tilting his head sideways so that he could look out into the room, and the drops from his little black rain cloud started to *plink! plink! plink!* into the bottom of the bucket.

There was a short silence while everybody except Measle glared severely at Iggy. Measle couldn't help grinning at him—Iggy looked so funny, bent over the bucket like that as if he was washing his hair.

Iggy, encouraged by being allowed into Nanny Flannel's domain, decided to start a conversation.

'I miss my little fing,' he announced, to nobody in particular. 'When's it comin' back?'

Measle saw Mr Bland and Mr Needle glance at each other, their eyebrows raised in query.

'He means Matilda,' he said. 'He likes Matilda.'

Iggy nodded vigorously, scattering drops of rainwater over the floor. Nanny Flannel cleared her throat loudly and Iggy froze again, holding his head stiffly motionless over the tin bucket.

'She is my ssspecial friend,' said Iggy, being careful not to move a muscle in his neck. 'When is she comin' home, Mumps?'

'Soon, Iggy,' said Measle.

'Good,' said Iggy. Then he said, 'Dere's a funny sssmell outside. It's quite a nice sssmell, actually. I dunno wot is makin' it.'

'A smell?' said Mr Needle, narrowing his eyes. 'What sort of smell?'

'A *nice* sssmell,' said Iggy.

Mr Needle's eyes stopped being narrow and he turned and smiled briefly at Mr Bland. 'The creature obviously likes Miss Flannel's excellent steak-and-kidney pie, Bland,' he said.

'No,' said Iggy, firmly, craning his head round to stare at Mr Needle. 'No, I don't like cake-and-ssskidly pie. Dat is 'orrible ssstuff, dat is. No, I mean anuvver sssmell, wot is *outssside*.'

'What does it smell like, Iggy?' asked Measle, trying to keep this conversation going, because conversations with Iggy were often quite funny. He was having a bet with himself about whether or not either of these brisk, efficient men from the Wizards' Guild ever actually laughed out loud.

'It sssmells like nice dead fings,' said Iggy. 'It sssmells like nice dirty teeth—an' like nice dirty feet—an' like nice sssoggy Sssprussel bouts—an' like old bread all covered wiv dat nice green furry ssstuff—an' like ... er ... um ... uvver fings like dat. I sssmelled it before, once—but I can't 'member when.'

Measle's curiosity got the better of him. He went to the kitchen door and opened it. He stuck his nose out into the cool evening air and took a sniff.

Nothing—just the smell of the countryside at night.

No—there! The faintest whiff of something disgusting—something foul and dead—or perhaps not dead, because there were sharp chemical smells mixed in with all the other horrible stinks. The smell seemed to be coming from a long way off, because there was still only the mildest trace of it on the soft breeze—

Measle pulled his head back into the kitchen. Carefully and calmly, he closed the door and then reached up and slid the heavy iron bolt into place. Then he turned round and said, 'Iggy's right. There's something out there—and I think I know what it is.'

Nanny Flannel, Mr Bland, and Mr Needle all stared at him with looks of deep concern on their faces.

'What did you see, dear?' said Nanny Flannel.

'I didn't see anything, Nanny,' said Measle. 'But I smelt something. And the thing is—I've smelt it before. Like Iggy did—but I *remember* where I smelt it, you see.'

'Where?' asked Mr Needle, sharply.

'In the Detention Centre,' said Measle. 'In the High Security bit, where my mum and dad were locked up. There was something in one of the cells and it smelt just like—well, just like whatever is out there. It's a horrible smell and, if you smell it once, I don't think you could ever forget it.'

'Yeah!' said Iggy, eagerly. 'Yeah—*dat's* where I sssmelt it! In de uvver place where de bad wraffmonks go!'

'But, what is it, dear?' said Nanny Flannel.

'I think it's called a Slitherghoul, Nanny. That's what Lord Octavo called it.'

The blood drained from the cheeks of Mr Needle and Mr Bland. Nanny Flannel's face remained its usual pink but a little crease of worry appeared on her forehead.

'Lord Octavo didn't think we need to worry about that, dear. He seemed more concerned about the escaped wrathmonks.'

Measle didn't answer, because he became aware that Mr Needle and Mr Bland, their heads close together, were holding a frantic, whispered conversation. Measle strained his ears and heard, '*. . . but why would it come here? . . . perhaps the boy is mistaken . . . Lord Octavo mentioned the distinctive odour . . . we should make sure . . .*'

Mr Needle and Mr Bland got up from the kitchen table. Both men plastered sickly smiles on their faces, in an attempt (Measle supposed) to reassure everybody that there was nothing to worry about. Their smiles were so obviously artificial that they had the opposite effect and, for the first time, Measle felt a small knot of fear in his stomach. Mr Needle crossed casually to the kitchen window. He opened it a crack and sniffed. Then, hurriedly, he closed the window again. He turned and threw a nervous glance across the room to Mr Bland—and Measle saw Mr Needle make a tiny nodding motion with his head.

Mr Bland let out a short, nervous laugh.

'I'm sure there's nothing to worry about, Master Measle,' he said. 'It's probably something quite harmless. Now, if you will excuse us, we had better report this to Lord Octavo—just to be on the safe side, you understand.'

Mr Needle and Mr Bland bowed slightly in Nanny Flannel's direction. Mr Needle said, 'An excellent supper, Miss Flannel. Many thanks.' Then he and Mr Bland turned and walked silently out of the kitchen.

There was a moment of silence. Then Nanny Flannel said, very quietly, 'Go and see what they're doing, dear. But don't let them see *you*. Understand?'

Measle understood. He nodded and slipped out of the kitchen, making his way as quietly as he could to the dining room. He crept over to the big jar of jelly beans standing on the sideboard. He took off the glass lid and fished out a couple of yellow ones that lay on the top of the heap. He would have taken more, but there wasn't time to dig for buried yellow beans so, clutching the two tightly in one hand, he tiptoed out of the dining room. Standing in the dark corridor, Measle heard the sound of voices coming from Sam's study. Measle crept along the wall, towards the study door. The door was open and warm lamplight spilled out into the dark passage. Measle edged closer—and now the whispering voices of Mr Needle and Mr Bland were as clear as bells.

'But—what can we *say*, Needle? How can we explain the loss of our mana?'

'We don't explain anything, Bland! Why give ourselves trouble? We simply report the odour and state that we have everything under control! Besides, it's probably nothing more than the scent of a dead animal, in which case we have nothing to fear!'

'But what if it *isn't*, Needle? What if it is in fact this Slitherghoul? The boy seemed fairly sure and so did the wrathmonk—'

'A small boy and an idiotic little wrathmonk! Why believe either one, Bland?'

'But if—'

'But, *if* what they are saying is true, then we simply make sure that the thing stays *outside*, while we remain *inside*, safe and sound! The doors and windows are barred and, as I understand it, the creature is nothing more than a small lump of jelly. I can't see a lump of jelly getting past the locks of Merlin Manor, can you?'

'I suppose not, Needle.'

'Of course not, Bland! Then, tomorrow, when our mana has returned, we will deal with it! It's just a matter of waiting it out, that's all.'

'Then why should we report anything at all, Needle?'

'Because, my dear Bland, Miss Flannel and young Measle and even that ridiculous Niggle creature already know that there might be something amiss. If we don't at least make some sort of report, it might appear that we were neglecting our duties.'

'Yes—yes, I see.'

'Good. Now, we'd better close that door. We don't want anybody eavesdropping, do we?'

Quick as a flash, Measle lifted his hand and popped a yellow jelly bean into his mouth. He bit down on it then stepped silently into the open doorway. Mr Bland was just a few metres away, approaching the door with his hand outstretched towards the handle and Measle, now as invisible as air, stepped sideways, pressing his back against the study wall. Mr Bland's eyes passed over Measle and saw nothing, of course. But he came very close and Measle held his breath as the man closed the door beside him. Then Mr Bland crossed back to where Mr Needle was standing by Sam's desk.

From the moment he'd bitten down on the jelly bean, Measle had started counting down in his head. He'd begun at thirty and now had reached twenty—

Nineteen, eighteen, seventeen—

He watched as Mr Needle took a small black notebook out of his breast pocket.

Sixteen, fifteen, fourteen—

Mr Needle opened the notebook and ran his finger down the page.

Thirteen, twelve, eleven—

Mr Needle picked up the telephone and, consulting the notebook, punched in a number.

Ten, nine, eight—

Mr Needle lifted the telephone to his ear.

Seven, six, five—

A puzzled look crossed Mr Needle's face and he took the phone receiver away from his ear and shook it gently.

Four, three, two—

Measle popped the second jelly bean into his mouth and, with the thought that in exactly half a minute he'd be visible again, started counting down from thirty.

Twenty-nine, twenty-eight, twenty-seven—

Mr Needle was jiggling the phone rest.

'Is something wrong, Needle?' asked Mr Bland, licking his lips nervously.

Twenty-six, twenty-five, twenty-four—

'There appears to be no dialling tone,' said Mr Needle.

'No dialling tone?' Mr Bland's voice contained a tremor of fear.

'None. It's dead. Listen for yourself.'

Mr Needle passed the telephone receiver to Mr Bland, who held it tight to his ear. Then Measle watched as Mr Bland, with shaking hands, slowly put the receiver back on its rest.

Fourteen, thirteen, twelve—

'Perhaps a coincidence?' muttered Mr Bland.

'Perhaps,' said Mr Needle. 'But we should assume the worst, Bland. Come along—we must be extra vigilant now.'

Measle pressed himself against the wall by the door as Mr Needle and Mr Bland walked quickly across the room towards him. Mr Needle opened the door and the two men hurried out—and Measle heaved a big sigh of relief, because his invisibility wore off only a few seconds after the men had gone.

Measle quickly went to his father's desk. He picked up the phone and held it to his ear.

Nothing.

Sometimes, the sound of *nothing* can be rather frightening.

This, Measle decided, was one of those times.

And then he decided it was an even *more* frightening time when, thirty seconds later, all the lights went out and he was plunged into pitch darkness.

THE SIEGE

It had been many months since Griswold Gristle, Buford Cudgel, and Frognell Flabbit had visited Merlin Manor, but they remembered it well.

After the Dragodon had been destroyed, together with his great dragon Arcturion, Griswold, Buford, Frognell, and Judge Cedric Hardscrabble had nothing left to lose. So, seeking revenge against the Stubbs family, they had ridden up Merlin Manor's long gravel drive on Cudgel's big black motorbike. They had attacked Sam Stubbs with every spell at their disposal. Shortly afterwards (and to their horrified surprise) they had found themselves bundled uncomfortably together in a magical silver net and carted away in a white van, which had driven them straight to the Detention Centre deep in the basement of the Wizards' Guild, where they'd stayed locked up ever since.

Their visit to Merlin Manor had been short and not at all sweet—but three of the wrathmonks had held a picture of the great house in their heads for all the long months of their imprisonment. Poor old Judge Cedric's mind was as fuzzy as ever, so he remembered almost nothing—but the others had minds that, while insane in their wrathmonk way, still worked reasonably well. Now, in front of them, the familiar shape of Merlin Manor was silhouetted against the night sky.

The Slitherghoul had stopped in a field about three hundred metres from the house, looking at the dark building through the eyes of Griswold, Buford, and Frognell and sensing the three wrathmonks' excitement at finally arriving at their destination. Then the Slitherghoul had switched to Toby Jugg's brain—and Toby Jugg was thinking something else entirely. Toby was thinking about how clever it would be to cut Merlin Manor off from the rest of the world.

The Slitherghoul had moved, using Toby's eyes to search. It started to look for a pole—a tall wooden pole, probably made from a pine tree, with many wires connected to the top of it.

There! At the edge of the field, where it ran by the side of the long gravel drive! A tall pole—

The Slitherghoul had slimed across the field at full speed. When it arrived at the base of the telephone pole, it reached up a long thin section of itself, stretching upwards towards the wires. It curled the tip of its jelly tentacle round the wires and pulled hard. For a moment, the wires strained and held—then they were wrenched out of their sockets with a twang! falling to the ground in a twisted heap.

Exactly a minute and a half later, Mr Needle had picked up the telephone in Sam Stubbs's study.

A dead telephone, because it was no longer connected to the outside world.

There were other cables up there at the top of the pine pole. Thicker cables. They would offer more resistance—*but they must come down too!* Under Toby's guidance, the Slitherghoul had reached for them—

First the telephone—now this! thought Measle, as he felt his way along the dark passage towards the kitchen. A little light from a full moon and a scattering of stars came through a skylight in the ceiling, so Measle could just about make out where he was, which meant he could hurry along a little faster than if the darkness had been total. By the time he got back to the kitchen, the ever-practical Nanny Flannel had lit several candles and stuck them in the necks of empty bottles and put them round the room. By their flickering light, Measle saw that Nanny Flannel was standing over Mr

Needle and Mr Bland, who were both sitting at the kitchen table, looking rather nervous.

'But what exactly *is* this creature?' Nanny Flannel was saying as Measle came into the room. 'And what is it doing here?'

Mr Needle and Mr Bland exchanged uncomfortable looks. Mr Needle was the first to speak.

'Nobody knows for sure what it is, Miss Flannel. Or what it does. However, I am certain that it poses no particular threat. It is, after all, quite small—'

'How small?' demanded Nanny Flannel, fiercely.

'As I understand, about the size of a coffee table, Miss Flannel. And made of some sort of jelly. Really nothing to fear.'

'Don't tell me what to fear and what not to fear, Mr Needle!' said Nanny Flannel sharply. 'There's an unknown something-or-other out there in the darkness, and now all the power is gone and we've no lights—'

Measle cleared his throat loudly and, when everybody had turned and was looking at him, he said, 'It's not just the lights, Nanny. The telephone doesn't work either.'

'What?' said Nanny Flannel, her eyes wide.

'Mr Bland and Mr Needle know,' said Measle. He turned to the two men and said, 'Don't you?'

'Um . . . there does appear to be a malfunction on the line,' admitted Mr Needle, reluctantly. 'I'm sure it's only temporary, though.'

'Nothing to worry about,' said Mr Bland, his eyes darting uneasily round the kitchen.

'Nuffink to worry about!' sang Iggy cheerfully, from his corner of the kitchen.

Then, without any warning, it began to rain heavily just outside the outer kitchen door. It didn't sound like ordinary rain. This rain sounded as if it was torrential—a steady, roaring sound of very big drops of water, very close together, hurtling through the night sky and crashing to the ground below. Before anybody could say anything, there came another sound—and it was just as frighteningly strange as the rain. A heavy, squelchy, sloppy-sounding THUMP! against the kitchen door. At exactly the same moment, the kitchen was flooded by the most horrible smell Nanny Flannel had ever smelt.

'Ugh!' she exclaimed. 'What on earth is that?'

'That's the Slitherghoul, Nanny!' yelled Measle. 'And I think it's a lot bigger than a coffee table!'

They all heard it now. Through the thunder of the rain, a slithering, sliding, grating sound came from outside as the Slitherghoul pressed its huge, slimy body against the outer wall of the kitchen. A yellowish-greenish-brownish slime spread across the window and the kitchen door creaked from the weight that was now pressing against it.

The Slitherghoul had started to look for a way in.

Mr Needle and Mr Bland jumped to their feet. They both had very frightened faces. Nanny

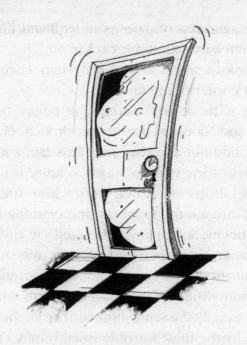

Flannel glared at them and said, 'Well, what are you doing just standing there? You're supposed to be guarding us all! *Do* something!'

'They can't, Nanny!' said Measle, raising his voice a little, because the slithering and the creaking sounds were getting louder. 'They can't— because they used up all their mana helping me with the swimming pool! They haven't got any magic left!'

Nanny Flannel's face darkened with fury. She took a couple of steps towards the men and Measle saw that she was going to give them one of her special scoldings. Nanny Flannel's special scoldings were very frightening. Only once had

Measle ever been on the receiving end of one—when he'd tried making pancakes on his own and had only succeeded in making a terrible mess of Nanny Flannel's kitchen—and he knew how awful they were. He felt suddenly a little sorry for Mr Needle and Mr Bland. Before Nanny Flannel could open her mouth and start, he blurted out, 'It's not their fault, Nanny! I asked them to help!'

Nanny Flannel took no notice. She lifted her finger and started to wag it under the noses of the two warlocks.

'You silly, silly little men!' she stormed. 'If you wanted to help, why didn't you just roll up your sleeves and dig in the ordinary way? How dare you waste your mana like that! How *dare* you!'

''Ow dare you!' yelled Iggy, who was getting wildly overexcited by all the noise and confusion. He had a big grin on his pale little face and the end of his long nose kept twitching—because the smell that was now flooding the kitchen was really, really *nice*! He'd lifted his head away from the bucket and now a little pool of water from his rain cloud was gathering on the kitchen floor.

Tinker was adding to the uproar by barking at the top of his lungs. He was facing the kitchen door, every hair on his body bristling with fury, every tooth in his head bared and gleaming. *Something out there! Something really, really smelly! Don't like it! Dangerous! Make it go away!*

'Miss Flannel—' said Mr Needle, wanting to start a long explanation about why it wasn't their fault that they had no mana—but the noise drowned out his voice. Outside, the Slitherghoul was starting to flex its great strength against the door and the window and now the timbers and the glass in both were creaking loudly at the strain. Inside, Tinker's barking was reaching fever pitch and Iggy had begun to prance around the kitchen in a strange, mad, hopping dance, shouting as loudly as he could, "OW DARE YOU! 'OW DARE YOU! 'OW *DARE* YOU!'

The last thing Nanny Flannel needed right now was a wet, overexcited wrathmonk dancing round her kitchen! She turned, marched over to where the mop was leaning against the kitchen wall and grabbed it.

'Stop this nonsense right now, Iggy!' she snapped.

Iggy was far too agitated to take any notice. He jumped up onto the kitchen table and started to hop about, his feet trampling all over the remains of supper. Several plates shattered and he kicked the pieces to the floor, all the time shouting, "OW DARE YOU! 'OW DARE YOU! *'OW DARE YOU!'*

Nanny Flannel realized that Iggy was so manic that he was out of control—and there was only one way to get him back to his senses. She marched across the kitchen, took careful aim, and swung the mop at Iggy's backside.

Whack! it went—and, with a yelp of surprise, Iggy jumped a metre into the air, clutching his bottom with both hands. A look of pure terror flooded his face. He stopped dancing and shouting. He dropped down from the table, scuttled to where Measle was standing and tried to hide behind him.

'You sssaid she wouldn't hit me wiv de mop, Mumps,' he whispered accusingly into Measle's ear. 'But she did—'an now I fink she is goin' to do it again!'

Nanny Flannel was glaring fiercely in their direction, the mop still held threateningly over her head, when suddenly the first pane of glass in the tall, floor-to-ceiling kitchen window cracked and splintered and fell to the floor with a shattering *crash!*

Everybody froze, staring with growing horror at the window. The whole frame was bending inwards, the wooden mouldings cracking, the panes of glass splintering—and the smell was now becoming almost more than anybody could bear without being sick.

Tinker's barking was becoming more and more frenzied, because *his* highly sensitive nose was being overwhelmed by the power of the stink. He couldn't believe anything could smell this strong! And this bad! Usually, Tinker didn't think anything smelt bad—just *interesting*. But this pong was beginning to choke him.

Mr Needle and Mr Bland put their hands to their faces and pinched their noses shut between finger and thumb. Apart from that, they didn't move. They were rooted to the spot and even their eyes seemed to be paralysed with terror.

Not so Nanny Flannel. The moment she heard the first pane of glass crash to the floor, she had turned and faced the horror, the mop held at the ready, as if it was a great two-handed sword.

'Measle dear!' she called, her old voice steady and firm. 'Measle, get out of here! Get out and lock the door behind you! Then run, dear! Run as fast as you can!'

Measle didn't move. He had no intention of leaving Nanny Flannel, or Iggy, or Tinker to their fates. He didn't mind so much about Mr Needle and Mr Bland, but he wasn't about to desert his friends! Besides, his curiosity was as strong as his fear. He wanted to see what this thing was—

He didn't have long to wait.

The pressure against the window was growing by the moment and, in the few seconds left before the whole frame gave way, Measle saw a very strange and horribly frightening thing.

He saw, by the light of the kitchen candles, that the whole of the outside of the window was covered by a thick film of yellowish-greenish-brownish slime which seemed to pulse and flex and slither against the weakening window. And then, without warning, a head—*a human head*—seemed to float past, buried deep within the transparent jelly—

And the head had eyes that seemed to be staring straight at Measle.

Eyes that glittered with a cold, calculating intelligence; the face framed by long, flowing hair and a short beard—

The face suddenly grinned at him. And, in that extraordinary moment, Measle knew who it was.

It was Toby Jugg.

THE WALLS ARE BREACHED!

There wasn't time for Measle to think about what this horrible sight meant, because a second later the entire window frame gave way with a creaking, splintering CRASH! It fell onto the kitchen floor in a jumble of broken wood and glass and the Slitherghoul fell in with it—or, at least, that part of the creature which had been pressing so hard against the glass. The rest of it was still outside but slowly it began to ooze its way through the gaping hole, adding to the slimy mass of jelly that lay in a great pile on top of the remains of the window.

Nanny Flannel took two paces forward, raised the mop high over her head and then brought it down hard on the leading edge of the Slitherghoul.

'Take that, you nasty thing!' she shouted. 'Take that! And that! And that!'

The stink inside the kitchen was overwhelming and Measle began to feel quite sick. Then he heard Iggy muttering in his ear.

'Coo! Dat sssmells ever ssso nice, don't it, Mumps? An' look at Miss Fwannel—she is bashin' de fing wiv de mop! I'm jussst glad she's not bashin' me!'

The Slitherghoul was getting bigger, as more and more of it slimed its way through the smashed window. It took no notice of Nanny Flannel's flailing mop, nor of Tinker's furious barking, not even when he darted forward and tried to nip at the very edge of the jelly. Instead, it simply oozed more and more of itself into the kitchen, lumping its enormous shape higher and higher, until the top of it brushed against the ceiling. Then, when most of it was inside the room, it acted—

Quick as a flash, before Nanny Flannel could react, the Slitherghoul whipped out a jelly tentacle and grabbed the old lady round her stout waist. It dragged her towards itself—

'Run, Measle! RUN!' yelled Nanny Flannel— then, a second later, the slime enveloped her and she was gone.

Measle stared with horror at the spot where Nanny Flannel had disappeared. It was the worst thing he'd ever seen—this great, stinking mound of jelly had simply swallowed his beloved Nanny

Flannel whole! She was gone—the one person other than his mum and dad whom he trusted with his life! And now all that was left between him and an identical fate were two useless warlocks, a wrathmonk who thought the smell of the monster was nice—and a faithful but very *small* dog!

Tinker kept up his furious barrage of barks and now had got up the courage to take several more nips at the leading edge of the jelly.

Poo! It tastes as bad as it smells! Horrible thing—get out of here!

Inside the Slitherghoul, something very interesting was taking place. For the last few moments, it had found itself using a different brain—

The reason the Slitherghoul was now looking out at the world through eyes that didn't belong to Toby Jugg was because of the extraordinary strength of Nanny Flannel's mind. The old lady had always been able to get everybody—even stubborn Sam Stubbs—to do exactly what she wanted them to do, so—after the initial shock of finding herself engulfed (*and then finding herself apparently still alive!*)—Nanny Flannel instantly tried to take charge.

For a few moments, she succeeded. She saw that Tinker was in imminent danger of being grabbed himself, because a finger of jelly was starting to extend towards him. Nanny Flannel, using all her power to overcome whatever was directing the creature, managed to pull the tentacle back and away from Tinker—

Instantly, she felt another mind—one at least as powerful as hers—push the tentacle forward again.

No! she thought. *No, I won't allow it!*

Once again, Nanny Flannel strained her brain—and, once again, the tentacle withdrew. Unfortunately, this action made Tinker even braver, because he assumed that the tentacle was pulling away from him because it was afraid, so he darted forward again, seized the smelly lump of jelly between his jaws and started to shake it furiously.

Instantly, Nanny Flannel's mind was overpowered—not just by Toby Jugg's but by several others' too. Nanny Flannel had no idea who these others could be, but Buford Cudgel, Griswold Gristle, Frognell Flabbit, and Officer Offal (all of whom had reason to hate the little terrier) joined their minds to Toby Jugg's and overwhelmed the thoughts of Nanny Flannel.

A second jelly tentacle whipped out and wrapped itself around Tinker. Tinker yelped and struggled—but then he too disappeared inside the Slitherghoul.

'NO!' screamed Measle.

It's not possible! he thought miserably. *My two best friends, gone! Just like that!*

Behind him, Measle heard Iggy snigger. Then he heard the little wrathmonk whisper, 'Coo! De nasssty old lady is gone! And de nasssty little doggie too! Coo! Disss is Iggy's lucky day!'

Measle was as unhappy as he'd ever been in his life, but he suddenly felt very angry too, particularly—at this precise moment—with Iggy Niggle. He was about to turn on the little wrathmonk when he saw what Mr Needle and Mr Bland were doing.

The two men were scrambling towards the door that led to the rest of the house. They each held a candle in a bottle. Mr Needle got to the door first. He grabbed the handle and wrenched it open, then he and Mr Bland, who was fighting to get past him, tumbled together out into the passage beyond. Measle saw Mr Needle push Mr Bland to one side—then he saw Mr Needle take hold of the edge of the door and, with one sweeping movement, slam it shut!

Measle reacted. He forced his legs into action—running quickly across the kitchen towards the door.

But, as he got close, he heard the distinct sound of a key turning in a lock—

Click.

Measle slammed against the door. He grasped the handle, turned it, and pulled hard—but the door didn't budge! He was trapped! Mr Needle and Mr Bland were so frantically desperate to get away from the monster in the kitchen that they had betrayed him!

'Open the door!' yelled Measle—but all he heard

was the pounding of two pairs of polished black shoes as Mr Needle and Mr Bland raced away down the corridor.

Measle turned round. If he was going to be swallowed by the Slitherghoul, he wanted to face it head-on.

The Slitherghoul seemed to be having some sort of problem. One minute it was pushing out a great jelly tentacle across the kitchen floor towards Measle, the next the same tentacle seemed to quiver and then withdraw, as if the huge, shapeless thing was unable to make up its mind.

Which was exactly what was happening.

Inside the Slitherghoul, a battle was raging. A battle of minds. On one side were the brains of Toby Jugg, Officer Offal, Griswold Gristle, Buford Cudgel, Frognell Flabbit, and Judge Cedric Hardscrabble—not to mention the rest of the wrathmonks from the Detention Centre, all of whom were quite happy to help in a venture, just as long as they were being really nasty and cruel to somebody.

On the other side of the battle stood Nanny Flannel. She wasn't entirely alone. Corky Pretzel, the young guard from the Detention Centre, was on her side. Corky was a good man but, unfortunately, he didn't possess a particularly strong mind. All the same, he knew instinctively which side he should be on and he matched his mind with Nanny Flannel's and, together, they fought as hard as they could—helped in no small way by the furious and determined doggy brain of Tinker, who certainly knew which side *he* was on.

But it was a losing battle. There were only three good minds on the friendly side and one of them belonged to a dog—with the result that, every time the Slitherghoul pulled itself back from attacking Measle, a moment later it would advance again. Each of these advances was twice the length of its retreats, which meant that the huge mound of jelly was moving, in a strange, jerky fashion, steadily across the kitchen floor towards Measle and Iggy Niggle.

There was no way out. The Slitherghoul's mass lay between them and the kitchen door and the *other* door—the one at his back which led to the rest of the house—was locked tight.

There must be something I can do! thought Measle desperately. *Or something Iggy can do—*

Of course! Iggy's got a spell! His lock-opening spell! It's the only one he can do, but it's perfect for this moment!

Measle whirled round and grabbed Iggy by the front of his old suit.

'Do your spell, Iggy! Do it now!'

Iggy wriggled uncomfortably in Measle's grip. 'Dat won't do nuffink on dat smelly fing,' he argued, his hooked nose twitching ecstatically.

'On the *door*, Iggy! Do your spell on the *door*!'

The Slitherghoul was inching closer and closer.

It extended a jelly tentacle towards Measle and Iggy, then, an instant later, it pulled it back inside itself again. The great mass jerked forward another half metre, then pulled back a little, before slithering forward again—

'On de door, Mumps?' said Iggy, in a puzzled voice. 'Wot door?'

'*This* one, Iggy!' yelled Measle, turning Iggy round and shoving him hard up against the wooden panels.

'Oh—dis one,' muttered Iggy. 'Okey-dokey. 'Ow many jelly beans will you give me?'

'A *squillion*!' shouted Measle, using Iggy's favourite number.

Iggy nodded eagerly and then looked expectantly at Measle.

'When you've done the spell, Iggy! I'll give them to you when you've done the spell!'

The stink in the kitchen was terrible. Measle glanced over his shoulder. The Slitherghoul was very close now and had, in fact, stopped moving forward. All it needed to do was extend a tentacle—

Inside the Slitherghoul, Nanny Flannel's brain screamed '*NO!*' It was a silent scream, of course— but a very powerful one. Corky Pretzel added his own thoughts and (in his own doggy way) so did Tinker—and the tentacle quivered and then withdrew again.

NO! GET HIM! shrieked Toby Jugg's mind and a

whole chorus of wrathmonk thoughts joined in: *Get him! Get him! Get him! Get him! GET HIM!*

And then Measle heard Iggy shout, '*Unka-sssshhhriek gorgogasssshhh plurgholips!*'—and, without waiting a moment longer, Measle leaned past Iggy and grabbed the door handle. He twisted it hard and pulled even harder—and the door flew open! Measle pushed Iggy through the gap and then jumped through himself, and, as he did so, he thought he felt the lightest touch of something on his shoulder.

Once through, Measle turned and, grabbing the edge of the door, he pulled it as hard as he could. The door closed with a *bang!* right on the tip of a long jelly tentacle that was waving its way through the air, headed straight for Measle's head. The tip of the tentacle was cut cleanly away from the rest of the slimy thing. It fell to the floor with a squishy plop—then Measle watched as it turned away from him and Iggy. It slithered across the floor like a little worm and, flattening itself to the thickness of a slice of bread, it wriggled under the door and back into the kitchen.

Measle quickly turned the key in the lock and heard the bolt slide home with a satisfying click.

'Ssscuse me, Mumps,' said Iggy, in a whiny voice. 'Ssscuse *me*—but if you want dis door *locked*, den why did you make me do my ssspell to *open* it? Huh? Huh?'

'That thing was going to eat us, Iggy!' hissed Measle.

Iggy shook his head firmly. 'No, it wasn't,' he said, his big round fishy eyes glowing in the darkness of the passage. 'It only eats nasssty fings, like Miss Fwannel and de doggie. It won't eat us, coz we is *nice*.'

Iggy often made silly assertions like this and Measle had learned not to argue with him. Besides, there were more pressing matters to attend to—*literally*. There was a squishy thump against the door and Measle heard, quite distinctly, the sound of the timbers creaking.

'Come on, Iggy!' he said, grabbing the wrathmonk's damp hand. 'Come on—that door won't hold for long!'

Together, Measle and Iggy tore down the dark passage. They passed the open door of the dining room—

Measle skidded to a stop and Iggy bumped hard into his back.

'Ow!' said Iggy and was about to start a long, whiny complaint about how he didn't like it when people stopped suddenly without any warning, when Measle grabbed him and dragged him back to the dining room door. He pulled Iggy over to the sideboard. Then, letting go of him, Measle took hold of the glass jar full of jelly beans and yanked off the top.

'Hold out your hands, Iggy!' he said. 'I'm going to give you your squillion jelly beans!'

'Wot—now?' said Iggy, in a surprised voice. It wasn't often that he got what he asked for quite as quickly as this.

'Yes! Right now. We're going to fill your pockets full!'

'And dat is a sssquillion, is it?' asked Iggy, a little suspiciously.

'Yes! When your pockets are full, that's a squillion!'

Iggy grinned in the darkness. He'd always wanted to know just exactly how many a squillion was—and now he knew.

The little wrathmonk held out both his hands and Measle poured a stream of multi-coloured jelly beans into them. Iggy stuffed the beans into both his trouser pockets and then held out his hands for more.

Measle went on pouring—and Iggy went on pocket-stuffing—until there was no room in any of his clothes for more.

'That's it, Iggy,' said Measle firmly, because Iggy, with his pockets bulging, was holding his hands out again. 'That's your squillion jelly beans.'

From down the passage, there was the sound of wood cracking. The kitchen door was beginning to give way. Hurriedly, Measle tipped the small number of remaining jelly beans into his own hands and, as quickly as he could, he sorted out the paler yellow beans and stuffed them into his pockets.

'Come on, Iggy!'

Measle and Iggy darted out of the dining room. Measle took a quick look down the dark corridor. There, at the far end, was a little ragged circle of light. As he watched, the circle grew suddenly bigger and there was the noise of wood being torn apart. In a flash, Measle realized what was happening—the bolts and hinges on the kitchen door had held against the Slitherghoul's attack and now the monster was trying to rip a hole in the panels that would be large enough to let it squeeze through.

Measle grabbed Iggy's hand. It felt sticky. Measle peered at Iggy in the gloom and saw that the wrathmonk's mouth was stuffed full and Iggy's jaws were chomping up and down. The thin little face was wreathed in a blissful smile.

'Don't eat them all at once, Iggy!' hissed Measle. 'Save some for later!'

Iggy shrugged and then brought his other hand close to his face. Measle saw that it was full of jelly beans. Iggy peered at the heap and then started picking out one, then two, then a third bean from the pile. These he stuffed into the small outer breast pocket of his damp and shabby suit. Suddenly aware that Measle was staring at him, Iggy muttered, 'I is pickin' out de green ones, Mumps. I don't like de green ones.'

Measle wondered how Iggy could possibly see which ones were green and which ones weren't—in this gloom, all the jelly beans looked pretty much the same colour to him. But there was no time to ask, because at the far end of the corridor there was another ripping, wrenching, tearing sound—and Measle suddenly remembered that he'd heard that sound before, when Basil Tramplebone had become a giant cockroach and, using the creature's sharp, curved claws, had tried to dig his way into the plywood tunnel where Measle and his friends were hiding.

Then—as now—that sound meant it was time to go.

Measle pulled Iggy after him as they ran away towards the door of Sam Stubbs's study. The door was closed, but Measle saw a faint sliver of yellow light beneath it. Measle hurled himself against the door and it flew open and he and Iggy tumbled into the room.

Mr Needle and Mr Bland, clutching their two candles, were huddled together on the far side, behind Sam's big desk—and their eyes opened very wide when they saw Measle and Iggy Niggle.

'Why—M-Master M-Measle!' stammered Mr Bland. 'You've escaped! Er . . . m-may I b-be the first to offer m-my congratulations—'

'I s-second that!' announced Mr Needle, smiling insincerely.

'We—we were just trying to see if the telephone was working again,' said Mr Bland.

'Unfortunately, it doesn't appear to be,' said Mr Needle. He was about to say more but the look on Measle's face stopped him dead.

Measle took a step into the room and glared at the two men. Then he said, 'You locked me in there! You locked me and Iggy in the kitchen!'

'No, no,' said Mr Needle, in a shocked voice. 'We would never do that, would we, Bland?'

'Never, Needle!' said Mr Bland and he smiled a sickly smile and started to fiddle with the telephone.

Measle shook his head in disgust. No matter how nice these two men tried to be, they still were never to be trusted. He said, 'Well, I thought you'd like to know that the Slitherghoul is just about through the kitchen door and is going to be heading this way any second! So perhaps you ought not to stay in here, because this door won't hold it back either!'

'An' den it will eat you,' announced Iggy triumphantly. 'Dat old Sssquiffypoo will eat you *bofe*—coz you ain't nice!'

A waft of stinking air tickled Measle's nose. He darted to the open study door and peered down the passage. He could just make out a section of jelly that was starting to ooze its way through the ragged hole in the door. Measle turned and looked over his shoulder at the two frightened men.

'Iggy and I are going now,' he said, quite quietly. 'Do you want to come with us?'

Mr Needle looked at Mr Bland and Mr Bland looked at Mr Needle. Then they both looked at Measle and shook their heads in unison.

'You are welcome to join *us*, Master Measle,' said Mr Needle. 'We intend to barricade the door.'

'We shall use the available furniture,' said Mr Bland, pointing at the big desk.

'I don't think that'll stop it,' said Measle. 'Not for long.' He glanced again down the passage and saw that most of the Slitherghoul seemed to be through the hole in the door. Its jelly mass filled the end of the corridor right up to the ceiling.

'Well, good luck,' said Measle, knowing that he didn't really mean it. 'Come on, Iggy.' He and Iggy backed out into the corridor; Mr Needle crossed the room and, with a small, fearful smile, the man shut the door firmly in their faces.

Measle and Iggy ran further down the passage, until they reached the great staircase of Merlin Manor. There were a lot of windows here in the hallway and Measle could see everything quite clearly. The only question was—which way to go?

Up had always been the direction Measle had chosen in the past. He'd climbed the Ferris wheel at the Isle of Smiles, he and Toby had climbed the immensely tall spiral staircase inside the Wizards' Guild—*and perhaps this Slitherghoul thing can't climb stairs!*—but, even as he thought that, Measle guessed it probably wasn't true. All the same, up seemed better than sideways or forwards at this moment, so he grabbed Iggy's skinny elbow and said, 'We're going upstairs, Iggy! Come on!'

Iggy had never been upstairs at Merlin Manor. He'd hardly ever been inside Merlin Manor at all and the idea of actually going upstairs was very exciting. He reached into his trouser pocket, pulled out a handful of jelly beans and, making sure there were no green ones among them, he stuffed them into his mouth.

Together they hurried up the great curving staircase, and, all the time, Measle was wondering, *And then what? Where do we go next?*

The moment Mr Needle had closed the door in Measle's face, he and Mr Bland had started to build the barricade. They had shot the bolt at the top of the door and then, together, they had manhandled Sam's big desk across the room and shoved it tight against the door. Then they had moved everything else—the chairs, the filing cabinets, the bookshelves, and even the fine Persian rug—and had piled them up in a great jumbled heap on top of and round the base of the desk. When there was nothing left in the room that could be moved, Mr Needle and Mr Bland huddled together on the bare floor, their backs pressed against the wall. They held their candles in trembling hands and waited.

They didn't wait for long.

The Slitherghoul pulled the last of itself through the ragged hole in the kitchen door. Buford Cudgel's head—which was bigger than the head of anybody else inside the monster—had become stuck for a minute and this had slowed down the Slitherghoul a lot. But now the Slitherghoul was free and clear.

But a supporting beam over the kitchen door was now badly damaged.

This beam was made of oak and it was very old. Ever since Merlin Manor had been built, the beam had held up much of the stone wall above it. Over the years it had slowly weakened, and now, with the sudden stresses and strain put on it by the forceful blundering of the Slitherghoul, the beam quite suddenly gave way.

There was a creaking, cracking sound, quickly followed by a thunderous roar that lasted about three seconds—then a rattling noise as small stones fell and tumbled down a great mound of dusty rubble—then, silence.

The Slitherghoul ignored the whole event. It was intent on what was in *front* of it, not what was *behind*.

It moved on stickily down the dark passage. It saw, through Toby's eyes, the faint glowing line of light at the base of the study door.

Somebody's in there! thought Toby's brain. *Possibly the boy! Or perhaps even his baby sister, the fabulous Mallockee!*

The Slitherghoul pressed the great weight of its body against the door and felt it bend inwards. *This one will give way quickly*, thought the collective minds of Toby and the wrathmonks, because it's easier to break down a door that opens *away* from you.

Inside the study, Mr Needle and Mr Bland had heard the thunder when the kitchen beam gave way, and now they heard the creaking of the door timbers and they huddled a little closer.

'Why has it not gone after the boy?' hissed Mr Needle into Mr Bland's ear.

'The light!' whispered Mr Bland. 'It sees the light under the door!' Both men took deep breaths and blew out their candles, plunging the room into absolute darkness.

But it was too late. The Slitherghoul was now bracing the rear section of its body against the floor, walls, and ceiling of the corridor and was beginning to press harder against the door. The wood creaked and the nails in the frame began slowly to tear away from the wall with a squealing sound. A moment later, the whole structure broke free and was pushed forward into the room, shifting the desk backwards a metre and dislodging the piled-up furniture, so that it all crashed thunderously to the bare floor.

Mr Needle and Mr Bland crawled into the furthest corner of the study. The room, with its heavy curtains drawn, was pitch dark and they couldn't see a thing. But they could smell—and the stink was so terrible that it made Mr Bland suddenly cough and choke.

'Quiet, Bland!' whispered Mr Needle. 'It will hear us!'

The Slitherghoul didn't need to hear anything. It pushed the heavy desk to one side, as if it was no bigger than a matchbox. Then it extended a fat jelly tentacle and slid it across the room. Slowly, carefully, it felt its way along one wall—then another—*ah! There! Something alive!*

Mr Bland gasped as the tip of the tentacle touched his ankle. Then, in the pitch darkness, he screamed as the tentacle wrapped itself round his leg and started to drag him across the floor.

'Needle! Help me!' he shrieked. But Mr Needle didn't help him. Mr Needle pulled his own body into a tight, trembling ball and he crouched in the corner, shuddering with terror and trying to make himself as small as he possibly could. In his paralysed mind, there was a tiny spark of hope—*Perhaps the thing will be content with Bland? Perhaps it won't come after me as well? Perhaps it thinks that Bland was alone?*

Mr Needle heard Mr Bland scream steadily all the way across the room. Then there was a squelching sound and the screaming stopped abruptly. For a moment there was silence and Mr Needle's hopes rose a little. Then he heard it again—the unmistakable sound of a slimy, slithering tentacle, coming nearer and nearer and nearer—and suddenly Mr Needle lost all control of his mind and started screaming himself, well before the tip of the tentacle even touched him—

Standing at the top of the staircase and leaning over the banister, Measle and Iggy listened to the distant screaming. It was a horrible sound and it was something of a relief to Measle when it suddenly stopped. But Iggy needed an explanation.

'Wot's 'appening, Mumps?' he whispered, fearfully.

'I—I think it's got Mr Needle and Mr Bland,' said Measle.

'Oh, goody,' said Iggy. 'I don't like dose men. Dey is quite nasssty.'

Measle turned on Iggy and hissed angrily at him.

'Sometimes, Iggy, you make me so *cross*! Mr Needle and Mr Bland were guarding us! Well, they were *supposed* to be guarding us—and now they've gone! And so have Nanny and Tinker! Now there's nobody left but you and me! And that thing is going to come for us next! Don't you understand? It'll be coming for *us*!'

As the echoes of his voice died away, Measle became aware of another sound—a slushy, squelching, slithery noise, coming from somewhere below him. He leaned over the balcony and peered down into the gloomy stairwell.

The Slitherghoul had reached the foot of the stairs and was starting to slime its way up the first of the steps. Even in the dim light, Measle could see that it was now enormous. Not only that, but the thing seemed to be moving faster than before—it slid smoothly up the stairs, the individual steps causing its great jelly body to ripple as it passed over them.

'Come on, Iggy,' muttered Measle. 'It's moving quite fast. We've got to stay ahead of it.'

'Where is we goin'?' said Iggy, peering doubtfully over the banister at the approaching mound of jelly. 'Where *can* we go, Mumps?'

'I don't know, Iggy,' said Measle. And whether it was the terrible smell that wafted up the stairs, or whether it was the awful realization that he really had no idea what to do, Measle suddenly felt quite sick.

There was a cracking sound beneath them, then the landing on which they were standing shuddered and lurched sideways, nearly knocking Iggy and Measle off their feet. The cracking sound grew louder—then there was a deafening BANG! quickly followed by a thunderous CRASH! from far below. Both Measle and Iggy grabbed the railing and leaned over, staring downwards.

Most of the bottom half of the staircase was gone. It lay in a great, dusty pile on the floor of the hall. For a moment, Measle had the happy thought that the Slitherghoul had fallen with it. But then his eyes became accustomed to the darkness and he saw, to his horror, that the creature was only a few metres below him. At the moment when its great weight had caused the staircase to crack and then break (at its weakest point, which was right in the middle) the Slitherghoul had managed to shoot out two thick tentacles of jelly and wrap them around the remains of the banister rail above it. The stairs had fallen away beneath it, leaving the Slitherghoul hanging in mid-air—and now it was slowly but steadily dragging itself upwards. Once it reached safety, it lay still for a moment, as if to make sure that no sudden movement on its part would cause the rest of the staircase to fall as well. Then, when nothing happened, it began to slither upwards again.

Measle realized it would only be a matter of seconds before the Slitherghoul was on them—

and, in the same moment, he knew that there was really only one place they could go now. There were no doors on the upper floors of Merlin Manor that were strong enough to keep the Slitherghoul away—and now there was certainly no escape back down the stairs. Besides, the idea of endlessly running from the monster *inside* the house was obviously pointless; which left only one possible escape route.

Measle grabbed Iggy's skinny arm and dragged him away from the stair head. Together, they ran down the long corridor, arriving, a moment later, at another, narrower set of stairs. Measle raced up them, dragging Iggy behind him.

'Where is we goin', Mumps?' gasped Iggy, stumbling to keep up.

'The roof, Iggy!' panted Measle. 'We're going to climb out onto the roof!'

ON THE ROOF

Measle knew a good way onto the roof. It was through his bedroom window.

Measle's bedroom was right at the top of the house, which was how he was able to get onto the roof from there, by climbing out through its tall window.

He wasn't supposed to do this, but he did, a lot. Or rather, he *had* done, until Sam found out that he'd been going up there regularly. It was one of the few times that Measle had seen him angry.

'Merlin Manor's roof is very old and a lot of the tiles are probably loose,' Sam had scolded. 'You step on one of those and you could easily slide off! And, last time I looked, you couldn't fly, could you?'

Of course, by the time that Sam had found out

that Measle had been climbing about on the roof, Measle already knew every inch of it.

And now the roof could be an escape route—

Measle burst into his dark bedroom and instinctively he reached out and flipped the light switch on the wall. Nothing happened. The room remained dark, but there was enough moonlight coming through the tall window to let Measle see his way across the floor. He pulled Iggy in and then shut the door and locked it.

'Is dis where you sssleep, Mumps?' said Iggy, looking round the room, his big fishy eyes round with wonder.

'Yes, Iggy.'

Iggy sniffed. 'It ain't very nice, is it?' he said. 'Not as nice as my little 'ouse. Well, ssstands to reason, don't it? It's rainin' in 'ere, ain't it? An' it *never* rains inssside my little 'ouse!'

It was true. Iggy's rain cloud had followed them as they moved through Merlin Manor and was now positioned directly over Iggy's head and dribbling its tiny drops down onto Iggy's woollen hat.

Measle marched over to the window and heaved it upwards. Without hesitation, he swung one leg, then the other, over the windowsill. Then he held out his hand and said, 'Come on, Iggy. It's quite safe—you can climb out too.'

Iggy scrambled through the opening and then stood close to Measle. They were on a narrow ledge, with a low parapet on the far side. Up here, all the windows led out onto this ledge, which ran round the whole house. The roof itself slanted steeply up behind them—and the ledge was the only flat part of the whole structure.

Measle leaned past Iggy and slid the window down. Then he peered along the side of the building, his eyes straining in the gloom. He leaned out further, but he still couldn't see what he was looking for.

'Come on, Iggy,' he muttered, moving a couple of metres sideways along the ledge and then leaning both hands against the steep tiles of the roof. 'We've got to climb up there. Do you think you can manage it?'

Iggy wrinkled his long nose in derision. '*Manage* it? *Courssse* I can manage it, Mumps!' he said, dismissively. 'I was a *burglarider*, wasn't I? I was de *bessst* burglarider in de whole world! I could climb anyfink, couldn't I?'

Measle had forgotten about Iggy once being a burglar. He grinned at the little wrathmonk in the darkness and then patted his damp shoulder.

'Come on then,' he said. 'Race you to the top!'

Iggy won easily. By the time Measle reached the pointed top of the roof, Iggy was already there, sitting astride the sloping tiles as if he was on a horse. Measle, panting slightly, joined him, sitting close behind him. This wasn't the highest section of Merlin Manor's roof—on the other side of the house there was a tower room that was quite a bit higher—but, even so, Measle was able to see all the way across the roof in every direction.

And then he saw what he'd thought he might see.

There, about forty metres away, hung a large, dense, and very black cloud, releasing a steady downpour of torrential rain onto the old tiles. The water streamed down the steep slopes in all directions, gurgling and splashing into the gutters and, in places, overflowing the channels before disappearing, in little glittering waterfalls, down into the shadows below.

The cloud was moving.

Measle saw that it was coming steadily towards them.

Just because he'd been running away—and thinking miserably about the horrible thing that had happened to Nanny Flannel and to Tinker— that didn't mean that Measle's brain had stopped working. The thought process had started the moment he'd seen Toby Jugg floating inside the jelly mass of the Slitherghoul.

If Toby's in there, then perhaps there are others? Perhaps that's where all the wrathmonks from the Detention Centre went—inside the Slitherghoul?

Another clue to this idea had been the sudden downpour of rain outside the kitchen door, only seconds before the Slitherghoul had started to try and force its way in—and that was why Measle had expected to see a wrathmonk cloud hovering over the Slitherghoul's position. The fact that his guess had been right didn't make Measle feel any better. In fact, the sight of the great, black, billowing cloud made him feel much, much worse.

'Coo! Wossat, Mumps?' breathed Iggy into his ear.

'That's a wrathmonk rain cloud, Iggy.'

'Ooh,' said Iggy, uncertainly. 'Dat must be a very big wraffmonk, Mumps!'

'It's not just one wrathmonk. It's *lots* of them. And they're the *bad* wrathmonks! From the *Other Place*, Iggy!'

Iggy didn't really want to have anything to do with bad wrathmonks from the Other Place since he'd promised to be on his best behaviour. This was the main condition that the Wizards' Guild had imposed on him, if he wanted to go on living at Merlin Manor with the Stubbs family, that is. And Iggy *did* want to—very much.

'But—what are ssso many bad wraffmonks doin' 'ere, Mumps?' said Iggy, twisting his head over his shoulder and talking out of the side of his mouth.

'I'm pretty sure that they're all inside the Slitherghoul.'

This concept was a bit too complicated for Iggy—but his little brain just managed to reason that, if the wrathmonks were *inside* something, then that might mean that they couldn't get at him or Mumps, and this made him feel much better.

'Oh, well, dat's all right, den,' he said, cheerfully.

Measle had been watching the cloud carefully. It was much closer now but it kept delaying its forward movement by a number of shifts sideways —first left, then right, then left again—

Measle realized what was happening. The Slitherghoul was investigating each room on the long corridor. Most of the rooms were empty, or were used for storage, which explained why the Slitherghoul didn't seem to be wasting much time searching them.

Measle heard the distant sound of breaking wood.

And now the leading edge of the rain cloud drifted over Iggy's head, and first Iggy and then Measle found themselves sitting under a drenching torrent of cold rain.

Measle had to shout over the noise of the downpour. 'It's in my bedroom, Iggy!'

The Slitherghoul was, indeed, just entering Measle's room. The fact that *this* door—unlike the others on the corridor—was locked was of considerable interest, and it had taken only a moment to smash the door down. But the room was empty and the creature was about to slime its way back out into the passage when something inside itself caught at its attention.

The something was Tinker. Tinker recognized the room immediately. *It was where he and the smelly kid slept!*

For a fraction of a second, Tinker's doggy mind was the strongest one there and it was this surge of thought that the Slitherghoul detected. Quickly, it switched to Toby's mind.

This is the boy's room! Might the boy still be here?

The Slitherghoul spread its mass over Measle's carpet, using a dozen extended tentacles to feel into every corner. One tentacle yanked open Measle's wardrobe and rummaged stickily among his clothes. Another felt carefully under the bed—

Not here! The boy is not here! thought Toby, irritably. Besides, he wasn't all that interested in the boy. It wasn't the boy he'd come for—it was Lee Stubbs and her little girl, the Mallockee! *Why waste all this time searching for a boy?*

Toby began to force the Slitherghoul to leave the bedroom.

Nanny Flannel's eyes were the ones that saw the little crack at the bottom of the window frame. Nanny Flannel knew all about Measle's expeditions onto the roof and the moment she saw the narrow opening she guessed where Measle and Iggy might be. Quickly, she wiped the idea out of her mind and started to join with Toby's mind in urging the Slitherghoul out of the room.

But another mind had caught her thought—

Griswold Gristle was deeply resentful of the way Toby Jugg had taken over everything. That a mere warlock should think he should be the one to lead them all! *No matter that his brain is more powerful than mine*, thought Griswold, furiously. *I should be the one to control where this creature goes and what it does!*

And what about me? What about what I want? came another thought, and Griswold recognized the brutish stubbornness of Buford Cudgel.

And me? came another, and this time Griswold heard the whiny tones of Frognell Flabbit.

Last—and very much least—came a feeble little thought from Judge Cedric Hardscrabble. *Griswold, dear friend—don't leave me! Don't leave me!*

Griswold sent a powerful brainwave out to his three friends.

We mussst ssstick together! he cried. *We mussst stick together by thinking together! There are other minds here, my friends, powerful minds! But if we ssstick together, we can be the masters here! Are we agreed?*

Yes! came the rumbling thought from Buford Cudgel.

Yes! came the whiny, scratchy thought from Frognell Flabbit.

Yes! We musst ssstick together, dear friends! came the mumbling, muddled thought from what passed for Judge Cedric's brain.

Very well! cried Griswold's mind. *Now, what is it that we four want?*

The boy!

The boy!

Oh, is that what we want?—and Griswold realized that this last thought was from his foolish old friend, the judge.

Yesss, Cedric. We want the boy!

All four wrathmonk brains were now thinking the same thought—and it was the power of their collective minds that stopped the Slitherghoul in its tracks.

No! screamed Nanny Flannel's mind. *Leave this room! There is nothing here!*

There are other, more important matters! shouted Toby's brain—and, for a moment, these two powerful personalities became dominant inside the Slitherghoul.

Who else is with us? shrieked Griswold. *Who else wishes to hunt down the boy? That evil boy, who has done usss all ssso much harm! That ssson of Ssstubbs, the mossst wicked family in the world! Come—join usss! Join usss!*

Immediately, several of the wrathmonks who had been locked up alongside Griswold and Buford and Frognell and Judge Cedric sent silent cries through the jelly—*YESSS! We will join you! The boy—hunt for the boy!*

Griswold recognized the cocky voice of Mungo MacToad among them—and then an unexpected voice joined in:

I want to get that young fellow, too! Count me in as well!

The voice was familiar to Griswold but, for a

couple of seconds, he couldn't place its owner. Then he realized who it was.

It was the voice of Officer Offal.

Officer Offal was mortally afraid of the wrathmonks who had been in his charge—and now he found himself floating among them! He had no idea if they could harm him under these circumstances but it had occurred to him that perhaps by joining them in their hunt for the boy (a boy he thoroughly detested, of course) then maybe they might soften their attitude towards him?

Ho, yes! he boomed. *I'm with you, lads! I'm on your side, wrathies!*

Griswold Gristle heard Officer Offal's falsely friendly offer—an offer from a person he loathed with every fibre of his soft white body! But he loathed Officer Offal a lot less than he loathed Measle Stubbs.

Why, thank you, Officer Offal! cried Griswold, trying to inject as much sincerity into his thoughts as he possibly could. *With your help, we shall undoubtedly sssucceed!*

And now there were just too many minds in opposition to Toby and Nanny Flannel. Besides, Toby and Nanny Flannel had entirely *different* reasons for wanting the Slitherghoul to give up chasing Measle, and that weakened their wills a lot.

As for Corky Pretzel—apart from being utterly confused by everything that had happened to them, he was a simple man who was accustomed to being *told* what to do by his senior officers, with the result that he lay quiet and still inside the Slitherghoul, hoping that nobody would notice him.

And Mr Needle and Mr Bland were doing pretty much the same, since they were now surrounded by a group of wrathmonks, most of whom they had personally escorted down into the depths of the Detention Centre.

So, for the foreseeable future, the wrathmonks were in control.

It was Frognell Flabbit who noticed the open window. A sudden gust of wind blew a scattering of rain in through the opening—and the Slitherghoul turned and slithered across the floor towards it.

SLIPPERY SLOPES

'We've got to move, Iggy,' said Measle, through chattering teeth.

The pounding rain had soaked through their clothes and both he and Iggy were shivering with cold. And besides, the thought that the Slitherghoul must now be directly beneath him made Measle want to put some distance between them.

Together, they started to move along the ridge, inching their way slowly over the tiles. Soon they came out from under the rain cloud and Iggy stopped moving but Measle pushed him gently between his shoulder blades and said, 'Go on, Iggy—we've got to get further away.' Iggy started moving again and only when they reached the far end of the ridge did Measle tap him on the back and say, 'OK, Iggy—that's far enough.'

In fact, they couldn't go any further even if they wanted to. This section of the roof ended here and in front of Iggy was a sheer drop to the ground below.

Measle twisted his body and looked back over his shoulder and saw, to his horror, that a slow-moving mound of jelly was oozing its way up the tiles, towards the spot on the ridge where they had just rested. The Slitherghoul was a good thirty metres away but, at the speed the thing was moving, it wouldn't be all that long before it would catch up with them.

For the first time in a long while, Measle had no idea what to do next. He and Iggy were trapped— and it was all his fault! Why had he imagined that they would find safety up here on the roof? Now there was nowhere to go—and there was nothing they could do to save themselves—

Measle felt Iggy wriggling behind him and he turned his head back in time to see the wrathmonk scrambling to his knees. Without a word, Iggy took hold of Measle's shoulders and then, very carefully, he clambered over Measle, so that he was between him and the slow-moving pile of slime, which had reached the ridge of the roof and was beginning to slither steadily towards them both. Iggy sat down again, his spindly legs hanging on either side of the ridge. He leaned forward and

began to scoot himself towards the Slitherghoul.
Measle caught hold of the back of Iggy's coat.

'What are you doing?' he hissed.

'I'm goin' to breave on it,' said Iggy over his
shoulder.

'*Breathe* on it? Why? What good will that do?'

'It won't do it *any* good, Mumps!' said Iggy,
irritably. 'Coz it's a bug, see? An' my breaving ssspell
kills bugs! Ssso I'm goin' to breave on it!'

'But, Iggy, that's not a bug!'

'Well, it *looks* like a bug, Mumps,' said Iggy.
'An' dat *makes* it a bug! Ssso *dere*!' The next
moment, he moved forward with a powerful jerk,
wrenching his coat out of Measle's grasp. Before
Measle could lean out and grab the coat again, Iggy
had managed to put a metre and a half between
them and now was moving along the ridge as fast
as he could.

'No, Iggy! Come back!' yelled Measle—but Iggy
took no notice. If anything, he scooted along a little
faster, rapidly closing the gap between himself and
the Slitherghoul.

Using the eyes of Griswold Gristle, the Slitherghoul
saw the strange little person coming steadily towards
it. Griswold's mind was momentarily puzzled; he
recognized the small wrathmonk from before and
saw no particular danger from him. *If needs be, we
shall absorb him*, he thought, *but we are after that
boy! That boy, sitting there at the end of the ridge, so
helpless! So exposed! We have him now!*

When Iggy got to within a couple of metres of the leading edge of the mass of jelly, he leaned forward, took a deep breath and breathed out as hard as he could. When nothing happened, he shouted, 'Ho! You want sssome more, you bad Sssquiffypoo, you!' And he took another breath and blew it out at the Slitherghoul—and the Slitherghoul simply kept moving forward—

Iggy took another breath—

The leading edge of the slime touched Iggy's knees—

From the far end of the ridge, Measle saw everything. He saw Iggy begin to try to scramble backwards. He saw the mass of the Slitherghoul rear upwards. He saw Iggy raise his arms to cover his head. He saw the jelly drop down and over the little wrathmonk, enveloping him completely. And then he saw that Iggy was gone and that the great slimy mass was advancing steadily towards him, much of its jelly body hanging down on either side of the ridge as it oozed its way along—

With Iggy swallowed up, Measle felt as alone as he'd ever felt in his whole life. More alone than when he was running from Basil Tramplebone! More alone than when facing the great dragon Arcturion! More alone than when he found himself betrayed by Toby Jugg! At least he'd had Tinker with him all those times! But now, he had nobody! All that stood between him and the Slitherghoul was a fast-diminishing length of roof!

I can't just sit here and wait for the end! thought Measle, desperately. *Perhaps—perhaps there's something I can throw at it!* Measle's hands scrabbled over the rough tiles, testing each in turn until he found one that felt a little loose. Measle pulled at it with all his strength. The tile shifted under the stress and, suddenly, it cracked in half. Measle felt a swift, searing pain across the palm of his hand. He looked down. There was a line of blood, oozing from what looked like a deep cut. Measle grimaced—*it really hurts!*

But there was no time to worry about a cut hand. The Slitherghoul was squelching closer and closer—

Measle lifted the broken tile. It felt heavy and solid. He raised it over his head and, using only his unhurt hand, he hurled the tile towards the Slitherghoul. It fell short, clattering onto the roof and then sliding rapidly down the steep angle. It hit the parapet and bounced, flying over the low wall and into the darkness below. Seconds later, Measle heard it break with a distant crash. Frantically, he pulled at another tile and, as he did so, the Slitherghoul suddenly paused in its forward motion. The back half of the thing lumped up against the front half and then, clumsily, slithered sideways, so that almost half of the mass of jelly was now draped over one side of the roof, with the front half still balanced across the ridge.

Measle, using both hands and ignoring the pain,

threw the second tile and this one struck the Slitherghoul square on its leading edge—and a little more of the mass of jelly slid sideways. Now, only a third of the creature clung to the ridge; the rest of it lay against the steep slope of one side of the roof. To his excitement, Measle saw that its great weight was slowly pulling it sideways and the torrential rain that poured down on the thing wasn't helping the situation either. The water was making the tiles slippery and the greater part of the Slitherghoul was having difficulty getting a grip on the slick surface.

Throwing stuff at it was working! Measle yanked at another tile and then threw it hard. It bounced off the Slitherghoul as if the thing was made of rubber and the Slitherghoul lost a little more of its grip on the ridge tiles, letting even more of its vast mass slide sideways.

There was a slow, rending, ripping sound, as the ridge tiles beneath the front third of the Slitherghoul were dragged out of their settings. They crumbled into fragments beneath the great weight of the creature and began to slide down the slope. With nothing to hold it in place, the mass of jelly lurched sideways and then slid, slowly at first but with gathering speed, down the steep and slippery slope of the roof. Measle watched with awe as it slithered—like a pat of butter in a hot frying pan— down towards the roof's edge. He saw it shoot out a number of jelly tentacles, waving them in a frantic bid to find something to cling to. Then he saw the whole huge mass pile up against the low wall of the parapet. More and more jelly gathered there in a growing heap, until the narrow ledge could contain no more. The excess jelly flowed over the top of the wall and, within three seconds, the rest followed, sliding soundlessly into the darkness below.

A moment later, there was a distant, squelching THUD!

Through all his feelings of misery and loneliness and pain, Measle couldn't help the sudden lightening of his heart. He'd done it! He'd saved himself!

And then the horror of the situation returned, plunging him back into frightened despair. There was no reason to think that the Slitherghoul was dead. A thing that could ooze its way through narrow holes, that could smash down heavy doors—a thing without a bone of its own in its entire body—a thing like that might easily survive a fall from a rooftop!

There was only one way to find out.

Measle sat quite still and watched the rolling billows of the nearby rain cloud. For half a minute it hung quite still in the night air, dropping its heavy fall of rain down onto the spot where the Slitherghoul had landed far below.

Then, with a sick feeling growing in the pit of his stomach, Measle saw the cloud start to drift slowly sideways. He watched as it moved along the side of the house, then it turned a corner and drifted out of sight behind the tall tower.

It could mean only one thing. The Slitherghoul was still alive!

What would it do now?

Trying not to use his cut hand, Measle scooted himself back along the ridge. When he got to the section where the tiles had been torn away, he found himself crawling along on the rough wood of an ancient beam. Measle could feel slime and his face wrinkled in disgust. Even the sticky trail that the Slitherghoul left behind stank to high heaven!

Soon, he was back at the point directly above his bedroom. Carefully, he turned onto his stomach and inched his way backwards down the steep slope of the roof. His toes touched the flat part of the ledge and he pushed himself upright. There, a couple of metres away, was the open window. Measle quickly stepped over the sill and dropped down onto the bedroom floor. In the gloom, he could make out the shattered remains of his door—and he could smell the terrible stink of the Slitherghoul's slime, which lay all over the floor in a thin film.

Measle shivered. He was soaked through and very cold. He pulled off his wet clothes and took clean dry ones from his wardrobe. He wrapped a handkerchief round his injured hand and tied it, using his teeth and his good hand to get the knot tight. He was just finishing dressing when he heard a sound from beyond the open window.

A scrabbling, scrambling, pushing, pulling, heaving sound.

To Measle's ears, it sounded as if something was climbing steadily up the outer wall of Merlin Manor.

Since there was nobody left at Merlin Manor but him, Measle realized what it must be.

His heart was thumping in his chest like a wheezy old pump and his legs felt weak. Slowly, without taking his eyes off the window, Measle started to shuffle backwards towards the smashed remains of his bedroom door.

Where can I possibly go this time? There's nowhere to hide, there's nowhere that's safe!

Measle's slow backward progress was halted suddenly when his heel caught against a smashed piece of wood on the floor. He staggered for a second, then lost his balance and sat down heavily among the remains of the door.

Something rose up above the parapet and filled the open window. A dark shadow blotted out the moonlight and loomed over Measle—it smelt really bad!—then it moved over the sill and flopped down onto the bedroom floor with a thud.

'Oh, dere you are, Mumps! I fort you might be 'ere ssstill—and you is! Dat was clever of me to fink dat, wasn't it? Huh? Huh?'

BRUISED
FEELINGS

'Iggy?'

'Wot you doin', Mumps? Sssittin' dere in de dark. An' wot you done to de door, huh? It's all sssmashed up. Coo—your dad's goin' to be ever ssso cross!'

Measle scrambled to his feet, ran across the room, threw both his arms round Iggy's neck, and hugged him fiercely.

'Iggy! I don't believe it! You—you were swallowed up! And now you're here! But *how*? How did you get out of the Slitherghoul?'

Iggy took hold of Measle's wrists and gently disentangled himself. Then he lifted his long hooked nose in the air, closed his

eyes, and took on the air of somebody who was deeply offended.

'I did not *get* out of de Sssquiffypoo,' he said, in a pained voice. 'De Sssquiffypoo *ssspitted* me out! Jusst like dat! Like I didn't tassste nice, or sssumfink! Jussst fink of dat, Mumps! Me, wot tastes luvverly! And dat ssstupid old Sssquiffypoo, it jussst spitted me out!'

Iggy took a deep breath and sighed heavily at the injustice of it all. Then he said, sorrowfully, 'It hurt my feelin's, Mumps. I never been ssspitted out before!'

Measle's happiness at finding Iggy alive and well and *outside* the Slitherghoul was tempered a little by the discovery that Iggy was covered from head to toe in a thin layer of smelly slime—and a lot of that slime had come off on him, too. Using his wet shirt, which he'd dropped on the floor, Measle started wiping the slime from both of them.

'But, Iggy—don't you see—it's *wonderful* that the Slitherghoul spat you out!'

'Huh!' said Iggy, dismissively. 'Well, *I* fink it was very rude!'

It took a while to persuade Iggy to get over his hurt feelings, but eventually Measle managed to get the story out of him. At the end of its long fall, the Slitherghoul had landed with a great squelching thump on the ground and had lain there, not moving, for several seconds. Iggy himself suffered no ill effects from the long fall and, in fact, felt rather comfortable floating about in the soft jelly. He'd sensed a number of minds reach out to him, but he'd pretty much ignored them—he was too busy wondering whether or not he liked this new experience. Apart from the vague thought that, if he was going to spend a lot of time inside this thing, then he might start to miss Mumps a bit, and then the stronger thought that he'd *certainly* miss Matilda a lot more, apart from those hazy feelings of loss, on the whole he was rather enjoying himself.

And then, quite suddenly, he'd felt a constriction round his body, a sudden shoving sensation against the top of his head, and, a moment later, he'd found himself squeezed, like toothpaste from a tube, out onto the cold wet ground. Iggy had sat there, a little dazed, and had watched the Slitherghoul turn away from him and then slime its way off alongside the wall of the great house, until at last it turned the distant corner and was lost to sight.

Like most people who have fallen a fair distance and survived, Iggy had looked up towards the roof high above him. His eye had been caught by a stout-looking iron drainpipe that ran from the gutters all the way down the wall to an open spout at the bottom. It was the type of drainpipe that Iggy had often used when he was a burglar—he could shin up one of those as easily as a monkey— and it crossed his fuddled mind that perhaps his buddy Mumps was still up there on the roof, waiting for him? Feeling more and more offended

at the way he'd been so
ignominiously ejected,
Iggy had started to
climb the drainpipe.
It was more difficult
than usual, because
of the slime that
covered his hands
and feet. That
made things terribly
slippery and several
times Iggy had
slithered a metre or
two back down the pipe.
But he was stronger than
he looked and his grip on the
iron pipe was like a steel vice
and, quite soon, he reached the
parapet. From there, it was a quick
hop over the windowsill and into
Mumps's bedroom.

'But—but why did the Slitherghoul
spit you out, Iggy?' asked Measle,
wiping the last of the slime from Iggy's coat.

'Coz it's got no *manners*, dat's why!' said Iggy,
firmly.

Measle threw the smelly, slimy shirt into the far
corner of the dark room. He was thinking furiously.

*There must be a reason! There must be a
reason why the Slitherghoul swallowed everybody*

else and kept them inside it, but not Iggy! Why? Why did it reject him and not any of the others?

Another thought occurred to Measle. It was to do with how he'd dislodged the Slitherghoul from the roof. It was all too *easy*! Surely a creature like that, which could change its shape, which could fall all that way without hurting itself, which could smash down doors and swallow any number of people whole—surely a monster as powerful as that wouldn't be bothered by a few roof tiles? And yet it had suddenly slumped to one side—

Then Measle remembered that it had slumped to one side *before* he'd ever hit it with a tile! Something other than a hurled tile had caused it to lose its grip. When it had slithered down the roof and piled its jelly mass against the low parapet, why hadn't it used its tentacles and grabbed hold, and hung on tight? Why had it simply allowed itself to flow over the top of the low wall and then plummet to the ground? It couldn't have been because of a few tiles.

Click, click, click, went Measle's agile brain.

The Slitherghoul had started to behave oddly immediately after it had swallowed Iggy ...

'I think you made it feel sick, Iggy!'

Iggy's eyebrows shot to the top of his head. He stared at Measle, a look of outrage plastered across his face.

'Wot? *Wot?* I did *WOT?*'

'Er ... I think you made it feel sick.'

Iggy glared at Measle for several silent seconds. Then he lifted his long, bent nose in the air and, staring haughtily up at the ceiling, he said, 'Ho! Dat is *charmin'*, dat is! Dat is de *nicessst* fing wot you 'ave ever sssaid to me, Mumps! Dat I make people sssick! Fank you! Fank you *ssso* much!'

It was strange how easily Iggy's feelings could be hurt. Measle realized he was going to have to do some fast talking if he wanted any co-operation from the little wrathmonk.

'Oh, I didn't mean you make *people* sick! We all love you, you know that!'

'No, I don't,' muttered Iggy, still staring up at the ceiling.

'Well, we *do*, Iggy! Look, what I meant was . . . um . . . the Slitherghoul spat you out because I think you tasted of something it doesn't like! And that makes you special, you see?'

'Ssspecial?'

'Yes! Very special! The Slitherghoul swallowed up a whole lot of people—good people as well as bad people—but it spat you out because you're special!'

Iggy lowered his gaze and looked at Measle out of the corner of one fishy eye. 'An' bein' ssspecial like dat—dat is a *good* fing, is it?'

'Yes! It's a *very* good thing! It means that you're safe from it! It means that it won't swallow you up, even if it wants to! It means . . . it means . . . it means that you're *stronger* than it is!'

Iggy—who in many ways was rather like a little boy—enjoyed being told how strong he was. He relaxed his stiff posture and nodded smugly.

'Well, *courssse* I is stronger dan dat old Sssquiffypoo, Mumps. I is ssstronger dan everyfing! I is ssstronger dan a Squiffypoo, I is ssstronger dan a car, I is ssstronger dan a train, I is ssstronger dan a . . . dan a . . . dan a—'

While Iggy was desperately trying to think what else he was stronger than, his hand crept to one of his pockets, dived in and came out with a fistful of jelly beans. Iggy poked around, removing the green ones and depositing them in his breast pocket. Then he threw the rest straight into his open mouth.

Iggy's mouth was smeared with sugar.

Click, click, click, went Measle's mind.

Can that be it? he wondered. *Could it be Iggy's awful diet of nothing but sugar that made the Slitherghoul spit him out? There are other wrathmonks inside the monster and it hasn't rejected any of them, and there are other ordinary people in there too, including a dog, and they haven't been spat out, either! Only Iggy— and the only thing different about Iggy that I can think of is what he eats, which I'm pretty sure isn't what any of the others trapped inside the Slitherghoul eat . . .*

'Maybe you taste too sweet, Iggy!'

The muscles in Iggy's face went into one of their wriggling, writhing contortions, as Iggy tried desperately to work out if Measle had said something nice, or something insulting. Eventually, Iggy decided that Measle was being complimentary.

'Ho—well, fank you, Mumps. I *is* quite sssweet, actually.'

Click, click, click . . .

'So, Iggy, if the Slitherghoul doesn't like sweet things, maybe we can find a way of making it go away! Of stopping it eating us!'

''Ow?' said Iggy, doubtfully.

'I don't know. Maybe . . . maybe we could throw sugar at it!'

The thought of throwing perfectly good sugar away was almost more than Iggy could bear and he started his facial contortions again. Then, seeing Measle's eager eyes staring at him, with excitement written all over them, Iggy's face muscles settled down and he said, 'Well, maybe we could throw jussst a *little* bit at it? Dat way, we could find out if it don't like it—an' if it don't care, den we won't throw any more, right?'

'Right!' said Measle, who was well aware of how important it was to Iggy that there was a plentiful supply of sugar at Merlin Manor.

'But all de sugar is in de kitchen,' said Iggy, in a pensive voice. In the back of his very small mind was the thought that, if they couldn't *get* to the distant kitchen, then they wouldn't be able to get to the *sugar*, which meant that there wouldn't be any sugar-throwing at all, which meant—

'Yes, Iggy,' said Measle. 'So, we're going to have to find a way down there, aren't we?'

'I come up de pipe fingy,' said Iggy smugly. 'Bet you can't do dat, Mumps.'

Measle walked quickly over to the window and leaned out as far as he could. He stretched his body across the narrow ledge and then looked down, over the low parapet. The thick, black, cast-iron pipe was right there and Measle peered along its length, seeing how the distance made it seem narrower and narrower the closer it got to the ground.

The ground was a very long way off.

The drainpipe looked smooth and slippery.

His hand was throbbing.

Normally, Measle was game to try pretty much anything, as long as it looked as if it might be fun. He even liked doing quite dangerous things, like climbing about on old roofs and going for motorbike rides with Nanny Flannel—but he also knew his limitations. While Iggy, a once-professional burglar wrathmonk, might be able to shin up and down drainpipes with ease, a twelve-year-old boy with a hurt hand was probably going to find it impossible.

Measle withdrew his head and rejoined Iggy, who was chomping away at another mouthful of jelly beans.

'You're right, Iggy. I don't think I can climb down that way. I've hurt my hand, too.'

Since he was a wrathmonk, Iggy didn't care a jot about people getting hurt, as long as it wasn't him. Or Matilda. He didn't like it when Matilda got hurt, but a lot of his concern for her was because of the terrible noise her powerful lungs could produce when she was upset about something. Iggy glanced briefly at Measle's bandaged hand and said, 'Huh! Dat is nuffink! Now, when Miss Fwannel hit me wiv de mop—dat *really* hurt!'

Measle knew better than to argue with Iggy. 'I bet it did,' he said. 'But the thing is—we've got to get down to the kitchen and, if I can't climb down, how are we going to do it?'

Iggy thought for a moment, his face muscles doing their usual contortions. Then he said, brightly, 'I could frow you off de roof?'

Measle sighed. 'Good idea—except that would kill me.'

'Not if I didn't frow you very hard.'

Measle shook his head, but Iggy's idiotic idea was leading him on to one that might just work.

'We could make a rope, Iggy! We could make a rope out of all the bedclothes, like escaping prisoners do! And then—then you could lower me down!'

'I could do *wot*?' said Iggy, doubtfully.

'You could lower me down to the ground, Iggy! You're very strong! Don't you remember rescuing me from that suit of armour that time? You pulled me up by my hair, didn't you?'

Iggy's face cleared. 'I did, didn't I?' he said, in a smug voice. 'Okey-dokey, Mumps. Let's do dat!'

For the next half hour, Measle and Iggy were very busy. They started with the bedclothes from Measle's bed—stripping off the two sheets and knotting the ends tightly together. Iggy couldn't help with the knotting, that was far too complicated for him, but he was quite happy trotting down the narrow stairs that led to the floor below and pulling the sheets off Sam and Lee's bed—and then another pair from Nanny Flannel's. He carried the bundle of linen back up to Measle's room and dumped it on the floor in a heap.

'Dat old Squiffypoo is back,' he said, carelessly, just as if he was announcing the arrival of a rain shower.

'What? *Where?*' said Measle, his eyes darting nervously round the room.

'Down at de bottom,' said Iggy. 'Where de ssstairs is all broked.'

'What's it doing?'

'It's not doin' nuffink,' said Iggy, stuffing yet another handful of jelly beans in his mouth. 'It's jussst lyin' dere, sssmelling *nice*, dat's all.'

Measle didn't really trust Iggy to know what the Slitherghoul was doing, so he hurriedly knotted the rest of the sheets together and then gathered them all up in his arms and headed for the door.

'Where is you goin', Mumps?' said Iggy, not budging.

'Down to the floor below. There's no point lowering me from up here, not if we can do it from down there! It won't be so far, you see?'

Iggy shrugged his skinny shoulders and followed Measle out of the bedroom. They walked quickly to the head of the narrow staircase, where Measle stopped. He listened for any noises from below. There was silence—apart from a faint drumming sound of heavy rain falling on a distant part of the roof.

Iggy's right! thought Measle. *The Slitherghoul is inside the house again!*

Careful not to make a sound, Measle and Iggy crept down the short flight of stairs. When they reached the landing below, Measle caught a faint whiff of the Slitherghoul's stench.

Measle put his mouth near Iggy's ear and whispered, 'Are you sure it was just lying still, Iggy? Are you sure it wasn't trying to climb up here?'

Iggy pulled his head away from Measle, stuck a finger in his ear, and waggled it irritably. 'I told you, Mumps! It wasn't doin' nuffink!'

Measle was about to move off again, when he heard it—a distant scraping, grating sound, of something heavy being pushed, or pulled, across a stone floor. Putting his finger to his lips, Measle grabbed Iggy's hand and together they tiptoed along the dark corridor, heading for the top of the great staircase. As they got nearer, the smell became stronger and stronger—and so did the scraping, grating noises.

Then, the noises stopped.

Measle and Iggy crept forward until they were able to peer down into the hall below.

The enormous pine table from the kitchen was now directly beneath them!

Measle frowned in puzzlement. What on earth was it doing there?

A moment later, the scraping sound started up again and Measle and Iggy watched as, slowly, another piece of furniture was pushed into position beneath them. This time, it was the polished mahogany table from the dining room— and now Measle and Iggy could see the dark, shifting shape of the Slitherghoul pushing its burden into place next to the pine table, making a kind of broad, uneven platform right below them.

And then Measle realized what the Slitherghoul was doing.

'It's trying to build a way to get up here!' he hissed.

Iggy stared down at the tables in admiration. He'd never think of anything as clever as that! 'Coo—dat mussst be a very sssmart Sssquiffypoo!' he whispered.

Yes, it must! thought Measle. *And that's kind of weird for a lump of slime!*

There was no time to do any more wondering.

Already, another large piece of furniture was being shoved into position. This time it was a sofa from Merlin Manor's living room.

The base of the Slitherghoul's structure was getting bigger by the second.

DEFENCE!

'Come on, Iggy! We'd better hurry!'

Measle and Iggy ran silently back along the passage, this time heading for Sam and Lee's bedroom. When they got there, Measle didn't linger. Instead, he walked quickly past his parents' bed—now stripped of its sheets—and pulled open the bathroom door. He went to the window, opened it, and leaned out as far as he could without falling.

'Here, Iggy!' he said, excitedly. 'We're going to get down to the kitchen from here!'

Measle made a loop at the end of the knotted sheets and wrapped it round his middle, tying it with a tight knot. Then he took the other end of the improvised rope and tied that round the base of the toilet. He pulled hard, to make sure that it wouldn't come loose. It seemed strong enough.

Measle turned to Iggy, who had been staring at his preparations with his eyes wide and his mouth hanging open.

'Right, Iggy,' said Measle, speaking in the slow, gentle voice he used whenever he wanted Iggy to do something. 'I'm going to climb out of the window and you're going to be holding tight to the rope—'

'Dat's not a rope,' said Iggy. 'Dat's just stuff you make cloves out of.'

'Yes, Iggy,' said Measle carefully, 'it is what you make clothes out of—but at the moment, it's *pretending* to be a rope, you see?'

Iggy's face cleared. *Pretending* was something he understood.

'Okey-dokey, Mumps. Ssso—wot was I doin' again?'

'You hold tight to the rope and, when I say, "Go, Iggy!" you start to let me down. Nice and slow— and, whatever you do, don't let go of the rope, right?'

Iggy nodded seriously. 'Don't let go. Right.' Then he frowned and said, 'Er . . . why don't I let go, Mumps?'

Measle sighed. Getting Iggy to do things could be very difficult and you never knew if he really understood or not.

'You mustn't let go because, if you do, I will fall all the way down and probably *die*! All right?'

This explanation seemed to satisfy Iggy, because he nodded again, more seriously than before. Then he picked up the knotted sheets and grasped them tightly with his strong, bony hands.

'Dere, Mumps,' he said. 'I is holdin' de rope.'

Measle said, 'Well done!' Then he swung his legs over the windowsill. He could feel the cool night air wash over his face. He looked down—the ground seemed a long way off. Measle took a deep breath and felt his fluttering nerves settle down a little.

'All right, Iggy,' he called, softly. 'You can start lowering me down!'

In the bathroom, Iggy, concentrating for all he was worth, slowly began to pay out the rope and, outside, Measle found himself slithering, centimetre by centimetre, down the rough brick wall.

Please don't let Iggy be distracted by something! thought Measle, knowing quite well that, if Iggy should suddenly feel the need for another mouthful of jelly beans, it was very likely that he'd simply stop whatever he was doing and—*and well, that would be a very bad thing!*

'You're doing great, Iggy!' Measle hissed, as loudly as he dared.

'I know, Mumps!' came Iggy's voice, floating out through the bathroom window.

Measle had obviously done a good job with the sheet-knotting, because the rope held and, sooner than he thought possible, Measle felt his toes touch down on the ground.

He slipped the loop of sheeting down over his hips and stepped out of it. Then, he hurried to the kitchen door and turned the handle. It didn't budge—

Of course! It's still locked!

It didn't matter. Getting into the kitchen was easy—Measle simply climbed through the shattered window, his feet crunching on the broken glass. There were several candles still burning and, by their light, he walked quickly to the pantry door and opened it.

Merlin Manor's pantry was big. Inside, stacked tightly on shelves, were packets and packets of sugar. There must have been several hundred of them—and they were all there just so that Nanny Flannel could supply Iggy with his daily ration of two hundred red jelly beans.

Measle stood there, staring at the bags and thinking hard. He realized that he hadn't thought this through—what exactly was he going to *do* with the sugar? What were the chances that his guess was right? How long could he stand here, wondering what to do, before the Slitherghoul completed its climbing platform?

Measle shook himself, clearing his head.

He saw a packet, nestling on a shelf down near the floor, which looked a little different from the others. He peered closer.

Sugar lumps.

Nanny Flannel must have bought them by mistake one day.

The thing about sugar lumps which makes them different from just plain sugar is the fact that you can carry them in your pockets.

They are also hard.

And square.

And exactly the right shape—

Click click click—

Measle grabbed the packet of sugar lumps and ran out of the pantry. Quickly, he hopped through the remains of the kitchen window. The sheet rope was still there, hanging from the bathroom window. Measle stuffed the packet of sugar lumps into the front of his jacket, then stepped into the loop that was coiled on the ground. He pulled it up round his chest. Then he looked up and called, 'Iggy! Iggy, are you there?'

Iggy's head popped out of the bathroom window and Measle could see his big round fishy eyes staring down at him.

'Wot d'you want?'

'I want you to pull me up.'

Iggy's face muscles started to wriggle and writhe and Measle sighed inwardly. Iggy was obviously *thinking* again—and, when Iggy thought, an awful lot of effort was expended with very few results.

Finally, Iggy's face settled down. He leaned out a little further and said, 'If you want to come back up, Mumps, den why did you go down in de firssst place? Huh? Huh?'

'I've got sugar, Iggy!' said Measle, knowing that the word 'sugar' would get rid of any objections Iggy might come up with.

Iggy's face split into a big grin.

'Okey-dokey, Mumps!' he hissed. 'I is goin' to pull you up now!'

Iggy's head disappeared and, a moment later, Measle felt the rope tighten round his chest.

It was amazing how strong Iggy could be when he wanted. Measle shot up the side of Merlin Manor as if he was in a lift. A few seconds later, he was scrambling over the windowsill and dropping down onto the bathroom floor.

'Where is de sugar, den?' said Iggy, his eyes glittering with greed.

Measle took the packet out and opened it. He gave a single sugar cube to Iggy who stuffed it into his mouth and crunched it up quickly with his sharp wrathmonk teeth.

'Gimme annuvver one, Mumps!' said Iggy, holding out a clawlike hand.

Measle shook his head. 'No, Iggy, not now. Remember, we're going to throw them at the Slitherghoul and see if that makes it go away.'

Iggy's face fell but he didn't take his eyes off the packet. Measle knew that he was going to have to keep a tight hold on it, or Iggy would simply grab it and then refuse to give it back. To keep Iggy from thinking of that idea, Measle took out another sugar lump and gave it to him.

'There, you can have one every now and then but we've got to save most of them for the Slitherghoul, and this is the only packet. All right?'

Iggy nodded slowly and without any conviction.

'How is we goin' to frow dem?' he said, his jaws crunching busily.

Measle didn't reply. He was busy searching in his chest of drawers.

It's in here, somewhere, I know it is! Now, where did I put it?

With a cry of triumph, Measle yanked something from the bottom of one of the drawers and held it up for Iggy to see.

'Wossat, Mumps?'

'It's my catapult! See, you put a sugar lump into this leather bit—like that, see—and then you pull it backwards like this and those bits get all stretchy, and then you take aim, and then you let go—'

The sugar lump whizzed across the bathroom, out through the open doorway and cracked against the door of Sam and Lee's wardrobe in the bedroom.

Iggy stared in amazement. Then he said, 'Can I 'ave a go wiv dat, Mumps?'

Reluctantly—because he knew that Iggy would nag him until he gave way—Measle handed Iggy the catapult and another sugar lump. Iggy raised the sugar lump to his mouth and Measle said, 'No, Iggy, remember, it goes in the pouch, doesn't it?'

'Ho, yesss, sssilly me.'

Iggy managed everything fairly well, until it came time to release the missile. Copying Measle, he took careful aim at the open doorway—then, instead of letting go of the pouch, he let go of the catapult's handle. The catapult flew backwards and smacked Iggy hard on his beaky nose.

'Owwwwww!' he squeaked, dropping the catapult and putting both hands to his bruised face. 'Ooooooooohhh! Dat cattybull fing is *'stremely* dangerous!'

Measle was sorry that Iggy was hurt—but he was also relieved, because now Iggy wouldn't want to have anything to do with operating the catapult. Measle had often found that it was best to let Iggy try something because, when he failed (and Iggy always failed), the chances were that he would never try again. This meant that Iggy would never again try to drive the big black motorbike; he would never again try to eat raw eggs; he would never again try to put his fingers in Tinker's ears; and would never, ever, be rude to Nanny Flannel. There were a lot of other things that Iggy would never try again—and now playing with Measle's catapult was one of them.

Measle had a quick look at Iggy's nose. There was no blood, so he gave Iggy six more sugar lumps to make him feel better and said, 'You're so brave, Iggy. I would have screamed my head off.'

Iggy looked pleased with himself and stopped snivelling and rubbing his nose. Measle realized that they really couldn't waste any more time. There was no telling how the Slitherghoul's platform was progressing—not without taking a look.

'Come on,' said Measle. 'Let's go and shoot at something, shall we?'

They left the dark bathroom, scurried silently over the thick carpet of the bedroom and out into the corridor. The Slitherghoul smell was strong out here. Measle took Iggy's bony hand and together they crept along the passage. As they neared the head of the stairs, they could hear the sounds of heavy objects being moved.

Carefully, Measle and Iggy craned their heads over the top of the banister rail.

The Slitherghoul was right beneath them, its stinking mass not more than a few metres away. It lay sprawled over the top of a great jumble of piled-up furniture and, even as they watched, it began to extend two thick jelly tentacles up towards them. Measle glanced over his shoulder and saw that the tentacles were aiming for a pair of massive stone pillars that stood at the top of the broken staircase. He knew, in that instant, that the pillars were going to be easily strong enough to support the creature's great weight—which meant there were only seconds before the Slitherghoul would be on their level! And, after that, where could they go?

Measle didn't waste another moment. He pulled out a sugar cube, fitted it into the leather pouch of his catapult, took aim, and fired.

The sugar lump struck halfway along the first of the two tentacles. It hit the outer skin of the Slitherghoul and then disappeared into the jelly, leaving no entry hole behind.

For a moment, nothing much happened, except that the tentacle stopped its upward movement and simply hung, quivering slightly, in the dark air. Measle quickly loaded another sugar lump and let fly—this time at the other tentacle.

Again, the little white cube just disappeared into the greenish-brownish-yellowish mass—and again, the tentacle paused.

Measle took careful aim and let go—and this sugar cube flew down and hit the main body of the Slitherghoul right between the bases of the two tentacles.

The effect was remarkable. The Slitherghoul seemed to shudder convulsively. Its two extended tentacles retracted at high speed, disappearing back into the slimy mass, which shifted uneasily on the great mound of furniture. The structure swayed with the Slitherghoul's sudden movement and there were several ominous creaking sounds from deep within the jumbled heap.

Measle fitted another sugar lump into the leather pouch and let fly.

The Slitherghoul shuddered again—and then it began to slide slowly down the stack of furniture. Its great weight slithered to one side, the stack swayed and creaked and swayed again—and then collapsed, with a thundering crash of splintering wood, down onto the stone floor of the hallway. The Slitherghoul could do nothing but ride the falling furniture mound all the way to the bottom. It thudded to the floor with a soggy, squelching *thump!* and then lay there, among the mass of broken furniture, quivering like a jelly.

It worked! thought Measle, excitedly. *Now, let's see if I can make it retreat even more!*

Measle started to shoot sugar lumps, one after the other, straight down at the great stinking mass and, to his great relief, the Slitherghoul began to heave its body out of the way of the missiles. It slimed over the remains of the furniture and moved away to the doorway of the living room, where it paused. But it was still in range of the whizzing sugar lumps—three hit it in quick succession—and it was forced to retreat even further, moving backwards into the dark living room until Measle lost sight of it in the shadows.

Iggy tugged at Measle's sleeve. 'Can we ssstop shooting de sugar now?' he asked, plaintively. 'Now dat de Sssquiffypoo has gone away?'

Measle took one last look down into the

darkness. Then he nodded and stuffed the catapult into his back pocket.

'An' can I have a sugar lump, Mumps?' whined Iggy. 'I'm ever ssso 'ungry.'

Measle felt in his pockets and pulled out the remaining lumps. There were very few left.

'We've got to save them, Iggy. It's the only way to keep the Slitherghoul away, you see.'

'Why can't you get sssome more from de kitchen?' muttered Iggy, anxiously.

Measle shook his head. 'I told you—there *aren't* any more. I looked. There was just that one packet. I think Nanny Flannel made a mistake when she bought them. There's plenty of sugar, just not any more in lumps.'

'Pl-plenty of sugar?' said Iggy, hopefully. He'd never been allowed into Nanny Flannel's kitchen, and so had never seen the pantry shelves sagging under the weight of bag after bag of sugar. The idea was terribly exciting.

'Can we go dere, den? To de kitchen? I wanna sssee all dat sugar, Mumps!'

Measle thought about this for a moment. It would mean returning to the ground floor, which was the same level as the Slitherghoul, and that was dangerous. On the other hand, they couldn't stay up here for ever and perhaps there was something they could do with that great store of sugar. Obviously, they weren't going to be able to shoot it at the Slitherghoul but perhaps there was some other way of using the stuff against the monster?

Measle was good at making up his mind in the shortest possible time. Briskly, he nodded and then got to his feet.

'Come on then, Iggy,' he said. 'We'll both have to go down the rope this time.'

They left the gaping hole in the landing that had once been the great staircase of Merlin Manor and went quickly back to Sam and Lee's bathroom. Measle explained to Iggy how he was to lower him down again and then, having done that, Iggy was to make sure that the sheet rope was securely fastened to the base of the toilet and then he was to climb down the rope and join Measle on the ground.

'Okey-dokey, Mumps.'

Two minutes later, Measle and Iggy were standing on the ground, close by the shattered kitchen window. They picked their way carefully over the windowsill and crunched across the broken glass to the pantry door. Measle fetched a candle from the mantelpiece and held it up, so that Iggy could see the glorious sight of all those bulging bags of sugar.

'It's all for you, Iggy,' said Measle and Iggy's face split into an enormous grin.

'All mine?'

'This is what Nanny Flannel makes your jelly beans out of. Well, mostly—I think there's some other stuff in them as well and of course there's the strawberry juice, too, but it's more sugar than anything else.'

Iggy couldn't take his eyes off the floor-to-ceiling stacks of sugar bags. He stared, entranced, with greedy eyes, and then he said, 'Can I eat sssome, Mumps?'

Measle shrugged. He couldn't think of a reason why not, and Iggy took his shrug as a 'yes'. He reached out one bony hand and pulled a bag right from the very middle of a stack. Instantly, the whole pile collapsed, several of the bags bursting and spilling their contents over the floor.

'Oops,' said Iggy, in a voice that sounded as if he didn't care a bit about the mess. He poked a hole in his paper bag with one sharp fingernail and then, holding the bag high in the air, he let a stream of sugar fall into his open mouth.

Measle stared at the glittering grains that lay scattered all over the floor. His first thought was— *Nanny is going to be furious at this mess!*—but then he remembered, with a sickening feeling, that Nanny Flannel wasn't going to be *anything* any more.

The sickening feeling turned quite suddenly into anger. Whatever this foul, stinking creature was, it had swallowed up two of his best friends in all the world and now seemed intent on swallowing up him and Iggy as well. Well, he wouldn't let it! *There must be something else I can do to it, besides shooting sugar lumps at it!*

Measle's mind started to work furiously.

All that sugar lying there—what if the Slitherghoul got completely covered with the stuff? What would that do to it? Would it do anything? And how could we get the Slitherghoul to cover itself with it in the first place? There's no question that it hates sugar! It hurts it somehow—so, the more sugar we can get on it, the more it'll be hurt! Maybe, with enough sugar, we might even be able to kill the thing! But, how to do it?

Iggy suddenly stopped pouring sugar into his mouth. He dropped the almost empty bag on the floor and the small amount of remaining sugar spilled out, adding to the mess already there. Iggy gulped, his fishy eyes wide. Measle thought the little wrathmonk's pale face looked even paler than usual and there was a sheen of sweat across Iggy's forehead.

'I is feelin' a bit sssick,' muttered Iggy.

Measle wasn't at all surprised—not with the huge amount of sugar that Iggy had consumed so far. Normally, Iggy was rationed to just two hundred red jelly beans a day and that would make most ordinary people feel pretty ill. But Iggy wasn't an ordinary person. He was a greedy wrathmonk who had eaten his entire ration of strawberry-flavoured jelly beans within a few minutes of getting them that morning, and since then he'd stuffed himself with many handfuls of other jelly beans from the jar in the dining room, plus poured almost a whole bag of sugar granules down his throat in one go. It was no wonder he was feeling queasy.

'Drink some water, Iggy,' said Measle and Iggy shambled over to the kitchen sink, turned on the tap and stuck his mouth under it. He'd turned the tap full on and the cold water shot out with some force, gurgling into Iggy's open mouth and splashing over his face, soaking his whole head. Iggy straightened up sharply and banged his head against the tap.

'Urrrgh! Owwww!' he squeaked, pulling off his woolly hat and dropping it into the sink. He rubbed his head with both hands.

Measle was about to sympathize and tell Iggy how brave he was being (which was something he always did when Iggy hurt himself, otherwise Iggy would complain for the rest of the day) when the smell hit him.

It must have been a sudden change in the wind direction outside, because one minute the stink wasn't there and the next it was—and it was very strong.

Quickly and silently, Measle stepped out of the pantry, his feet crunching on the spilled sugar. Beyond the broken window the darkness lay heavy against the house. Measle ran to the jagged opening and carefully peered out—

The Slitherghoul was sliding fast across the kitchen yard and now Measle heard the thunder of its massive rain cloud overhead.

Measle turned away from the window, his eyes searching desperately for a way out. His first thought was for the door that led to the corridor and he dashed across the kitchen and grabbed Iggy by one wet hand. He dragged the little wrathmonk towards the shadows on the far side of the kitchen. His candle guttered in his hand, the dim flame lighting up the doorway—

Which was completely blocked by a great pile of rubble that reached from floor to ceiling.

No Way Out

They were caught like rats in a trap.

When the old oak beam had given way, it had brought down a whole section of the kitchen wall and part of the passage ceiling too. The pile of plaster, bricks, and wood was jammed tight in the opening. The only other way out of the kitchen was through the shattered window—and now the Slitherghoul must be almost directly outside.

There was only one thing that Measle and Iggy could do.

Measle blew out his candle and dropped it to the floor. Then he dragged Iggy back to the pantry and together they pressed themselves into the shadows of the back wall.

Measle reached into his pocket and took out a

yellow jelly bean. Then he grabbed Iggy by the lapels of his mouldy old jacket and pulled him close. Before Iggy could say a word, Measle stuck his hand deep into the breast pocket of the mouldy jacket and extracted a green jelly bean. He held the green bean in front of Iggy's face and hissed, 'Eat it, Iggy!'

Iggy was still rubbing the bruised spot on his head. He blinked a couple of times and then said, 'I told you, Mumps, I don't like de green ones!'

'I don't care, Iggy!' hissed Measle. 'You've got to eat it!'

Stubbornly, Iggy shook his head and, at the same moment, he compressed his lips tightly, showing clearly that he had no intention of letting the nasty green thing anywhere near his mouth.

Measle peered desperately over Iggy's shoulder. Beyond the broken window, a dark shape moved in the shadows. The smell of the Slitherghoul flooded the kitchen.

Measle made a fist out of the hand that was holding the green jelly bean and then, quite gently, he bopped Iggy right on the end of his bent and beaky nose.

'Owww!' yelped Iggy, opening his mouth wide to wail. Instantly, Measle opened his fist and crammed the jelly bean into Iggy's mouth. Measle put one hand on the top of Iggy's soggy head, the other under Iggy's bottom jaw and then pushed both hands hard together.

Iggy's mouth closed with a snap and, right before Measle's eyes, the little wrathmonk disappeared.

Measle couldn't see Iggy, but he could feel him. He could feel Iggy's chest lift, as Iggy filled it full of air—and he knew in that moment that Iggy was going to yell out some sort of protest at this cruel treatment. Measle instantly put his hand over Iggy's mouth. At the same moment, he popped the yellow jelly bean into his own mouth and bit down hard.

If anybody had looked into the kitchen then, they would have thought that nobody was there, apart from some faint, gurgling, grunting noises coming from deep inside the pantry. The noises sounded exactly as if somebody was trying to say something but couldn't because somebody *else* had their hand pressed tightly across their mouth.

The Slitherghoul slimed up to the jagged opening of the kitchen window and, using several wrathmonk eyes, it peered into the room. It had been attracted here by a light flickering in the distant shadows and several of the wrathmonk minds had cried, *He's there! The horrid boy is there!*

In the dim light of the remaining candles, all the Slitherghoul could see was an empty room and the dark rectangle of the pantry door. It was about to turn away and search somewhere else when the sound of running water reached the ears of every one of its victims. Iggy had left the tap running at full force and the water in the sink wasn't draining away. Iggy's woolly hat was lying where he'd dropped it—at the bottom of the sink, blocking the drain hole, and the water was rising fast. Soon it would spill over the edge.

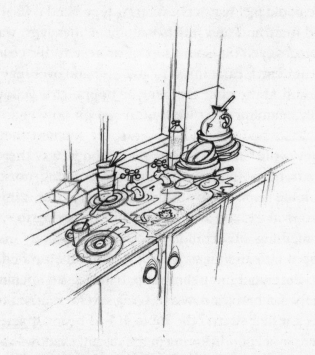

The Slitherghoul paused and then peered into the flickering shadows and Toby Jugg's mind cried out, *Why? Why is the water running?* And then Griswold Gristle's mind joined in and hissed, *I think the boy is there!*

We don't sssee anything! came a chorus of other wrathmonk voices, and the weight of their opinions began to turn the Slitherghoul away from the window again—but Griswold's mind shrieked, *No! He's there, I tell you! We have sssseen thisss trick before! The boy has the ability to disappear into thin air! We mussst feel for him!*

The vast, stinking bulk of the Slitherghoul pressed up against the hole where the window had been and part of its body bulged through the opening and spilled onto the broken glass on the kitchen floor. Measle and Iggy, pressed hard against the back wall of the pantry, watched through their invisible eyes as a fat tentacle of slime extruded from the body of the creature. Slowly the tentacle started to stretch out across the floor, its tip sweeping backwards and forwards in wide arcs. Slowly, horribly, the tentacle came nearer and nearer.

Measle and Iggy didn't move a muscle. Iggy had frozen into a statue at Measle's side and Measle had felt confident enough to take his hand away from the wrathmonk's mouth. He needed one hand to get another green jelly bean out of Iggy's pocket and he needed his *other* hand to get a yellow one out of his *own* pocket and hold them in readiness.

This time, Measle had been too scared to count down from thirty, so he was forced to guess how much longer they had. Well before the half minute was up, he slipped his yellow jelly bean between his lips. Then he felt for Iggy's mouth and pressed the green jelly bean past Iggy's unresisting teeth, quickly clamping his hand over the wrathmonk's jaw.

This time, Iggy seemed to understand why he was being made to eat the nasty green ones, because Measle felt him bite down on the jelly bean without any protest at all.

But invisibility wasn't going to help them. Not this time. Four of the wrathmonks had experienced Measle's disappearing trick twice before and it was they who were leading this search, causing the tentacle to slither back and forth across the whole width of the kitchen, a hunt which Measle knew would end in their discovery.

The sound of running water changed from the roar of a wide open tap to something more splashy, as the sink suddenly overflowed. The water cascaded over the lip of the basin and dropped, in a miniature Niagara Falls, onto the kitchen floor. Quickly it spread across the tiles in an ever-widening puddle. The tip of the tentacle swept through it, brushing the water from side to side and sending little tidal waves rolling towards the pantry.

Measle and Iggy huddled together, watching helplessly as the fat, wriggling tentacle came nearer and nearer.

A tiny wave of water, no more than a couple of centimetres high, washed through the open pantry door. It reached almost to the feet of Measle and Iggy, flowing over the crystals of sugar on the floor—and the grains melted and dissolved.

The tentacle had felt its way all across the kitchen floor and now only the dark pantry was left. There was an absolute certainty in Griswold

Gristle's mind—*We have him, dear friends!* he cried. *There is only one place he can be! Push on—push on into the darkness!*

The tentacle wriggled its tip through the opening of the pantry door and slithered across the floor, its tip sliding from side to side through the shallow puddle of water.

The Slitherghoul felt a sudden, stinging pain.

None of its internal victims felt the pain and, when the tentacle stopped its forward motion and started hurriedly to reverse out of the pantry, the minds of Griswold and Buford and Frognell and Judge Cedric all cried out, *No! Don't ssstop! Go forward! He's there, we tell you! He's there!*

But the Slitherghoul paid no attention. Its own brain was small and crude and pathetic next to the minds of its victims, but when it felt pain, or suspected its existence was in any sort of danger, it reacted instinctively, overpowering any alien thoughts that might try to control it.

None of its victims understood the reason for the extraordinary retreat from the dark pantry and the Slitherghoul's hurried exit back out through the kitchen window.

No! No! NO! screamed the thoughts of the four wrathmonks—and now several other minds joined in and tried to make the Slitherghoul return to its search. The creature ignored them all and slithered away over the gravel path by the side of the house. Cooling drops from the rain cloud fell heavily onto its heaving body, slowly washing away whatever it was that had caused the stinging sensation. The Slitherghoul paused in its flight and lay still, letting the rain thunder down. In its primitive mind, a new sense—a sense of *danger*—lay like a lead weight, and it was a sense the Slitherghoul had never experienced before. If a brain as small and as crude as the Slitherghoul's could be said to feel uneasiness, then that was what the Slitherghoul was now feeling—and no amount of urging from the minds of its victims was going to budge it until that feeling went away.

Inside the pantry, the effects of the jelly beans were wearing off. Measle and Iggy reappeared in the darkness. Both turned to stare at the other in wonder and Measle saw that Iggy's eyes were even rounder and fishier than ever.

'Coo,' said Iggy, quietly. 'Dat old Sssquiffypoo just went away. Why did it do dat, Mumps?'

Measle knew why. It was the sugar, of course. The water from the sink had dissolved the crystals that were scattered over the pantry floor, making a sweet solution which the Slitherghoul had found unpleasant to the touch—perhaps even painful! Certainly the creature seemed desperate not to have any further contact with the stuff . . .

Click, click, click, went Measle's brain.

A vague idea for a trap formed in his head. It was a big idea, full of doubts and uncertainties, and certainly very hard to achieve, but it was the only one he'd got at the moment—*and it must be better to do something than just wait around for the creature to catch up with them! The only question was, where could they set the trap?*

'Is—is dat old Sssquiffypoo comin' back, Mumps?' asked Iggy, peering out into the kitchen.

'I don't know, Iggy. I hope not, anyway. But look, I've got an idea and I'm going to need your help.'

Iggy sniffed suspiciously. Sometimes Mumps's ideas meant a lot of hard work. 'Do we have to dig again?' he said. 'Coz, if we do, den I'm not helpin', and dat's final!'

Measle didn't reply. He stepped out into the kitchen, sloshing through the water on the floor. He reached out and turned off the kitchen tap, then he fished in the water and pulled Iggy's sodden hat out. The drain gurgled and the water began to drain away. Measle watched as the level in the sink fell and he didn't take his eyes away until the last of the water had disappeared down the hole.

Click.

I know where the trap can be!

Measle turned excitedly to Iggy but, before he could say anything, Iggy grabbed at the sodden hat in Measle's hands and said, 'Ooh, I was wonderin' where dat was, Mumps! Fanks!'

Iggy stuck the cap on his head and the water dribbled down his face and neck.

'There's no digging, Iggy,' said Measle, thoughtfully.

Iggy's face brightened. 'Okey-dokey, den.'

Stepping as silently as possible across the debris on the kitchen floor, Measle and Iggy went to the window and peered out into the darkness. The smell of the Slitherghoul was faint. Measle looked from side to side, his eyes searching the dark sky. *There!* About fifty metres away, the dense rain cloud hung close to the side of the house and, beneath it, Measle could just make out the low hump of the Slitherghoul. It didn't seem to be moving.

Measle grabbed Iggy and dragged him back to the pantry. He positioned the little wrathmonk next to the shelves and pulled Iggy's arms straight out in front of him.

'Now, look, Iggy, this is what we're going to do. We're going to load you up with bags of sugar and we're going to see how many you can carry, OK?'

'Ooh, is dis a game, Mumps?'

'Well, it's a *sort* of game. A very special sort of game, which is going to help us get rid of that old Squiffypoo. So you're not going to complain if you have to carry rather a lot, are you?'

Iggy shook his head firmly, sending drops of water flying. He liked doing things which showed off how strong he could be. Digging, he'd decided, wasn't one of them, but carrying heavy stuff probably was. He held his arms stiffly in front of him and Measle started grabbing bags of sugar off the shelves and piling them high against Iggy's chest. Quite soon, the stack was up to Iggy's eyes.

'Right!' said Measle. 'That's enough for one load.'

He took hold of Iggy's elbow and led him out of the pantry and across the kitchen. A couple of times Iggy almost fell, tripping over some of the fallen bricks and plaster that littered the floor, but Measle steadied him each time and they reached the shattered window without dropping a single bag.

Measle paused at the window and peered out. The Slitherghoul was still there, a dark hump under a torrent of rain. There was no way of telling in which direction the creature was looking, so Measle wasn't going to take the risk. He reached into his pocket and took out a yellow jelly bean. Then he did the same to Iggy, pushing his hand past the stack of sugar bags and wriggling it into Iggy's breast pocket. He pinched a green jelly bean between his finger and thumb and pulled it out.

'Now then, Iggy,' he whispered, 'when I say go, we're going to eat our jelly beans, all right?'

'All right, Mumps,' said Iggy, reluctantly. 'But I ssstill don't like de green ones.'

'Well, I don't like my yellow ones much either, but that's part of this game, you see. When we're invisible, we're going to run as fast as we can. And we're going to try and not drop a single bag.'

'Dat is easy-peasy for you to sssay,' said Iggy, scornfully. 'Coz you isn't *carryin'* any bags, is you?'

'No, I'm not,' said Measle carefully. He didn't want to start an argument with Iggy—not at this moment, certainly. 'But I'm in charge of these jelly beans, you see. I've got to be able to get them out of our pockets quickly, and I need both hands for that, don't I?'

Iggy nodded. Even his little brain could see the logic of that.

'Ssso—where is we goin' to run to, Mumps?'

'There,' said Measle, pointing out into the darkness. 'We're going to run out there.'

Baiting the Trap

'Er . . . dat's where de old Sssquiffypoo is, Mumps,' said Iggy, a little nervously.

'I know, Iggy. That's why we're going to eat our special jelly beans. We'll be invisible and the Squiffypoo won't see us, will it?'

Iggy's face cleared and he grinned. 'Okey-dokey, Mumps.'

'But we'll have to be very quiet, otherwise the Squiffypoo might hear us, and that would be almost as bad as it seeing us, Iggy. So, we have to run like little mice, all right?'

'Okey-dokey, Mumps.'

'Now, when we run out there, you won't be able to see me and I won't be able to see you. So I'm going to keep hold of your collar, Iggy, all the way.'

'All de way *where*?'

'All the way to our swimming pool.'

Iggy's eyes narrowed suspiciously. 'I fort you sssaid we wasn't goin' to do no more diggin'?'

'We're not. In fact, what we're going to do is see if we can fill it up again.'

Iggy's face started its wild grimacing so, to prevent an endless discussion about nothing, Measle said, hurriedly, 'Just do whatever I tell you to do, and everything will be fine. And, if we get separated, just run as fast as you can back to the kitchen, understand?'

Iggy's face settled down and he nodded, slowly.

Measle held up the green jelly bean and said, 'Now, I'm going to stick this in your mouth, but don't bite on it yet. Wait until I say "GO!"'

Iggy nodded again and opened his mouth and Measle put the green jelly bean on Iggy's tongue. Then he popped his yellow bean into his own mouth and tucked it into his cheek.

'Ready?' he said, reaching out and taking hold of Iggy's damp collar.

Iggy nodded again, his eyes wide with the effort of not biting into a jelly bean, even if it was one of the green ones.

Measle took a deep breath.

'GO!'

Measle watched as Iggy's jaws clamped down on the jelly bean. At the same instant, Measle slipped his own jelly bean out of his cheek and bit down hard—and, together, he and Iggy disappeared in wisps of grey smoke.

'Right, Iggy, now let's run!'

Measle, clutching tight to an invisible collar, scrambled over the jagged windowsill. He could feel Iggy moving next to him as they dropped down onto the stones of the kitchen yard and, the moment Measle sensed that Iggy was with him on the solid ground, he started to run as fast as he could, dragging Iggy along beside him.

The edge of the lawn was just a few metres away but a good seven seconds had passed before Measle's feet touched the grass. Keeping hold of an invisible little wrathmonk who was staggering under a heavy load of sugar bags was slowing him down badly.

Out of the corner of one eye, Measle was watching the distant hump that was the Slitherghoul. It still wasn't moving.

Just let it stay there! thought Measle, beginning to pant a little now. He and Iggy stumbled silently over the grass, towards the dark rectangle of their swimming pool and, by the time they reached the edge of it, another ten seconds had passed.

They were more than halfway through their invisibility.

Measle skidded to a halt on the damp grass and he felt Iggy do the same at his side. The muddy pit was directly in front of them.

'Throw the bags in, Iggy!' hissed Measle.

'*Wot?*' came Iggy's voice, from somewhere near Measle's left ear.

'The bags, Iggy! Throw them in the hole!'

'Frow dem in de hole? *Frow dem in de hole?* Are you *potty*, Mumps?'

Measle felt Iggy's body stiffen, as if the little wrathmonk was about to utter a strong protest— *but there isn't time for that, Iggy!*—so Measle, still firmly clutching the back of Iggy's collar, reached out with his other hand and began to scrabble at the bags in Iggy's outstretched arms. He couldn't see them, but he could *feel* them, and a moment later his scrabbling took effect as several of the topmost ones slipped from the pile. Measle heard them fall, with soggy thumps, into the muddy bottom of the pit.

Iggy gasped and Measle felt him take a step backwards, away from the edge of the pit. *That's no good!* thought Measle desperately. There was only one thing to do, and Measle did it. He grabbed Iggy's collar with both hands and pushed hard, forcing Iggy back to the edge and almost shoving him over, and Iggy, desperate not to fall in, forgot all about the load he was carrying and started to flail his arms about, just like people do when they feel their balance going. Immediately, Measle heard the sound of a large number of invisible sugar bags thumping down into the pit—and, at the same moment, came a wail of despair from Iggy.

'Noooo!'

Measle moved his hands off Iggy's collar and up over his invisible mouth and Iggy's wail was instantly cut back to a muffled moan.

'Sshhhh, Iggy! Not a sound!' Measle hissed. 'We don't want the Squiffypoo to hear us!'

To Measle's horror, right front of his eyes, a long, pointed ear started to take shape out of grey smoke. The jelly beans were wearing off! Measle took one hand away from Iggy's mouth and fumbled for Iggy's front pocket. He yanked out a still invisible jelly bean and stuffed it into Iggy's mouth.

'Bite it, Iggy!'

As Iggy chomped down on the jelly bean, Measle was already pulling one of his own from his pocket and popping it into his mouth.

They were only just in time. The grey smoke took only moments to solidify and by the time the second jelly beans took effect, both Iggy and Measle could be seen quite clearly, looking like a pair of grey ghosts out in the middle of the vast lawn.

Measle peered towards the lump in the shadows. Neither it, nor its rain cloud, seemed to be moving.

'We were lucky that time, Iggy,' he whispered into the darkness, and, out of the darkness, came Iggy's plaintive whisper back at him, '*Lucky?* We ain't lucky, Mumps! We jussst frew away all dat puffickly good sugar!'

'And we're going to do it again, Iggy. Lots more

times, in fact! Come on, let's get back to the kitchen before our jelly beans wear off again.'

Getting from the pit back to the kitchen was a quicker business than getting from the kitchen to the pit, because now Iggy wasn't burdened by armfuls of sugar bags but, even so, they only just made it back inside the relative safety of the kitchen before both of them materialized out of grey smoke.

The moment Iggy appeared in front of him, Measle realized that the little wrathmonk was upset. Iggy's face was wriggling and contorting more wildly than usual and he was even paler than normal. His fishy eyes were huge and almost completely round and he was glaring at Measle with an expression of bewildered fury.

'Wot—wot does you fink you is *doin'*, Mumps?' he sputtered, angrily. 'Miss Fwannel will kill usss! Frowin' away puffickly good sugar like dat! Dat is not funny!'

Measle kept his voice calm and quiet. 'Nanny Flannel has gone, Iggy. So has Tinker. So have Mr Needle and Mr Bland. Mum and Dad and Tilly are all a squillion miles away. We're all alone here, and we have to try to save ourselves.'

'Dat is all very well, but frowin' away puffickly good sugar—'

'We're not throwing it away, Iggy. We're building a trap.'

'A trap?'

'Yes, a *sugar* trap.'

Iggy's face was as blank as a sheet of white paper and Measle knew that there was no point in trying to explain things to him—not now. Later perhaps, but right now he just needed Iggy's strength.

'Look, Iggy, you've just got to trust me,' said Measle, gently. 'I know what I'm doing, but I can't do it without your help. So, will you help me, without asking any questions and without getting all cross?'

Measle's calm and soothing voice had a remarkable effect on Iggy. His wriggling face muscles settled down, his eyes got a little less round, and his whole skinny body seemed to relax a fraction. He sniffed and said, 'No diggin'?'

'No digging, Iggy. Just more throwing sugar. Lots more. All right?'

Iggy was very, very silly, but, deep in his heart (and not caring to admit it) he knew that Measle was clever. He knew that Measle was cleverer than he was, which was why, most of the time, he would let Measle take charge of things during their adventures at Merlin Manor. And now his friend had a very serious look on his face and, in that instant, Iggy decided to do what Measle was asking.

'Okey-dokey, Mumps.'

They made that hurried trip ten more times and, now that Iggy knew what was expected of him, they did it faster and faster.

By the time the pantry shelves were bare, both

Measle and Iggy were very tired. And, while Iggy's breast pocket still bulged with green jelly beans, Measle's pocket was almost empty of yellow ones.

'I fink I like diggin' better, Mumps,' panted Iggy, leaning against an empty shelf. He was staring at the floor, bent double, with both hands grasping his knees, in an attempt to catch his breath. 'All dis runnin' about,' he grumbled, 'bein' ingrizzible, frowin' away puffickly good sugar. Ho, yesss, I definitely likes diggin' better!'

'Well, we don't have to do either any more, Iggy,' gasped Measle. He too was bent over, his hands on his knees, panting for breath. 'Now, we've got to do something else, but I promise it won't be *nearly* so tiring.'

SETTING THE TRAP

When Measle and Iggy had got their breath back, Measle crept to the kitchen window and peered out. The dark lump of the Slitherghoul was there, fifty metres away but now it was moving again, slowly sliming its way across the lawn, the rain cloud hovering overhead.

With a sickening feeling in the pit of his stomach, Measle saw that it was heading straight for the swimming pool.

Not yet! thought Measle, panic rising in his chest. *The trap's not ready yet! It mustn't see it! It mustn't see what we've done!*

Measle's mind raced.

Distract it! We've got to distract it!

Measle came to a sudden decision. He knew

191

what he had to do. At the back of his mind, he knew it was a hideously *dangerous* thing to do but they had no choice.

Measle darted back to the pantry and seized Iggy's hand. Dragging him across the littered kitchen floor, he hissed, 'Come on, Iggy! We've got to do some more running!'

Iggy opened his mouth to object, but then he remembered that he'd decided to be helpful. He allowed himself to be pulled along and, at the same time, he dipped his fingers into his breast pocket and pulled out one of the few remaining green jelly beans. He was about to pop it into his mouth, when Measle saw what he was doing.

'No, Iggy! Not this time! This time, we have to be *visible*!'

Iggy got as far as saying, 'Grizzible? *Grizzible?* But, if we is *grizzible*, den dat old Sssquiffypoo is goin' to sssee usss, and den—'

He didn't get any more out, because Measle dragged him through the broken window. Once outside, Measle started to jump up and down, waving his free arm and yelling, 'OVER HERE! OVER HERE! COME AND GET US—WE'RE OVER HERE!'

Out on the dark lawn, the Slitherghoul slowed and then stopped, a good three metres short of the edge of the swimming pool pit. Ponderously, it moved its huge slimy body round. Measle yelled even harder.

'COME ON, YOU HORRIBLE OLD SQUIFFYPOO, YOU! COME AND GET US!'

The Slitherghoul seemed to pause for a moment. In fact, a small battle was going on inside it. Nanny Flannel was trying to hold the Slitherghoul back, but the four evil wrathmonks joined their minds to Toby Jugg's and, with the help of several of the other released prisoners, they were urging the Slitherghoul to give chase.

Nanny Flannel did her best, but the others were too strong for her. The Slitherghoul began, slowly at first, to slime its way across the lawn towards the kitchen yard. Gradually it gathered speed.

'Come on, Iggy!' hissed Measle. 'Now we've really got to run!'

Together, Measle and Iggy raced down the long side wall of Merlin Manor. Their feet crunch-crunched on the gravel path. Halfway along the wall, Measle dared a quick glance over his shoulder.

I—I don't believe it! That great slug thing is gaining on us! How can it move so fast?

Indeed, the Slitherghoul was catching up—and catching up fast. Measle remembered the time when Basil Tramplebone, in the guise of a giant black cockroach, had been chasing him and Tinker along the railway lines of the great table-top train set. Basil the cockroach had been about the same size as this terrible creature and *he'd* been able to move fast, too.

Measle remembered another thing: if a great mass such as this wanted to stop suddenly, or change direction, it took time and space to do it. So, the trick was to dodge and weave—

Measle and Iggy reached the corner of the house and they darted round it. Here was the front of the house, with its great circle of gravel driveway. For a moment, Measle and Iggy paused, gulping in lungfuls of breath.

Across the driveway, set in an enormous area of closely-cropped grass, was one of the glories of Merlin Manor.

The main rose garden.

Partly because of the great pride that Sam took in them, and the care he lavished on their upkeep—but mostly because of Iggy's breathing spell, which killed the bugs that threatened to harm them—the roses of Merlin Manor were spectacular. Bushy and dense and healthy, every summer their stems were heavy with flowers of every colour and every scent. They grew tall and very wide and overhung the narrow grass paths that intersected the beds, so that, at first glance, the rose garden looked almost like an impenetrable jungle. But the paths were there and Measle knew them well. If there was dodging and weaving to be done, the paths in the rose garden were the spots to do it.

A soft night breeze brought the stink of the Slitherghoul to Measle's nostrils. He looked back over his shoulder again—the monstrous mound of slime was slithering over the gravel path at an impossible speed. It was no more than a few metres away!

Measle leapt forward, pulling Iggy with him. Silently, they ran across the drive, then onto the lawn. The rose garden loomed dark in front of them. There was just enough light for Measle to see the beginning of one of the paths that led towards the centre of the garden and he headed for it as fast as his legs—and the weight of a dragging wrathmonk—would let him.

They made it just in time. Only seconds after Measle and Iggy darted between the first of the overhanging rose bushes, they heard the sound of the Slitherghoul barging into the same gap. There was the sound of breaking branches.

Measle and Iggy ran deeper and deeper into the rose garden. They dodged left—then right—then left again—their heads slung low and their backs bent as they scurried between the overhanging plants. Behind them came a terrible noise of ripping stems as the Slitherghoul forced its giant body along the same paths. But it was slowing down. Measle could hear the sounds slowly diminishing.

'It can't turn corners like we can!' he panted in Iggy's ear. 'It's slowing down! Come on—round here!'

He hardly needed to give Iggy directions. The

little wrathmonk knew the rose gardens better than anybody, since he spent so much time there. At first, Iggy hadn't liked the roses much. It's not in the nature of a wrathmonk to like nice things, particularly nice things that smell so good; wrathmonks prefer the stink of rotting meat to the scent of roses. But slowly Iggy had got used to his job and, while he never really liked the flowers much, he did get quite fond of the *thorns*. The longer and the sharper the thorns were on any particular rose bush the better as far as Iggy was concerned. He always spent a little longer breathing on those rose bushes that grew the best set of thorns than on those whose thorns were smaller and blunter—with the result that the biggest and best rose bushes in the gardens of Merlin Manor also possessed the biggest and best thorns.

The sound of breaking branches behind Measle and Iggy not only grew quieter as they put more and more distance between themselves and the Slitherghoul, the noise itself also seemed to have stopped moving at all. Now, the only sound they could hear was a distant thrashing, thumping, ripping.

Measle paused for a moment and turned round. He stood on his tiptoes and tried to see over the tops of the rose bushes, but they were too high.

'Come on, Iggy, let's get to the sundial!'

The sundial was made of brass and it stood on an old stone pillar in the centre of the great rose garden. A few more twists and turns brought Measle and Iggy to the circular bed, where the sundial stood.

'Quick, Iggy, lift me up!'

Iggy hastily stuffed the jelly beans he'd just taken out of his pocket into his mouth and, chewing busily, he hoisted Measle up, so that Measle was high enough to pull himself onto the top of the stone pillar. He carefully stood upright on the small platform and then stared out across the rose gardens.

It was pretty dark, but he could just about make out the dark lump of the Slitherghoul. It appeared to be about six metres within the border of the rose garden—and it appeared to be stuck. Measle watched as the lump heaved and rippled and he saw, to his puzzled satisfaction, that the lump didn't seem to be advancing by even a centimetre.

His puzzlement only lasted another second.

'It's stuck, Iggy!' Measle called down. 'And I think it's the thorns that are sticking it!'

Anybody who has tried to walk among rose bushes knows just how grabby a rose thorn can be. They stick in your clothes and you really have to pull hard to get free. There were a thousand thorns sticking in the soft, slimy jelly of the Slitherghoul's body and, while the creature felt no pain, it found itself making almost no headway whatsoever. It strained and pulled—and a hundred thorns popped away from its sides—but a hundred more fastened into the soft substance, so that its forward motion was slowed down to mere centimetres a minute.

It looked to Measle as if it was going to be stuck there for quite a time.

'Dat is a clever plan, Mumps,' said Iggy, standing at the base of the pedestal and staring up at Measle with a look of admiration on his pale face. '*Ssstreemely* clever, ssstickin' dat old Sssquiffypoo wiv de prickles.'

Getting the Slitherghoul stuck in the rose bushes hadn't actually been part of Measle's plan, but he decided to let Iggy think it had been. Right now, he needed all the admiration he could get, if only to persuade Iggy to do whatever he said, without any of the usual arguments.

Measle jumped down from the pedestal.

'Right,' he said, firmly, 'I think we've got a little

time before that old Squiffypoo gets free. Come on, we've got work to do!'

'Not diggin' again, Mumps?' said Iggy suspiciously.

'No, Iggy, *not* digging! *Fun* work! Come on!'

Together, Measle and Iggy ran quickly through the rest of the rose garden, putting more and more distance between themselves and the sounds of the thrashing Slitherghoul. Soon, they were out the other side, racing towards the far wing of Merlin Manor. They rounded the corner and ran on, down the long side of the house, then round another corner, and there lay the back lawn of the house and, right in the middle of it, the darker shadow of the swimming pool pit.

'Coo!' panted Iggy, running fast at Measle's side. 'We has gone all round de *whole* house!'

Measle led Iggy back to the kitchen yard. There, on the wall close by the door, was a tap. Fastened to the tap was a garden hose. It was coiled over a hook and Measle, using all his strength, lifted the whole coil off the hook and dropped it to the ground. Then he grabbed hold of the brass nozzle and started to drag it across the yard.

'Come on, Iggy!' he yelled. 'Give me a hand with this!'

'What is you doin' wiv dat pipe fing?' said Iggy, standing there and not helping at all.

'We've got to get this end all the way to the swimming pool! Come on, help me pull!'

Iggy didn't move. He sniffed and put his nose

in the air and said, 'Huh! Dat pipe fing won't reach.'

'Yes it will, Iggy! I measured before! When we were doing the digging! It reaches fine! Now, come *on*!'

Reluctantly, Iggy took hold of the hose and together they dragged it all across the kitchen yard, then onto the grass. The further they pulled it, the heavier it became, but finally they reached the edge of the pit. Both of them were breathing hard.

'Iggy, I want you to run back and turn on the tap. Can you do that?'

Iggy sniffed scornfully. 'Of courssse I can do dat!' he said. 'Wot do you fink I am—a ssstoopidy-poopidy?'

'No, I don't think you're a stoopidy-poopidy.'

'Good,' said Iggy, firmly. 'Den I will do it.' He paused, his face wriggling in thought. Then he said, 'Er . . . wot was it you wanted me to do, Mumps?'

'Turn on the tap, please.'

'Ho, yesss. Okey-dokey.'

Iggy shambled away towards the house and Measle bent down and put his hand on the brass nozzle. A few moments later, he felt the whole hose move and stiffen as it filled with water. Using both hands, Measle twisted the brass nozzle and a hard jet of water blasted out of it. He directed the stream down into the bottom of the pit and heard the water spray across the scattered bags of sugar. It made a sort of *blatting* sound as it smashed against the paper bags.

'Wot is you doin' *now*?' squealed Iggy, who had trotted back to Measle's side and was staring, with horror, down into the dark pit. 'Wot is you *doin*'? You is makin' all dat lovely sugar all *wet*! And den we won't be able to *eat* it, Mumps!'

'I'm filling up our swimming pool, Iggy!' said Measle, putting all the enthusiasm he could muster into his voice. 'And it will be lovely to swim in, won't it? Because, you see, the water will taste all sweet, like your jelly beans! In fact, it'll be like *swimming* in jelly beans!'

Measle saw Iggy's face break into a wide smile.

'Coo, dat will be nice, doin' swimmin' in jelly beans!'

The water roared down into the hole. The seconds, then the minutes, ticked by and Measle began to realize that filling a large hole in the ground with water was going to take quite a long time. The *blatting* sound of water smashing against paper bags had changed to a loud splashing noise, so Measle guessed that the level of the water must have risen just higher than the scattered sacks, but even so, at this rate, it was going to take an age to fill the pit.

'Iggy, could you go and see what that old Squiffypoo is doing?'

'Wot, now?' said Iggy.

'Yes, now! It may have got free—and we've got to get a lot more water into the pool before we can have our swim!'

'Okey-dokey,' said Iggy, and he trotted off into the darkness.

'Be careful!' yelled Measle, but Iggy didn't reply.

Measle held tight to the brass nozzle and directed the jet of water into the black pit. He didn't dare let go of the thing—he knew what happened when you let go of a hose when water was running through it. He and Iggy had been playing with it one day, seeing how high they could make the jet go and then, when they got bored with doing that, squirting water at each other—and Iggy had made the mistake of dropping the hose. Spraying water everywhere, the hose had started to wriggle and writhe all over the lawn, like a crazy snake, and it had taken Measle and Iggy a good three minutes to catch the thing again. By the time they did, they were both soaking wet.

Measle's hand started throbbing. He'd forgotten all about it in the excitement and terror of the chase but now, with the fingers of both hands clutched tightly around the brass nozzle of the hose, he could feel the pain. All of a sudden the discomfort, the darkness, the loneliness, and the danger of his situation seemed to lump together in a great heavy weight—and the weight settled on his shoulders like a big black slab of misery and fear that pressed him down towards the muddy ground.

Where's Iggy? Is he doing what I asked him

*to do—or has he forgotten all about me and is
off somewhere, gobbling the rest of his jelly
beans?*

I wish he'd come back.

I wish Tinker was here.

I wish Nanny was here.

I wish Mum and Dad were here.

But they're not.

And—I'm scared.

The minutes ticked away. The splashing sound
had a deeper note to it now, as if the water itself
was getting deeper. It was too dark to see into the
pit, so Measle had no way of knowing just exactly
how high the level of the water was, but he knew
it couldn't be very high. Not yet at least.

''Ello, Mumps.'

Measle almost dropped the hose. He twisted his
head round and here was Iggy, his face gleaming
pale in the surrounding darkness.

'Iggy! You nearly gave me a heart attack!'

'Did I?' said Iggy, his face splitting into a proud
grin. He had no idea what a heart attack was but it
sounded a pretty important thing to give people
and, since Mumps was his best friend, he was
pleased he'd nearly given him one.

'Did you see the Slithergh— I mean, the
Squiffypoo?' Measle asked.

'Ho, yesss,' said Iggy, his eyes wandering over the
dark rectangle of the pit. 'I saw 'im all right. Can we
ssswim yet?'

'Soon, Iggy. What was the Squiffypoo doing? Is it still stuck in the rose garden?'

Iggy shook his head. 'No, it's not ssstuck. Not no more, no how.'

'It's not? Well, what's it doing, Iggy?'

'It ssstarted to follow me, ssso I runned away, didn't I?'

'That was sensible, Iggy. So—where is it now?'

'Wot, de old Sssquiffypoo?' Iggy jerked his thumb over his shoulder. 'It's right behind me.'

Sugar and Slime

Even as Iggy spoke, Measle caught the first faint whiff of the horrendous Slitherghoul stench. He looked over Iggy's shoulder and there—rounding the far corner of the house and slithering over the gravel of the kitchen yard—it came.

The Slitherghoul seemed to pause for a moment. Then, it obviously saw Measle and Iggy, because it jerked forward towards the edge of the lawn, gathering speed as it slimed its way towards them.

Just for a second, Measle found himself paralysed with fear. He and Iggy were out in the open, with nowhere to hide—and the trap wasn't ready yet! The only weapon he had was the hose—and it wasn't much of a weapon, not against a creature that seemed oblivious to the drenching rain that cascaded against its body! Instinctively, Measle turned the nozzle away from the pit and aimed it straight at the fast-advancing creature.

The water blasted out in a great glittering arc but the Slitherghoul was still well out of range. Measle lifted the nozzle higher—

Then suddenly, the pressure in the hose relaxed and the jet of water from the nozzle died away to a trickle.

Measle stared down at the hose in disbelief. At the same moment, he heard the distant sound of water splashing down hard against gravel.

He looked up and saw that the Slitherghoul was speeding in a direct line towards him and Iggy, and the direct line lay exactly over the top of the hose that was stretched along the grass. The weight of the Slitherghoul must have forcibly yanked the other end of the hose clean off the tap.

Measle dropped the nozzle and took a step backwards. Immediately he felt the muddy ground crumble beneath his feet. He waved both arms wildly, in an attempt to keep his balance, but it was no good. The edge of the pit slipped away, carrying Measle with it, down into the darkness.

SPLASH!

Measle landed on his back, sending a great spray of water up into the air. The water quickly flooded through his clothes. He struggled and his feet found the muddy bottom. He stood up. The water came to just above his knees. Something pale floated by.

'Dat old Sssquiffypoo is comin', Mumps!' called Iggy's voice from somewhere above him. 'It's comin' fassst! It's nearly here! I don't fink dis is a good time to go ssswimmin'!'

Measle floundered in the icy water. The bottom of the pit was slippery with mud and there were lots of the pale, floating things scattered across the dark surface—the sodden remains of the paper sugar bags.

Then, without warning, there was a tremendous SPLASH! right at Measle's side and Measle received a great wave of water directly in his face. Sputtering, he cleared his eyes.

In the dimness, he could just make out Iggy, who was sitting in the mud looking crossly at the water that reached halfway up his chest.

''Ere—I do not *like* dis ssswimmin', Mumps,' Iggy announced, making no effort to get to his feet. 'I is all wet—*all over*! I don't like bein' all wet—not all *over*!'

Measle lunged and grabbed Iggy's sleeve.

'Come on, Iggy, we've got to get out of here!'

Iggy didn't respond. He was thoughtfully sucking one of his claw-like fingers.

'Dat's funny,' he mumbled. 'Dis swimmin' water tastes quite nice. Maybe dis ssswimmin' ain't ssso bad after all.'

It was obvious Iggy had completely forgotten everything Measle had told him about the plan and there was no time to explain it all over again.

207

Measle pulled hard at Iggy's sleeve, causing the finger to pop out of the little wrathmonk's mouth.

''Ang, on Mumps! I wasn't finished!'

'Come *on*, Iggy!'

His feet slipping and sliding on the muddy bottom of the pit, Measle started to drag Iggy towards the sloping shallow end. Together, they sloshed their way through the black water, the masses of sodden, floating paper bags making their progress even harder. They'd only got about halfway there, when Measle once again caught the dreadful stench of the Slitherghoul. He whipped his head around.

There, at the far end—where the pit was deepest—silhouetted against the dark sky, loomed the Slitherghoul. Measle could see that it was poised right at the edge of the pit and, even without any visible eyes, appeared to be staring down at them.

It had never been part of the plan to be in the pit themselves but Measle realized in that instant that the accident that had put him there was probably a bit of unlooked-for luck. The problem of getting the Slitherghoul into the pit was something that had bothered him and he'd pushed the whole thing to the back of his mind, in the hope that, when the time actually came, he'd have a solution. But here—cold and wet and muddy though it might be—*was* a solution! And it was so *obvious*.

Measle let go of Iggy's sleeve and started to

wave both his arms frantically over his head. He jumped and splashed and screamed as loud as he could.

'Here! I'm down here, you old Squiffypoo! Come and get me, you stinky thing! Last one in the pool's a weedy sissy!'

The dark mass of the Slitherghoul seemed to shiver. Then, without a sound, it heaved itself forward, over the crumbling edge of the pit. The entire creature half fell, half slithered down into the water, making a wave that almost knocked Measle off his feet. For a moment, the Slitherghoul seemed to disappear beneath the surface but then, a second later, Measle saw the great mound of slime rear itself up again. Sodden scraps of paper bags festooned its jelly sides.

'Come on, Iggy! RUN!'

Iggy had been bending over, his face close to the muddy water, surreptitiously slurping the sweet stuff into his mouth when Measle grabbed him and started to drag him away. He slipped and fell but Measle kept on dragging him through the water and Iggy, lying prone, took the opportunity to swallow a few more mouthfuls. He felt himself being hauled up a slope, and now it was hard for his mouth to reach the surface of the water, because the water was getting shallower and shallower.

Measle was almost at the top of the slope and his feet were clear of the water. Held tight by one sleeve, Iggy was still lying there, his head bent sideways in a final attempt to get just one more swallow. With a last effort, Measle heaved Iggy clear of the water.

Measle paused for a second, panting hard.

They both heard the hissing sound at the same moment. Measle turned and Iggy lifted his head and they both stared down into the pit.

The hissing sound came from the Slitherghoul —or rather, it came from the Slitherghoul's skin. The creature made no sound, but plumes of steam seemed to be rising from the muddy water that surrounded it. The monster itself was writhing and rippling and shuddering and floundering, causing a succession of large waves to splash against the sides of the pit—and those same waves, rebounding off the walls, swept back and over the top of the struggling mound of jelly, *which was gradually getting smaller*.

There was no doubt about it. As it flopped and struggled in the muddy water, Measle could see that the Slitherghoul was slowly shrinking.

Then a very strange thing—even stranger than the shrinking—happened.

Two yellow bubbles, like nasty zits only much, much bigger, swelled up on the outer surface of the Slitherghoul. As Measle and Iggy watched, the bubbles grew and then burst wetly, exposing a pair of slime-covered heads. The heads twisted and turned in what looked like an effort to drag themselves clear, and the attempt seemed to work, because, next, two pairs of shoulders were exposed, then four arms. A moment later, he and Iggy could see two waists, then four legs.

Mr Needle and Mr Bland fell, with a double splash, away from the quivering surface of the Slitherghoul and into the muddy water. Both men disappeared beneath the surface for a second or two, then their heads rose back out. Mr Needle and Mr Bland coughed and spluttered and wiped the slime from their eyes. Then they turned and saw the great quaking mound of jelly behind them.

Mr Needle screamed—and so did Mr Bland. Slipping and sliding and bumping into each other in their panic, they scrambled away from the creature as fast as they could. They stumbled up the slope, seeming not to see Measle and Iggy at all. They simply blundered past them, their clothes and hair soggy with muddy water and stinking slime. When they reached the top, both men stared wildly in all directions, then ran away into the darkness.

Measle pulled Iggy to his feet and they both stared down at the slowly diminishing monster. It was still enormous—it filled the deep end of the pit completely—and it displaced a huge amount of water, so much so that the level of the sweetened liquid reached about three quarters up its rippling sides. It seemed incapable of forward movement, because it made no effort to drag itself out of the stuff that was hurting it so badly, and Measle wondered if, somehow, it was paralysed. But, whatever else was happening to it, the gradual shrivelling continued.

Another bubble appeared on the skin of the Slitherghoul. This time, the shape of the bubble wasn't round, like the ones that had contained the heads of Needle and Bland. This bubble was smaller and roughly rectangular. When it burst, it exposed something that, beneath the slime, seemed to be covered in hair—white and fuzzy hair.

With a yelp, Tinker's little body slipped out of the slime, slid down the flank of the Slitherghoul, and splashed into the water. His nose bobbed up and he sneezed twice and shook his head furiously—then, seeing Measle and Iggy standing at the top of a long, muddy slope, he dog-paddled towards them. A moment later, his paws touched down on solid ground and he raced up the incline and jumped into Measle's arms.

Like all dogs, Tinker had—in the past—done his fair share of finding disgusting things to roll in and then, having worked as much of the disgusting stinky stuff into his fur as he possibly could, had run indoors to show off his new smell to everybody. Measle had always felt sorry for him when Nanny Flannel had dragged him off for a forced bath. This time, Tinker could smell as bad as he liked, because Measle's joy at finding the little dog alive and well knew no bounds. And Tinker stank. He stank really badly, and his fuzzy white fur was matted with slime—but Measle didn't care.

Even as his face was being licked frantically by a doggy tongue, Measle's mind was working overtime. The Slitherghoul seemed to be giving up its victims! *First, Mr Needle and Mr Bland, then Tinker, so, who'll be next to emerge?* He remembered the sequence—*the Slitherghoul swallowed Nanny Flannel first, then Tinker, then Needle and Bland—and it was letting them out in reverse order, which meant that the next victim to appear ought to be—*

Even as he was working it out, the stout shape of Nanny Flannel was rising up out of the shrivelling jelly. Her glasses were askew and her hair had come loose—and the moment her feet were free, she rolled and tumbled down the side of the Slitherghoul and splashed into the muddy water. But there was no pause for spluttering—not from Nanny Flannel. She found her feet and, without a backward glance, strode firmly through the sloshing water and up the slope to Measle's side.

'Oh! Look at the state of me!' she said, smiling cheerfully into Measle's eyes and trying to wipe some of the slime from the front of her dress. 'I won't try to kiss you, dear—I see Tinker's already doing that and the last thing you need is to be covered with any *more* of this foul stuff. Now, I don't know how you did it, Measle, but I can't tell you how nice it is to be outside that disgusting thing!'

Measle was speechless with happiness. He couldn't do much of anything except grin with delight. Nanny Flannel seemed to understand his silence, because she began to try to clean her glasses on her dress, but all she managed to do was transfer slime from one surface to another. She gave up and popped the smeary spectacles into her pocket.

'I can't see a thing, dear,' she said. 'What's happening?' She peered short-sightedly down into the darkness of the pit.

Measle and Iggy peered too. There was movement—a lot of movement—down there. It was too dark to make out exactly what was happening, but all over the shuddering slimy body of the Slitherghoul small bubbles were forming, some no bigger than the head of a pin, some as large as a man's fist—and, as Measle and Iggy watched and Nanny Flannel squinted in horrified wonder, the bubbles began to burst, releasing whatever was inside. It was too dark to make out the small objects that were now streaming down the flanks of the Slitherghoul—but within a few moments, the surface of the surrounding water started to bubble and heave with activity.

'Whatever is going on?' said Nanny Flannel. A

moment later, Measle understood what was going on, because some of the larger objects that were disturbing the water in the pit began to move towards the shallow end. Once they found solid ground, they pulled themselves out of the water and ran up the slope, rushing past Measle's feet.

Rats. Mice. Several voles. Some tiny shrews. Three rabbits. A weasel—

'They've all come out of the Slitherghoul!' said Measle. 'It must have swallowed them too!'

They all looked back at the shrinking creature flopping and floundering in the muddy water. The surface of the pool was still alive with activity, but whatever the animals were that were causing the movement, they didn't seem to be moving anywhere in particular.

'Insects!' whispered Measle. 'They don't know which way to go. The Slitherghoul must have swallowed up thousands of them!'

'Time to go, dear,' said Nanny Flannel firmly. She took Measle's hand and pulled him gently, and Measle dragged his eyes away from the extraordinary spectacle down in the bottom of the pit and allowed himself to be led out onto the grass. Iggy shambled after them.

'Now then, Measle,' said Nanny Flannel, 'there are other creatures inside that nasty thing and I imagine it won't be long before they escape too. I don't know what or who they were, because inside that monster I could only *sense* their presence, but I know that most of them mean you harm—'

'I think I know who they are, Nanny,' said Measle. 'Toby Jugg is in there—I know that because I saw him—and I think all the wrathmonks from the Detention Centre are in there too, including the four who hate me most—Griswold Gristle and Buford Cudgel and Frognell Flabbit and that stupid Judge, too—'

Nanny Flannel interrupted him. 'Then, dear, let's get away from here as fast as possible,' she said. 'Because, if you're right, then they should be making their appearances any minute now!'

Even as Nanny Flannel stopped speaking, a larger bubble was forming on the top of the Slitherghoul and, a second later, the head of a young wrathmonk with red hair and protruding ears popped out. All over the Slitherghoul's body, other lumps and bubbles were rising out of the slime.

'Come on, dear!' said Nanny Flannel, raising her voice—and Measle and Iggy didn't need any further encouragement. Measle put Tinker down on the grass and, together, the four of them ran quickly across the lawn, towards the looming shadow of the house. When they got to the kitchen yard, the sound of splashing water reached their ears. The tap in the wall was still running at full force and Nanny Flannel marched over to it. She took her filthy spectacles from her pocket and held them under the stream. Then she shook the water off the lenses and turned the tap off.

'No point wasting water,' she muttered to herself. She reached deeper into her pocket and took out a handkerchief and dried the glasses. Then, perching the glasses on the end of her nose, she turned to Measle and said, 'Now then, dear, you're usually very good in this sort of situation. Any idea what we do now?'

For once, Measle was at a loss. So many things had happened so quickly over the last few minutes he hadn't had time to plan ahead. And plan for what? What was going to happen next anyway? Gloomily, he shook his head and said, 'Haven't a clue, Nanny.'

'Pity,' said Nanny and Measle detected a note of grimness in her voice. 'A great pity,' she repeated, 'because I can just about make out a couple of shapes coming out of your swimming pool—and they both look quite human, I'm sorry to say.'

Measle whipped his head round and peered out across the expanse of grass. Dimly, he could make out two figures on their hands and knees crawling up out of the pit. It was too dark to see who they were.

Measle squinted, trying desperately to pierce the gloom. As he strained his eyes, he saw a third figure emerge from the pit—and this figure was huge and hulking and Measle remembered only one huge and hulking figure from the Detention Centre.

'I think one of them is Mr Cudgel!' he whispered urgently. 'And that means—'

'And that means the other brutes won't be far behind!' said Nanny Flannel. 'We must find somewhere safe. Not the house—that's the first place they'll look!'

As if they all had the same thought, Measle, Iggy, and Nanny Flannel crept as silently as they could to the corner of the kitchen yard, putting a little more distance between themselves and the distant pool. By the time they reached the spot, two more shapes had crawled out of the pit and had joined the others. At the moment, all of them were still on their hands and knees, their heads hung low, and Measle could just make out the faint sounds of gasping and coughing and spluttering.

Nanny Flannel tapped him on the arm. 'Measle, dear, the big question is—have they still got their wrathrings on?'

It dawned on Measle that this was indeed the Big Question. Without their wrathrings, the escaped prisoners were absolutely deadly. But, if they still had their wrathrings round their necks, some of the danger they threatened was reduced. The wrathrings would stop their major enchantments—but it would do nothing for their breathing spells. However, for a wrathmonk to perform his breathing spell, he had to be very close to his victim. There was no way of telling if the distant figures had dull silver rings around their throats and Measle had no intention of going any closer to them than he was right now.

'I don't know about the wrathrings, Nanny,' he said. 'But, either way, we've got to get away from here. I know Mr Gristle and Mr Cudgel would both like to try out their breathing spells on me and I'd rather they didn't get the chance.'

'Come on then, dear,' said Nanny Flannel. 'You too, Iggy. Stay with us, mind. They may be wrathmonks just like you but they're much, *much* nastier and you're not to go anywhere near them. Do you understand?'

'Yes, Miss Fwannel,' muttered Iggy obediently.

'Where are we going, Nanny?' asked Measle, relieved that, from now on, somebody else would be making the decisions.

'I don't like the idea of being caught out in the open, Measle. So I think we ought to barricade ourselves in somewhere. The garage, perhaps? That's got a good strong door and no windows. Assuming they have their wrathrings on—and let's hope they do!—we ought to be able to hold out in there for quite a while—and, with any luck, they won't find us anyway.'

Measle nodded slowly. There really was nowhere else to go.

'Good,' said Nanny Flannel, decisively. 'Let's go! Quickly now!'

Hurriedly, they turned the corner and ran along the side of the house, towards the distant garage.

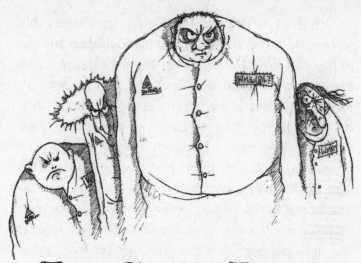

THE SLIMY BUNCH

Under a steady downpour of icy cold rain, a crowd of wrathmonks was gathering on the muddy grass by the side of the pit.

Most of them were on their knees, coughing and spluttering and spitting and not taking notice of anything much, other than concentrating on clearing their eyes and noses and throats of the stinking slime that covered them from head to foot. They all felt strangely weak as well, with arms and legs that seemed to be made of softened wax. The wrathmonks had been cradled in the comfort of the Slitherghoul for several days now, without being able to move even a fingertip, and the result was that their muscles had become flabby with disuse. They felt sick and confused as well.

221

Griswold Gristle was the first to recover his senses. He sat on the damp lawn and looked around in the darkness. He could see Buford Cudgel, a few metres away, bent double and gasping for air. Frognell Flabbit knelt nearby, scraping slime from his head and wiping his hands on the grass. Judge Cedric Hardscrabble lay on his back by the very edge of the pit, his bowler hat over his face. He seemed to be fast asleep.

The rest of the wrathmonks were slowly dragging themselves up and out. In the darkness, they looked like dead people rising from their graves—or, in this case, from one giant communal grave.

'Mr Cudgel! Mr Cudgel!' croaked Griswold, climbing unsteadily to his feet.

'What?' growled Cudgel, lifting his big, bullet head and glaring angrily at Griswold.

'Would you be ssso kind and look down into the hole and sssee what has become of the creature? I would not care to be ssswallowed up inssside it again!'

Cudgel grunted and then crawled to the edge of the pit and looked down. He was quite still for several seconds and Griswold began to wonder what was keeping him so interested. Then Cudgel swung his head and rumbled, 'It's got sssmall, Griswold. Not much bigger than a table.'

'And what is it doing, dear Mr Cudgel?'

'Sssplashing about. It looks a bit feeble, if you asssk me.'

'Not moving out of the water?'

'No.'

Griswold shivered. His clothes were soaked with slime and water and he was getting very cold.

'Mr Flabbit! Cedric! Come to me, please! You too, Mr Cudgel, if you would be ssso kind?'

Buford and Frognell shambled over to where Griswold was standing. Judge Cedric stayed where he was. He raised his bowler hat off his face and said, in a faint voice, 'What a mossst extraordinary dream I've just had, dear Griswold! Let me tell you all about it! There was thisss enormous lump, mossst peculiar it was, of what I can only dessscribe as yellowish-brownish-greenish jelly—'

'Cedric!' snapped Griswold. 'Be quiet and come here!'

Slowly, his ancient bones creaking with the effort, Judge Cedric Hardscrabble dragged himself to his feet and, his legs wobbling unsteadily beneath him, he stumbled over to join the group.

The other wrathmonks from the Detention Centre simply sat about on the grass and stared round with bewilderment. Never having been to Merlin Manor before, they had no idea where they were. They noticed, vaguely, that there was a small group of four wrathmonks over to one side, who seemed to be engaged in an urgent, whispered conversation.

Separated from them were two figures who seemed, somehow, different from the rest.

Toby Jugg huddled on a pile of mud, his knees drawn tight against his chest, both arms wrapped round his legs. He was gazing wild-eyed down at the edge of the pit. Nearby, Officer Offal was squatting on his haunches, having a hard time wiping the slime from his broad, pink face.

Toby's long hair was soggy with slime and water and it lay plastered flat against his head, exposing both of Toby's ears. The Gloomstains—those dark, greyish-blackish discolourations that showed the world that he was a powerful warlock—had disappeared from the tips of his ears and now, instead, Toby had a brand new and impressively large rain cloud hovering a few metres above his head. He appeared not to notice the drenching rain that beat down on him, but Officer Offal, with one eye finally cleared of the stinking slime, noticed it. Offal peered a little closer at the figure under the cloud and saw, with a sudden start of fear, that Toby's ears were clear of the Gloomstains. He experienced a sudden, sick feeling. The evidence was right before his eyes and Officer Offal knew exactly what it meant.

Toby Jugg was no longer a very powerful warlock who had been reasonably friendly towards him.

Toby Jugg was now a very powerful *wrathmonk* —and who knew what the insane creature's attitude would be now?

Officer Offal didn't want to wait to find out. He shuffled backwards hurriedly.

The movement caught Toby's eyes. They were now an unpleasant shade of yellow. Slowly, Toby turned his head and his yellow eyes rested on the figure of Offal as he tried, as unobtrusively as possible, to edge away into the shadows.

'Ah—there you are, Offal,' said Toby, gently, and Offal stopped trying to shuffle away and sat, as still as a statue, a weak little smile hovering on his mouth.

'I feel sssomewhat ssstrange,' said Toby, hissing like a snake. His eyebrows rose in surprise at the sounds he was making. Then he lifted his big, lion head and stared upwards at the black cloud that hovered overhead.

'Ah,' he said, slowly. 'Now I undersssstand. How very interesssting. I wonder—'

Toby broke off. Tentatively, he reached up and touched the dull silver wrathring round his neck. His eyes narrowed with anger and frustration. Then his face relaxed. He opened his mouth, took in a small breath and puffed it out—and a tiny cloud of glittering particles appeared in the still night air. Toby smiled a small, secretive smile. Then he said, 'Officer Offal, would you be ssso kind and come over here? I have missed you ssso much. I would like you to sssit bessside me. Come, Officer Offal.'

Offal licked his fat lips nervously and Toby said, 'I won't hurt you, Officer Offal. I promise I won't hurt you.'

Offal smiled a sickly smile. Knowing there was

nothing else he could do, he crawled slowly and reluctantly across the wet grass and sat down a metre from Toby's side.

'Thank you, Officer Offal,' said Toby. He grinned wolfishly at Offal and Offal saw, quite clearly, the two sets of pointed teeth on either side of Toby's mouth glowing white in the darkness.

And then Toby broke his promise. He whispered, 'You're my own little guinea pig, Officer Offal. My own, fat little guinea pig. And I'm a wicked liar.' He took a deep breath, leaned towards the tubby ex-guard, and *blew* at him.

Toby's breath glittered white in the darkness. It was a pale, gleaming cone of vapour that spread out from his lips and washed over Officer Offal's head like a wave crashing over a rock.

Instantly, Offal's face froze; not only in the sense that it stopped moving, but also quite *literally*. His sickly grin remained plastered across his face as a fine layer of frost spread across his pink cheeks, turning them a ghostly white. Tiny icicles formed on his bushy eyebrows and his dying eyes shone with a thin sheet of ice film. Toby went on breathing softly over Offal and his frigid breath spread the freezing effect over the whole of the guard's body, until he was completely covered with a layer of frost, and icicles hung from his chin. Beneath the film of white, Offal's skin had turned a pale, ghostly blue.

Toby stopped breathing. He stuck out one finger

and prodded Offal's chest. It was as hard as stone. Toby pushed a little harder. Slowly, the frozen body of the guard toppled sideways and fell, with a solid-sounding *clunk!* onto the grass. Toby peered closer. There was no movement at all, not even the rise and fall from the man's chest, that would show he was still breathing. Offal might as well have been made of granite.

Toby smiled. Then he muttered, 'Hmm. Remarkable. Inssstant death by freezing! Not at all a bad exhalation enchantment! A sssplendid one, in fact! But no less than was to be expected with a warlock of my ssstanding!'

He turned his handsome head, sweeping his yellow eyes over the wretched collection of wet, shivering wrathmonks. Then his gaze centred on a group of four wrathmonks, a little separated from the rest, their heads huddled together. There was something about them that was vaguely familiar to Toby, as if he'd seen them somewhere before, but couldn't quite work out where. One of them was a great giant of a man, with a bullet head and a massive, bulldog jaw; one was small, with tiny black eyes and a shiny, billiard-ball head. The third had a red, lumpy face and a long hank of greasy hair combed over his forehead to disguise his baldness; the fourth was very old, with a great bush of frizzy white hair sticking out from under an ancient bowler hat. All four wrathmonks wore white prison jumpsuits, which meant that they, too, had been captives in some section of the Detention Centre.

Toby shook his head, trying to remember where he might have seen them before but there seemed to be something wrong with his brain. He didn't usually have this trouble with thinking or remembering—and then he realized what he was. *I'm a wrathmonk! Which means I'm insane! Which means my mind won't work as well as before—but perhaps the advantages will outweigh the disadvantages! But, first things first—I shall need some friends!*

Staggering a little on weak and wobbly legs, Toby rose to his feet and stumbled towards the four huddled wrathmonks.

Down at the bottom of the pit, the thrashing, writhing, rippling movements of the Slitherghoul were weakening. Buford Cudgel had been right: it was now no bigger than a dining table. The muddy water that surrounded it now sometimes washed clear over the top of the mound of jelly, sloshing round yet another bubble of slime that was rising out of the creature. The bubble popped—and Corky Pretzel's head emerged, quickly followed by Corky Pretzel's big, muscle-bound body. There was now no distance for Corky to fall—he simply flopped sideways, hitting the water with a gentle splash.

Corky—just like everybody else—was keen to get as far away from the foul creature as he possibly could. But, even as he began to struggle towards the shallow end, Corky heard voices from somewhere up above.

They were voices he recognized: two of his prisoners from the Detention Centre.

'But—dear Griswold—' bleated the quavering voice of Judge Cedric Hardscrabble, and instantly came back, 'No, Cedric!' in the oily, irritated tones of Griswold Gristle. 'I cannot provide you with an umbrella and, even if I could, I wouldn't bother! We have more pressing matters to attend to, than finding you a ssstupid umbrella!'

Corky froze. He pressed himself tight up against the muddy wall of the pit, as far away from the Slitherghoul as possible, with only his head showing above the water. While he'd been considerably kinder and more sensitive than Officer Offal had ever been, he was still the Detention Centre guard and the voices that were floating down to him were the voices of his prisoner wrathmonks, every single one of whom would be happy to see him dead.

The Slitherghoul itself took no notice of him. It simply continued to flounder and thrash, its movements becoming progressively weaker and weaker. It was now no bigger than a coffee table.

'Gentlemen,' came another voice from above and Corky listened even more intently than before because there was something odd about the voice. He *thought* he recognized it but there was something a little different about it, something he couldn't quite put his finger on—

'Gentlemen—forgive me for interrupting you, but you four ssseem to have collected your wits about you sssomewhat more quickly than those other poor wretches over there. And, sssince I too appear to have a greater underssstanding of our circumstances than they do, I thought I would approach you and introduce myssself. I am Toby Jugg—at your ssservice, gentlemen!'

Corky wasn't clever but he knew the difference between a warlock and a wrathmonk. He'd also been down in the bowels of the Wizards' Guild long enough to know all his prisoners by name and it wasn't longer than five seconds before Corky worked out that the hissing sounds he could hear in Toby Jugg's voice meant only one thing. Corky didn't need to see Toby's rain cloud—he knew with a certainty that it would be there, hovering a few metres over Toby's head.

'What do you want with usss?' said Griswold, coldly—and Corky remembered that wrathmonks were not naturally drawn towards others of their kind, unless those others could somehow be of benefit to them. Indeed, Corky knew that wrathmonks often heartily detested each other.

'I would like to know if it was any of you that was interesssted in the Ssstubbs boy,' said Toby, his voice relaxed and genial. 'If ssso, then you should know that it was I who joined my mind with yours and helped you in the pursuit.'

'Really?' said Griswold, his voice still sneery with distrust. 'And why should we believe you?'

'Were you not aware that another mind—and a ssstrong one, too—was allied to your efforts?'

Reluctantly, Griswold conceded that they had felt a certain encouraging presence and Judge Cedric said that, to him, the additional mind intruding on his thoughts had felt a bit like having a scratchy little kitten inside his head.

'Yesss, yesss, Cedric!' snapped Griswold, irritably. 'We don't wish to hear about kittens! Thisss fellow is claiming an interessst in the Ssstubbs boy. Well, what is ssso different about that, may I asssk? Any wrathmonk worth his sssalt would have the sssame interessst—a desire to wreak revenge on the Ssstubbs family! What makes you ssso different, Missster Jugg? And another thing—why were you not in the Detention Centre, along with the ressst of usss, eh?'

Corky strained his ears. He knew the answer, of course, but he wanted to hear it from Toby Jugg himself.

'I am new to your ranks, gentlemen,' came Toby's easy-going, friendly voice. 'Until very recently, I was but a lowly warlock, imprisoned in the High Ssssecurity block of the Detention Centre, along with a fellow I am sure you remember. A fellow by the name of Officer Offal?'

There was a hate-filled hissing from the four wrathmonks. Toby's voice came again, drowning out the sounds of enraged snakes. 'You'll be happy to hear that I have dealt with him on your behalf. He's over there, closely resembling a frozen Chrissstmas turkey—the result of my newly-discovered exhalation enchantment. Please feel free to examine him.'

Corky heard shuffling sounds as the wrathmonks moved away. He was about to move himself—about to get himself out of this freezing, filthy water, about to get away from the wriggling mound of jelly—when a sudden gust of wind swept across the lawns of Merlin Manor, driving rain from the various wrathmonk clouds sideways. Corky received a splattering of drops on his upturned face and, immediately, he huddled back against the muddy wall of the pit, staring anxiously upwards. The rain on his face meant that there was still a wrathmonk nearby. Then he heard a strange little noise. It took him several moments to work out what it was—Toby Jugg was humming cheerfully to himself.

There were three small splashes in the water next to the Slitherghoul and Corky switched his gaze from the rectangle of dark sky above his head. Three little creatures were swimming towards the shallow end of the pool and Corky could just about make out what they were.

Two rats and a mouse. The mouse seemed to be

having difficulty steering towards the shallows and, once or twice, it even went in small circles—almost as if there was something wrong with its eyesight. All three animals swam slowly, their legs moving stiffly and weakly through the water but, eventually, all three made it to shallow water and, once their paws found solid ground beneath them, all three staggered—like little drunk men—up the muddy slope and out of sight.

Then came the sounds of the four wrathmonks returning and Corky, switching his gaze back up to the rectangle of night sky, shrank further back into the shadows and tried hard to stop his teeth from chattering.

'Not bad, Missster Jugg,' came Griswold's oily voice, and now there was a note of respect in it. 'Not bad at all. Of courssse, we four were hoping to have the pleasure of dealing with that oaf Offal in our own ways but you ssseem to have done the job for usss—in a fairly effective manner, I sssuppose. Ssso—that is your exhalation enchantment, is it? Breath of ice?'

'It ssseems to be,' said Toby.

'Hmm. You should consider yoursssself fortunate,' said Griswold. 'Only a very few wrathmonks are possessed of *fatal* breathing spells.'

'Is that ssso?' said Toby. 'Then I am indeed fortunate! And what, may I ask, are yours?'

'Boils!' came Judge Cedric's reedy voice. 'Sssplendid boils and ssspots and pimples, all over!'

'Toothache!' said Frognell Flabbit, in his pompous, important voice. 'Agonizing toothache. Mossst effective, if I do sssay ssso myssself!'

'Mine is of the more *fatal* variety,' drawled Griswold, in a superior tone. 'My exhalation enchantment has the effect of rapid and total dehydration. It dries out all the body's natural fluids, leaving behind—I'm delighted to sssay—nothing more than a little, shrivelled, desiccated corpse!'

There was a pause and then Corky heard Toby say, 'And you, sssir? Although, I must sssay, your great sssize and ssstrength would almost be all that you need, I should imagine.'

'Mine is fatal, too,' came Buford Cudgel's rumbling voice.

'Unfortunately for Mr Cudgel,' squeaked Griswold, 'and jussst between oursssselves, you undersssstand, he is quite unable to use it!'

'Shut your mouth, Gristle!' barked Cudgel and Griswold's voice stopped dead. Corky strained his ears harder. This was the first he'd heard about Buford Cudgel being unable to use his exhalation enchantment and he hoped he'd hear more. He wasn't disappointed.

'I'm ssso sssorry to hear that,' said Toby. 'Why, it mussst be an *extraordinary* enchantment indeed! I am mossst interesssted—do *please* tell me about it.' And Toby used such a friendly, concerned, and interested voice that Buford Cudgel appeared to soften towards him, because Corky heard the giant wrathmonk mutter, 'It's because it's too dangerousss, even for me, sssee?'

'Too dangerousss? How amazing! How is it too dangerousss?'

'It makes all the germs and bacteria in my victim grow to the sssize of insssects,' said Cudgel, and Corky detected a note of pride in the voice that sounded like distant thunder.

'And,' interrupted Griswold Gristle, 'poor Mr Cudgel has only ever used it once—when he first achieved wrathmonkhood—and that was on a little bluebottle which was buzzing round his head. He breathed on it—and what do you sssuppose happened next?'

'Who's telling thisss ssstory, Gristle—you or me?' rumbled Cudgel.

'Why, *you* are, my dear Missster Cudgel,' said Griswold in a wheedling voice. Then he added, in a voice that was tinged with sarcasm, 'But, perhapsss you might do it *quickly*, sssince we are all sssomewhat cold and wet and I for one would prefer that to be otherwise!'

'Right. Well, I found out how many germs a fly has on it—and *in* it,' said Cudgel, his enormous frame shuddering at the memory. 'It's billions— *trillions* even! The whole room filled up with these horrible things and then they overflowed into the hall and up the ssstairs. They were crawling everywhere, biting and ssstinging and chewing—I only jussst got out of there alive. The whole house burssst open like a rotten apple and they ssstarted filling up the back yard—'

'It was lucky that their life ssspan outside their host is quite short,' interrupted Griswold. 'Also, there happened to be a cave nearby, full of bats! There must have been a couple of million of the dear furry creatures! They came out and ssstarted to eat the germs as fassst as they could. It took them a whole week and at the end they were the fattest bats you've ever sssseen—'

'They could hardly fly at all!' said Cudgel, gloomily. 'Sssince then, I never dared use my breathing ssspell.'

'Sssuch a pity,' breathed Griswold. 'One would ssso like to sssee it in action.'

'Ssso would I,' whispered Toby, respectfully. 'Ssso would I!'

There was a long silence, while the wrathmonks savoured the thought of Buford Cudgel's unusable spell. Then Toby, injecting an even more respectful tone into his voice, said, 'How wonderful, to be wrathmonks of sssuch great experience! How I should be honoured to learn from you all!'

This seemed to have the right effect, because Griswold said, in a brisk, business-like voice, 'Missster Jugg, you mentioned earlier you were interesssted in the Ssstubbs boy meeting an unpleasant end. Ssso are we. Perhapsss you would care to join forces with us? In an inferior capacity, of coursse—but perhapsss we can teach you sssomething of our wrathmonk ways!'

'I would be ssso very grateful,' said Toby. 'Perhaps —dare I sssuggessst this—we might move to sssomewhere a little drier? Perhaps we could find a room in that house there, where we could dissscuss matters?'

This suggestion obviously met with approval, because Corky heard a rumble of agreement and immediately the group of wrathmonks moved away, out of his earshot. Corky waited. When he'd heard nothing from above for several minutes, he was about to wade through the muddy water towards the shallow end when a sudden splashing sound reached his ears. The noise was quite different from the floundering sounds of the Slitherghoul, which seemed to have stopped altogether.

Corky looked into the shadows and saw, to his surprise, that the Slitherghoul had disappeared. In its place was the figure of a pale, skinny young man, in a long black robe. The young man was splashing feebly in the water, his eyes tight closed, his mouth opening and closing like a dying fish. He had long, stringy black hair and a nose that was so big it seemed to be crowding out all his other features. Corky watched as the young man's head suddenly disappeared under the water, then rose again, coughing and spluttering. He was obviously so weak as to be in danger of drowning and, while he was rather an unpleasant looking specimen of humanity, Corky had no intention of letting that happen.

Corky waded over and scooped the thin body out of the water, cradling it in his arms. The young man's eyes opened momentarily, then closed just as fast. A soft moan emerged from his mouth, then his head flopped sideways and he stopped moving. Corky bent and pressed an ear to the man's skinny chest. The beating of his heart was there—slow and very faint—but it was regular and, with the small rise and fall of the man's chest, Corky thought that there was a good chance the man might simply have fainted away.

'Come on, then, you,' muttered Corky, hoisting the slimy little body onto one shoulder with no more effort than if it had been an empty sack. 'Come on, whoever you are. Let's see if we can get ourselves up and out of here, eh?'

Corky waded silently to the shallow end. He stepped carefully on the slick, slippery mud, moving up the slope until his eyes could peek over the top. He turned slowly, peering into the empty darkness. The lawn appeared to be deserted. *No! There! Over by the looming shadow of the great house—a bunch of white-suited wrathmonks! It looks like most of 'em! And they're just about far enough away not to see us if I'm careful.*

Corky crept up the slope and out onto the grass. Then, hunched low, he began to move quickly away from Merlin Manor and towards a distant line of trees.

THE GARAGE

The garage of Merlin Manor had once been a great stone barn, where the hay that had been cut at the end of the summer months was stored. It had been converted into a garage many years ago, by a predecessor of Sam Stubbs—a predecessor with lots of money, a passion for rare cars, and an equally strong passion for security. It had huge steel doors across the front, and no windows for a car-thief to climb through, other than a small, heavily-barred skylight set high up on the roof. Inside, Sam's predecessor had kept his splendid collection of new and antique automobiles—all fifty of them—so now there was more than enough room for the long, green Stubbs car *and* Nanny Flannel's motorbike. In fact, there was enough space inside the building for two or three school buses and a small plane as well. Like all garages, there was the usual sort of clutter around the walls. There were shelves with tools and old oil cans and rusty pitchforks and, running the length of the back wall, there was a sort of loft high up under the sloping roof, which could only be reached by climbing a rickety ladder.

In almost total darkness, Measle, Nanny Flannel, Iggy, and Tinker were huddled together up in the loft, half concealed in a pile of dusty hay. Their clothes were slowly drying out and their teeth were no longer chattering but they still felt cold and damp and uncomfortable. The slime was stiffening in Tinker's wiry fur, itching as it contracted, and the little dog was scratching himself busily with a back paw.

'Can you hear anything out there, dear?' asked Nanny Flannel, in a hoarse whisper.

'No, Nanny—Tink, keep still!—no, not a sound.'

'Where can they all have got to?' muttered Nanny Flannel.

'Well, I know where dey is *not*, Miss Fwannel,' hissed Iggy. 'Dey is not in *'ere*!'

Not yet, thought Measle.

The enemy wasn't very far away.

Toby had led Griswold Gristle, Buford Cudgel, Frognell Flabbit, and Judge Cedric Hardscrabble away from the pit and across the grass to the kitchen yard. When the other wrathmonks saw this party of five walking with purpose towards the house, it had seemed like a good idea for them to follow, if only to see what the group had in mind. What Toby had in mind was, first, get out of the incessant rain and, second, go in search of Measle—because Measle was the most likely person to know where the Mallockee was. And when Measle had told Toby where she was, then there was no further reason to keep the boy alive . . . *But I mussst tread carefully*, he thought, *I mussst let the Gristle fellow think he is in charge—at leassst for the time being . . .*

The crowd of wrathmonks almost filled the ruined kitchen, but at least they were out of their rain. Some drops occasionally splashed in through the broken window, but the wrathmonks were already so wet, they didn't notice. They huddled together and listened while Griswold outlined his plan. When he'd finished, there was a silence.

'I don't sssee why we should help,' said Mungo MacToad, defiantly. His ginger hair was matted against his head, making his protruding ears look more pronounced than ever. 'It's nuthin' to do with usss.'

'I ssseem to remember that you were quite keen to join usss while we were all inssside that horrible creature,' said Griswold severely. He glared at the young wrathmonk through his tiny black eyes, his pasty white forehead furrowed in a frown.

'Yeah, well,' muttered Mungo, staring at the kitchen floor, 'that was when we was inssside, wasn't it? We was ssstuck, wasn't we? Nothing else to do. But now we're *free*, ain't we? And I for one ain't got no time to go hunting no boy.'

'Not even a *Ssstubbs* boy?' rumbled Buford Cudgel, clenching and unclenching his enormous fists.

Mungo sniffed and said nothing. He was mortally afraid of the giant wrathmonk.

'What about the ressst of you?' called Griswold, looking round at the crowd. 'Who among you would be ready to join usss in our hunt?'

There was a lot of shuffling of feet and staring at the littered kitchen floor, but not a single wrathmonk said a word.

Then Toby, in a small, humble voice, began to speak—and there was something about this big, broad-shouldered wrathmonk, with his yellow eyes and his great mane of grey-flecked hair, which made each member of that huddled crowd listen to every word. He spoke quietly and reasonably and his eyes made contact with each member of his audience in turn, so that every single wrathmonk felt that Toby was speaking to him, and him alone. And what Toby said made sense. He talked about the monstrous Stubbs family, and how it was the *duty* of every self-respecting wrathmonk in the world to exact revenge against every member of that family. He told them a little about the Mallockee, and how incredibly valuable she would be to the Wrathmonk cause. But mostly he spoke about Measle Stubbs, that terrible boy, who seemed to take pleasure in destroying their kind—he even ticked off the names of those whom Measle had killed. 'Our old friend Basil Tramplebone and his pet, Cuddlebug, Mr and Mrs Zagreb, young Ssscab Draggle—they all met terrible deaths at the hands of that unnatural boy!' Toby followed that with the list of those whom Measle had caused to be imprisoned. '*Wise* Judge Cedric Hardscrabble, *intrepid* Frognell Flabbit, the *great* Buford Cudgel, and the *brilliant* Griswold Gristle, not to mention myssself and perhapsss sssome of you as well? And, if it wasn't the boy who caught you, then it was mossst likely the foul Sssam Ssstubbs, was it not?'

At first, Griswold Gristle was annoyed that this newcomer to their ranks should take it upon himself to do all the persuading. But the more Griswold listened, the more he fell under Toby Jugg's spell and, by the time Toby finished speaking, Griswold had (without being fully aware of the fact) pretty much resigned the leadership of his group.

In fact, there wasn't a wrathmonk there who *didn't* fall under the spell of Toby's cheerful, persuasive voice and, when he fell silent, every fishy wrathmonk eye was staring at him with awe and admiration.

'Ssso, what do you want usss to do?' rumbled Buford Cudgel.

'Find Measle Ssstubbs,' said Toby, leaning elegantly against the cold kitchen stove. 'It shouldn't be difficult.'

'He is a ssslippery child,' said Griswold. 'He's very good at hiding, Missster Jugg.'

Toby eased himself off the stove. 'I don't doubt it, Missster Gristle. But tell me this—' And here Toby raised his nose and sniffed delicately at the still air—'am I wrong in thinking that, with the onset of thisss glorious wrathmonkhood, my sssense of sssmell has improved dramatically?'

'That's true enough,' said Frognell Flabbit. 'Your sssense of sssmell does get a lot better. Why?'

'Because,' said Toby, grinning cheerfully, 'using our noses, it would ssseem an easy matter to dissstinguish between Measle and all the ressst of us. Am I not right in thinking that Measle is the only living creature around here who has *not* been ssswallowed by the monster? And, if that is ssso, then am I not right in thinking that he will be the only living creature around here who will not sssmell of this ssstinking ssslime that covers usss all from head to foot?'

Several of the younger wrathmonks gave small, embarrassed grins. They thought the smell of the Slitherghoul quite pleasant on the whole . . .

'And therefore,' continued Toby, 'would it not be a sssimple affair to detect the sssmell of a fairly clean human boy, from the ssstench of all the ressst of us?'

There was a murmur of admiring assent from the wrathmonks. Logical thought was something very few wrathmonks went in for—mostly, they just did the first thing that came into their heads. Toby, sensing he now had them all in his power, herded them out to the kitchen yard, where they stood in a circle, under a downpour of rain, sniffing the night air.

'I got a whiff of sssomething jussst then,' said Mungo MacToad. 'I think it came from over there.' He pointed off to the side of the house. Toby said, 'Come, let usss follow our noses!' He set off in a purposeful, commanding manner and the wrathmonks fell in behind him, sniffing furiously. As they got closer to the distant garage, more and more wrathmonks picked up the scent—and now the excitement among them was rising.

'There, Missster Jugg!' exclaimed Griswold, pointing at the dark shape of the garage. 'I do believe he might be in there!'

Mungo MacToad sniffed harder than anybody. He said, 'No quessstion about it! He's in there!'

When they got to within five metres of the building, Toby paused and the rest of the wrathmonks came to a halt behind him. Toby scanned the tall stone wall, taking in the giant steel doors, with their massive hinges. Carefully, he walked all the way round the building and the crowd of wrathmonks followed respectfully in his footsteps. When he got back round to the front, Toby nodded in satisfaction. There were no other doors in the garage, and no windows at the back either. There was a small skylight set high in the slanting roof, but there was no way that any of them were going to be able to reach that. The only way in and out was in front of him. He approached the spot where the doors joined together. There was a pair of handles on either side of the join and Toby grasped them in his big hands and tried to pull the doors apart. He grunted with the effort, but the doors wouldn't budge.

'Let me try,' said Buford Cudgel, elbowing his way through the crowd. Toby stepped aside and Buford took hold of the handles, bunched the muscles in his broad back and strained—

The doors didn't even creak.

Toby motioned all the wrathmonks to move back several paces. Then he bent his head close to the door and called, 'Look, Measle, old ssson, I know you're in there! Now, don't be afraid, I don't mean you any harm. I jussst want to know where the Mallockee is, that's all! And your mother, of course! You tell me where the Mallockee is, and where your mother is, and I'll leave you alone! I'll leave all of you alone!'

Inside the garage, high up in the gallery, Iggy shivered under the hay. That was the voice of his old master, Toby Jugg! He'd always done what Toby

Jugg told him to do. For a moment, Iggy forgot all about the fact that Toby had been found guilty by the Court of Magistri and had been sent to rot deep in the bowels of the Wizards' Guild and that therefore he—Iggy—no longer owed any loyalty or obedience to his old master.

Iggy cupped his hands round his mouth and before either Measle or Nanny Flannel could stop him, he yelled, 'DE LITTLE FING AIN'T 'ERE, MISSSTER JUGG, SSSIR! DE LITTLE FING IS FAR, FAR AWAY, DOWN IN DE SSSOUTH HOLE! SHE'S— mmmmmph! mmmmmmph! mmmmmmph!'

Measle had managed to get his hand over Iggy's mouth just after Iggy had yelled 'Sssouth Hole!' but the damage was done. Toby's voice came back through the iron doors—

'Is that you, Missster Niggle? How interesssting to hear your voice again! And thank you ssso very much for the information!'

Outside, Toby straightened up, his face a mask of disappointment. He believed what Iggy had told him. There was no reason not to. Besides, he'd heard something about the upcoming South Pole conference from his guard, Corky Pretzel, and it made perfect sense that Sam Stubbs, the new Prime Magus of the Wizards' Guild, would take his magically-gifted daughter with him. And that meant that Lee Stubbs had most probably gone with them.

No Mallockee. No Manafount. This entire expedition was a waste of his time!

Griswold Gristle was tugging at his sleeve and Toby looked down at the small, bald wrathmonk with distaste.

'What do you want, Missster Gristle?'

'That persssson who ssspoke,' Griswold bleated, 'there are sssome among usss who believe he might be a wrathmonk—'

Toby shook off Griswold's clutching hand. 'He *is* a wrathmonk. His name is Ignatius Niggle, and he is a *traitor*, Missster Gristle! He is in league with the boy! He helped to imprison me! He's a weak, pathetic little turncoat! And, if you're going to kill Measle Ssstubbs, then I think he should die as well!'

Griswold Gristle shuddered with delight. The prospect of the imminent death of Measle Stubbs was just too wonderful for words, and, if that meant killing a treacherous little wrathmonk too— well, that hardly mattered at all!

'You will help usss, Missster Jugg? You will help us break down the doors?'

Toby stared up at the tall, windowless walls and the massive steel doors. It looked impossible, but a leader gives orders when his followers ask for them.

'Find tools. Hammers. The heavier the better.'

Griswold Gristle gathered the wrathmonks and explained what was needed. They scattered in all directions, searching the nearby outbuildings. Within minutes, they were back, clutching what they had found. Buford Cudgel held a big sledgehammer, the kind used for smashing concrete.

The rest of them had found a variety of tools, mostly quite useless. Toby curled his lip in contempt when he saw that Frognell Flabbit was carrying a small electrical screwdriver and he almost laughed out loud at Judge Cedric's find—a large tin of white paint.

The wrathmonks stood around, looking at Toby expectantly. He waved a hand at the steel doors and immediately the wrathmonks started to attack them with everything they'd got. Only Buford's hammer made any impression at all—a series of dents in the thick metal. Mungo MacToad scraped an old chisel viciously across the doors and Griswold Gristle pounded at them with a small spanner. Judge Cedric banged his tin of paint weakly against the barrier until the lid flew off and a great splash of white flew out and cascaded over his head.

Judge Cedric wailed and dropped his paint can and Mungo MacToad sneered and said, 'Oh, yeah, a definite improvement, I don't think!'

After five minutes of useless exercise, the wrathmonks gave up. Panting, they fell back from the doors and stared at them in disgust. Only Toby, who had taken no part in the attack, still breathed easily. He was mildly amused at the pathetic efforts of his little band of followers, but enough was enough. They would be expecting results from their leader and he must not disappoint.

Toby stepped near to the battered, paint-splashed

doors. He peered closer and saw for the first time that, in one of them, there was a large keyhole at waist level. There was no key in it. Toby bent and put his eye to the hole. He saw nothing but blackness. There was a piece of straw by his foot. Toby picked it up and pushed it into the keyhole. The straw met no resistance.

Toby straightened up. He turned to the clustered crowd of wrathmonks and his eyes singled out the hulking figure of Buford Cudgel.

'Missster Cudgel? A word, please?'

Buford lumbered forward, elbowing his way through the crowd.

'Yeah—what?'

Toby pointed to the keyhole. 'It occurred to me that your devassstating exhalation enchantment might jussst work in thisss sssituation, Missster Cudgel. Sssee, there is a sssmall hole through which you can blow—'

Buford shook his head. 'No, it's no good. I told you—it's too dangerousss! There's ssso many germs, the weight of 'em sssmashes down walls and breaks through doors—'

'I doubt *these* walls, Missster Cudgel,' said Toby, pointing upwards at the massive blocks of stone that comprised the walls of the old barn. 'And not these doors either. I think we have proved jussst how ssstrong they are. Besides, we shall ssstand well back, ready for flight should the need arise.'

'I dunno—' said Buford, uneasily.

Toby grasped Buford's arm. It was like grabbing hold of a tree trunk. 'But Missster Cudgel, wouldn't you like to try out your amazing exhalation enchantment once again? Especially on sssuch deserving victims!' Toby turned and looked out at the pale faces of the other wrathmonks. In a few words, he described the effects of Buford Cudgel's breathing spell and, by the time he'd finished, every face had taken on a look of respect and anticipation.

'I daresssay that would be sssomething we would all like to sssee!' said Toby and every head nodded vigorously. Nobody had such a devastating breathing spell as that!

'Go on then, Missster Cudgel!' said Mungo MacToad, whose own exhalation enchantment was little more than the ability to turn everything he breathed on a nasty shade of purple. 'Give usss an exhibition!'

Buford glanced at Griswold Gristle and Griswold nodded excitedly. 'A grand way to dessstroy our enemies, Missster Cudgel,' he squeaked. 'Imagine the potential devassstation of thisss whole area! Merlin Manor and its lands will be ruined for ever! And, if we all ssstand well back and are prepared to flee, as Missster Jugg has sssuggested, I sssee no real danger for us thisss time.'

Buford nodded his great bullet head. 'All right, then,' he rumbled. 'But I dunno if it'll work. You're sssupposed to be really close to your victims and I

don't even know where they are, do I? Ssso, if it
goes wrong, don't blame me.'

He approached the door and bent double and
put his mouth to the keyhole.

'Ho there, Measle Ssstubbs!' shouted Buford, his
voice like a splitting clap of thunder. 'Remember
me? It's Buford Cudgel! I've come to sssay
goodbye! We've all come to sssay goodbye—
Missster Gristle and Missster Flabbit and the judge
and me—and a whole lot of other wrathmonks,
too! Do you remember my breathing spell, Measle?
If ssso, then you know what happens next, don't
you? And here it comes! Goodbye, Measle Ssstubbs,
from all of usss! HAVE A NICE DEATH!'

Mungo MacToad sniggered. 'Good one, Missster
Cudgel!' he yelled from a safe distance.

Buford took a deep, deep breath and started to
blow steadily through the keyhole.

GERMS!

The pounding against the steel doors had been deafening for those huddled inside the garage and it had gone on for what seemed an age before finally stopping. Ever since, there had been an eerie silence from outside.

Until now.

Tinker heard it first.

His fuzzy ears cocked forward and he turned his head in the direction of the sound and growled softly deep in his throat. Iggy's long, pointed ears were the next to pick up the faint noise of somebody blowing through a keyhole and then Measle heard it too. It sounded like wind whistling round distant chimneys. Only Nanny Flannel, who was beginning to go a little deaf, didn't hear anything at all.

Measle froze. He'd recognized the voice of the giant wrathmonk and he remembered the moment, back at the Isle of Smiles Theme Park when he was surrounded by his enemies and Buford Cudgel had described the awful effects of his breathing spell.

Germs and bacteria, that lived inside the victim's body, growing in an instant to the size of small insects—

'What's happening, Measle?' whispered Nanny Flannel. Measle shook his head, pretending he didn't know. It was probably best that nobody knew but him. He braced himself and waited for the horror that was coming.

The interior of the garage at Merlin Manor was a huge space and the stinking breath of Buford Cudgel was almost immediately diffused in the surrounding air, losing much of its potency and failing, as yet, to reach the nostrils of any living creature, let alone the noses of Measle, Iggy, Tinker, and Nanny Flannel, who were huddled together high in a distant corner of the loft, just about as far from the garage door as it was possible to be.

But, eventually, the foul but diluted air had to find *something* alive and it did—in the shape of a small, black beetle, which was scurrying across the concrete floor in search of something to eat.

The beetle didn't have nostrils, but it did have primitive organs that could absorb and react to the filthy, magical breath of Buford Cudgel. The effect was immediate. The beetle stopped dead in its tracks, as if it had walked into a wall. Then its legs curled up under its body and it slumped, dead, on the floor, and, at the same time, it started to swell. It was only a second or two before the pressure inside its corpse caused the outer shell to split open.

A mass of wriggling, shapeless *growing* things spilled out onto the concrete floor. More and more of them burst through the split in the insect's body and, within moments, the beetle's corpse had disappeared under a mounting pile of squirming, writhing movement.

From his vantage point up in the loft, all Measle could see was that something appeared to be moving down on the concrete below. What it was, he had no idea but it was definitely growing—it was spreading over the floor and rising up in the air and, all the time, its dark surface was shifting and rippling, as if it was somehow alive—

It's germs! thought Measle. *It's bacteria—and they're growing, just like Cudgel said! And any second now, they're going to reach us!* Panic caught at him, like a giant hand squeezing his chest and, for a moment, he couldn't breathe. He felt Iggy crawl closer to him in order to peer down at the dark mass below them, and he heard Tinker's familiar growl a little further off. Nanny Flannel was lying by his other side and she tapped him on the arm and said, 'What on earth *is* that down there, Measle?'

But Measle was so frozen with terror that he couldn't even open his mouth to tell her.

Outside, Buford had finally run out of breath. He straightened up, turned, and said, with a shrug of his massive shoulders, 'Well, that didn't work, did it? I told you ssso—you've got to be right next to your victim for these things.'

'Ssso, what now, Missster Jugg?' squeaked Griswold, who by now had utterly relinquished the role of leader.

Toby peered up at the tall building. While not particularly interested any more in what became of Measle Stubbs, he was still intrigued by a challenge. Of course, there were any number of ways of getting into the barn—they could drive a tank through those doors, or blow them up with a small bomb, or even cut down a tree and have Buford Cudgel use it as a battering ram—but all these solutions would take time and trouble. Besides, they seemed so *clumsy*.

There had to be a more—well—*interesting* way of breaking through.

Inside the garage, the entire floor was now covered by a heaving, seething sea of blackness—

and the sea was getting deeper every second, the shifting, squirming surface rising fast towards the loft. Already, the Stubbs family car and the motorcycle and sidecar combination were out of sight. There was a soft hissing sound as millions of shapeless things moved against each other.

'Coo, dat is funny lookin' ssstuff, Mumps,' muttered Iggy, and Measle caught a whiff of wrathmonk breath from Iggy's lips.

The idea popped in his head like a bursting bubble.

Of course! Why didn't I think of that before?

'Iggy—breathe on it!'

'You wot?'

'Breathe on it, Iggy! It's *bugs*! Billions and squillions of bugs! And your breath kills bugs, doesn't it?'

'Ho, yesss,' said Iggy proudly. 'My breaf is de *bessst* breaf for killin' bugs! My breaf is ssso 'orrible, it can kill bugs de sssize of *eggylumps*! De sssize of houses! De sssize of mountains! De sssize of—'

Measle knew that, once Iggy started on one of his lists detailing how brilliant he was, it was difficult to stop him, so he grabbed Iggy's damp collar, pulled him close and yelled directly in his face.

'No time, Iggy! Tell me later! Right now, I need you to breathe on them! Breathe on them *NOW*!'

Iggy had heard that tone from Measle before and he knew better than to argue with him. He leaned over the edge of the loft floor and took a deep, deep breath. Measle could hear the long, drawn-out sound of air being sucked into wrathmonk lungs. Puffing his cheeks, Iggy blew out hard, spraying his breath downwards towards the rising surface that seemed to boil with movement.

Outside, an idea had occurred to Toby Jugg.

He was staring closely at the giant hinge that held the lower half of the left-hand door to the stone wall of the garage. The hinge was dusted with a light coating of rust. Toby reached out and dragged a forefinger across it—the surface wasn't smooth, like formed steel. It was slightly rough, as if the metal had been shaped in a mould.

Cast-iron!

A possibility!

Toby beckoned to Buford Cudgel and the giant shambled to his side.

'Missster Cudgel, dear fellow, I need your great sssstrength, and your great hammer, too.'

'What's the point?' grumbled Buford. 'Didn't work the last time.'

'But it might *thisss* time, Missster Cudgel. Now, if you would be ssso kind as to raise that hammer and then bring it down as hard as you can against thisss hinge—*no!* Not *yet*, Missster Cudgel! When I sssay, and not before! There is sssomething I mussst do firssst!'

Buford paused, the sledgehammer held in beefy hands high over his head. He watched as Toby bent his head close to the hinge—and then he frowned in puzzlement as Toby took a deep breath and began to blow gently against the ironwork.

Instantly, the brown rust colour that covered the hinge turned white, as a fine layer of frost congealed on the surface. Toby went on blowing—but nothing else happened.

Nothing that could be seen, at least.

In fact, what was happening was this: the chilling cold from Toby's exhalation enchantment was penetrating deeper and deeper into the cast-iron hinge, bringing the temperature of the metal lower and lower and lower, until the whole thing was colder than the coldest part of the deepest of deep freezers—

And Toby went on blowing.

'What's 'e doing, Missster Cudgel?' said Mungo MacToad, who had sidled up close to Buford's side.

'I dunno, do I?' said Cudgel, edging away from the red-haired wrathmonk. He'd never cared for Mungo MacToad—a nasty, know-it-all piece of work in Buford's opinion.

'All right, Missster Cudgel,' called Toby, straightening up and wiping his mouth with the back of his hand. Buford noticed that Toby's lips had turned a pale shade of blue. Toby said, 'Now, hit that hinge as hard as you can, please!'

Buford raised his sledgehammer and brought it down with all the force that his enormous muscles could muster.

The iron hinge shattered into a thousand pieces, little shards of ice-cold metal whizzing off in all directions, like shrapnel from an exploding grenade. One of them struck Frognell Flabbit's leg and he yelped and moved away to a safer distance.

''Ere—that's clever, that is!' said Mungo MacToad, admiringly. He stepped closer and stared down at the remains of the hinge. ''Ow did you do that, Missster Jugg?'

'If metal gets very cold, it becomes brittle,' said Toby. 'Ssspecially cast-iron. I thought everybody knew that.'

'*I* knew that, Missster Jugg,' said Griswold Gristle, eagerly, although in fact he didn't.

Toby wasn't listening. He had moved across to the other door and was blowing down at the lower hinge there. After a short while, he beckoned to Buford Cudgel and, a second later, that hinge was shattered too. Now, with their lower supports gone, both doors sagged a little. Toby looked up at the top hinges. They were out of his reach. Once again, he beckoned to Buford.

'Can you lift me on your shoulders, Missster Cudgel?'

Buford put down his hammer and hoisted Toby up onto his shoulders as if he was no heavier than a toddler. Wobbling slightly, Toby leaned forward and started to breathe against the third hinge.

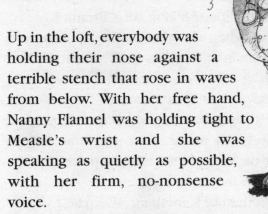

Up in the loft, everybody was holding their nose against a terrible stench that rose in waves from below. With her free hand, Nanny Flannel was holding tight to Measle's wrist and she was speaking as quietly as possible, with her firm, no-nonsense voice.

'You *must*, dear,' she said, and Measle shook his head for the third time. Nanny Flannel tightened her grip.

'Don't shake your head at me, young man. You have no choice. Those doors aren't going to hold much longer.'

'But—'

'No buts, Measle. It's you they're after and we can't help you—so you have to run, don't you see?'

'But—but I can't just leave you, Nanny!'

'Yes, you can, dear. Now, how many yellow ones have you got?'

Measle reached in his pocket and pulled out the few jelly beans that were left. It was hard to see the different colours in the dim light that filtered through the skylight but he could just about make out a few that were paler than the rest.

'A couple, I think, Nanny.'

'And you, Iggy?'

Iggy tapped the front pocket of his jacket and said, 'I got about a sssquillion, Miss Fwannel.'

'Good. So, when the time comes, I want you both to use them and get away, if you can. Is that understood?'

There was a thunderous *CRASH!* from outside and the left-hand door shuddered and slipped sideways by half a metre. Now its whole weight was resting on the ground, held in place only by the central locking device.

Measle thought of something. 'Why can't you do the same thing, Nanny?' he asked, excitedly. 'What's *your* least favourite jelly bean?'

'That's no good, dear,' said Nanny Flannel, sadly. 'You see, I don't like *any* of them—and you've got to have a clear least-favourite for the magic to work.'

'What about Tinker? He probably likes jelly beans, doesn't he?'

Nanny shrugged her narrow shoulders. 'The trouble with Tinker is he likes them *all*, so it doesn't work for him either, for the same reason. And no, dear, you can't carry him. He'll slow you down and that's the last thing you need right now. Tinker and I will be fine—won't we, Tinker?'

Tinker wagged his stubby tail a couple of times and crawled a little closer to Nanny Flannel's side. His mind was taken up with other matters though—

So many really big smells! Really, really BIG ones! And the fact is—and I never thought I'd say this—but a dog can have too much of a good thing . . .

Toby had finished breathing on the final hinge. He tapped the top of Buford Cudgel's bullet head and Buford reached up and lifted him off his shoulders and put him back on the ground.

Toby looked up at the tall doors, noting the new, sagging angle of both of them. Thoughtfully, he moved sideways, positioning himself well to the right of the doors—and Griswold Gristle saw him do it. Not knowing quite why he should feel the need to copy Toby, Griswold went and stood at his side, like a trusty lieutenant. He turned and motioned to Frognell Flabbit and Judge Cedric, gesturing that they too should move closer to him. When Judge Cedric hesitated, Frognell grabbed the old wrathmonk's skinny arm and hustled him to Griswold's side. The rest of the wrathmonks, mesmerized by what was going on, simply stood in a huddled group directly in front of the doors and gaped up at the last remaining hinge.

Buford raised his hammer high—

'Hit it from the side, Missster Cudgel!' squeaked Griswold, for he had suddenly seen the possible danger to them all—a danger that Toby Jugg had also obviously realized, because he had been the first to station himself off to one side. *And yet, he said nothing!* thought Griswold. In that instant, he realized that Toby Jugg was not to be trusted a jot.

Buford stepped to one side and raised his hammer high. He swung his arm back and then swung it forward with all his might. The hammer head connected with the final frozen hinge, shattering it with a CRASH!

For a moment, nothing happened. Then there was a creaking, groaning sound of protesting metal and the tops of the doors separated from the stone lintel and began to fall fast away from the garage walls.

It all happened too quickly for the small group of gawking wrathmonks who were standing directly in the path of the falling doors. Before any of them could think of moving out of the way, the great steel panels were upon them.

There were no screams, no crunching of bones —just a pair of dull THUMPS! as the doors hit the ground, obliterating the group of gaping wrathmonks beneath them.

In the very next moment, the great doors themselves were obliterated. A tidal wave of black, slimy sludge poured out of the opening, washed sluggishly over the flattened doors and then spread out across the yard in a stinking layer several centimetres thick.

'What—what on *earth* is this ssstuff?' said Griswold, stepping back hurriedly to avoid any of the black sludge touching his shoes. He and Toby —and Frognell Flabbit, Buford Cudgel, and Judge Cedric Hardscrabble—stationed as they were on either side of the garage doors, had experienced nothing worse than a quick blast of air as the doors fell past them. The black sludge, after its first wave had been released, flowed slowly, giving them time to move backwards and away from its path; but all of them peered in puzzlement as it ran past, and all of them wrinkled their noses in disgust at the stench—a swampy mixture of bad eggs, rotten meat, and mud.

'It would appear that your exhalation enchantment worked after all, Missster Cudgel,' said Toby, straightening up from examining the black tide. 'Thisss material, unless I'm missstaken, is dead bacteria. Dead bacteria grown to extraordinary sssize. The only question is—why are they dead ssso sssoon? Didn't you sssay it took sssome time for them to expire?'

Buford nodded. 'And who did it kill? That's what I want to know.'

'That's what we *all* want to know, Missster Cudgel,' muttered Toby. He glanced down at the spot where the small mob of wrathmonks had been standing. All that could be seen of the two metal doors, which had crushed them flatter than pancakes, were the vague shapes of a pair of huge, slime-covered, rectangular slabs.

'It would ssseem that your—ah—your *great strength* has killed a few *other* unfortunates too,' went on Toby, without a trace of sympathy in his voice. 'Entirely by *accident*, of course,' he added hurriedly, because Buford was glaring angrily in his direction.

'Well, they will hardly be missed,' sniffed Griswold disdainfully. 'A very low-grade ssselection of wrathmonks, in my opinion. Frankly, we will be better off without them.'

And that was the last thought, of *any* kind, that they gave to their former fellow wrathmonks.

Iggy's breathing spell had worked and the bacteria hadn't stood a chance. His breath had washed over the rising sea of germs, killing them instantly. Iggy, with the extraordinary lung capacity that wrathmonks possessed, had kept on blowing down at the rising, seething black mass below him until the mass had stopped rising and stopped seething and become, instead, a sludgy lake of dissolving, decomposing matter, held back only by the great steel doors, which acted like a dam across a river.

The black sludge had finally stopped flowing. Toby and the rest of the wrathmonks peered cautiously round the sides of the opening and into the darkness of the garage. The smell was very strong. They could just make out the shapes of the Stubbs car—and the motorcycle and sidecar—half buried under a thick layer of black slime.

'Is anybody there?' called Toby, and his voice echoed round the great interior of the garage. 'Anybody *alive*, that is?'

Up in the loft, Nanny Flannel took her hand away from Measle's wrist and put it on his shoulder. She put her other hand on the back of Iggy's scrawny neck.

'Now, dear!' she hissed. 'And you, Iggy! NOW!'

Measle and Iggy bit down on their jelly beans. The moment they were both invisible, Nanny Flannel pushed them, giving them the impetus they needed. Measle couldn't see Iggy and, as he stepped out into space, all he could hope for was that Iggy wouldn't jump towards the same spot that he was aiming for—the sludge-covered roof of the family car, several metres below.

Measle landed, with a squelchy thump, on his hands and knees. The layer of black slime on the top of the car was about ten centimetres thick—

too thin to cushion his fall much. It was also very slippery and Measle found himself sliding forward across the roof, then down over the windscreen and onto the long, rakish bonnet. He flailed in the darkness, just managing to grab hold of what he thought must be one of the windscreen wipers, halting his forward movement with a jerk. Off to one side, and from somewhere lower than where he was, he heard a soggy splash and then, a moment later, a muffled 'Oooowwww!' from an invisible Iggy. He had obviously miscalculated his jump, a jump which should have taken him to the top of a stack of shelves, but which instead had let him drop all the way down to the floor, where the slime was deepest.

But there was no time to worry about Iggy. Already, a whole lot of wrathmonk heads were visible on either side of the opening and Measle knew that twice as many wrathmonk eyes were busy scanning the shadows for the cause of the two distinct sounds they had just heard.

'Is that you, Measle, dear boy?' called Griswold Gristle, his voice eager with anticipation. 'Are you still among the living? If ssso, how lovely for you! And how lovely for all of usss too! All your old friends, Measle—all jussst *dying* to sssee you!'

It was lucky for Measle that not one of the surviving wrathmonks was prepared to start wading through the black sludge in order to investigate the interior of the garage. Instead, their heads remained quite still, poking round the two sides of the opening. Measle slipped soundlessly off the bonnet of the car and down onto the garage floor. He could hear Iggy off to one side, muttering miserably to himself, 'Ooooh! Dis is disssgussstin', dis is!' Measle waded through the muck towards the sound, feeling in the darkness with his hands. But Iggy must have moved away from the spot where he'd fallen, because Measle heard him again, his muttering, grumbling little voice now coming from the other side of the motorcycle.

'*Nasssty* ssstuff! Not nice, like de Sssquiffypoo ssstuff! Dis is '*orrible* ssstuff!'

'Iggy!' hissed Measle into the darkness. 'Get out of here! Run, Iggy! Run!'

The muttering stopped suddenly and a moment later Measle heard the sound of legs wading hurriedly through sludge. The sound was heading towards the open air—*and that's where I ought to be heading too!* thought Measle, turning quickly and pushing his way through the slimy mess. He guessed that he had a few seconds of invisibility left.

There was no point trying to be quiet. His movement though the sludge could be seen quite clearly—a pair of troughs disturbing the black surface, two furrows that moved steadily out of the garage and past the wrathmonks' puzzled gazes.

'It's him!' squealed Griswold, pointing a pudgy,

trembling finger at the moving furrows. 'The boy! He's *invisible*—an old trick from Measle Ssstubbs!'

'And—and there's another one!' howled Frognell Flabbit, his long comb-over hanging lankly down onto his shoulder. His finger was pointing too, at another set of tracks that were sloshing past them through the muck.

Mesmerized by the strange sight, none of the wrathmonks moved. Instead, they simply stood on the sidelines, watching the progress of the two sets of furrows crossing the garage yard. As the furrows neared the edge of the sludge, they seemed to separate—one set moving off in the direction of the long driveway, the other heading towards the back of Merlin Manor.

'Quickly!' shouted Toby suddenly, galvanizing the other wrathmonks out of their paralysis. 'We mussst catch them! Sssplit up. Missster Cudgel and Missster Flabbit, you come with me! Missster Gristle and the judge—follow that ssset! Quick—after them!'

When really frightened, Iggy could run fast. Iggy ran fast now. He scuttled like an invisible spider towards the only place he really knew—the rose garden at the front of Merlin Manor. Every few seconds, as instructed by Measle and Nanny Flannel, he reached into his top pocket, pulled out a green jelly bean and swallowed it and so remained invisible all the way to the rose garden. Once he reached its outer edge, Iggy plunged deep into the heart of it, finding a spot where the bushes grew thickest. Then he crawled on his stomach, beneath the clinging thorns, finding his way to a little space he knew about, right in the very centre. It was a place where he hid sometimes, when Nanny Flannel was cross with him, and it was the one place he felt reasonably safe. His little black rain cloud didn't give him away, either—it was so small, it hovered close above his head, so there was nothing for his pursuers to see, other than the dark shapes of hundreds of rose bushes covering most of the huge lawn in front of Merlin Manor.

Toby, Frognell, and Buford had been following a trail of small, black, slimy footsteps, which Iggy had left behind him. The trail grew fainter and fainter as the slime wore off Iggy's shoes, and it petered out altogether just short of the rose garden, bringing the three wrathmonks to a halt.

'Use your noses!' barked Toby, sniffing wildly at the night air. Buford and Frognell obeyed, lifting their noses and smelling for all they were worth.

'Well?'

'All I can sssmell is thisss ssslime,' muttered Frognell, trying unsuccessfully to smooth back his drooping hank of hair. 'And that could jussst be usss, couldn't it?'

'You don't sssmell the boy?'

'Flowers!' rumbled Buford. 'Jussst ssstinking flowers! And ssslime! That's all! There's nobody here, I tell you!'

Toby stared long and hard at the rose garden then, reluctantly, he turned away.

Deep inside a thicket of thorns, Iggy went on chewing his green jelly beans.

Dat's funny, he thought to himself, *dey don't taste all dat bad, actually*.

If anything, Measle ran even faster than Iggy, because he was in the greater danger. He had only one jelly bean left.

As they'd hurriedly planned it up in the loft, the idea was that—once outside—he and Iggy should run in opposite directions, in the hope that their pursuers would then split up into two smaller groups, which might give both of them a slight advantage.

Measle had reached the kitchen yard and now he paused, wondering frantically which way to go next. He had only a few moments of invisibility left before he'd be forced to swallow his last bean—and then what? He glanced up at the dark shape of the house. There was nowhere he could hide in there, not with the staircase gone, the upper storeys out of reach and the kitchen little more than a cave.

Where? Where to go now?

Measle turned away from the house and looked out across the enormous lawn. *There! On the far side—the line of trees where the forest begins— perhaps I could hide in there!*

Without giving it another thought, he raced away from the house, heading across the lawn towards the distant trees. Behind him, he heard the crunch of feet on gravel. Frantically, he burrowed in his trousers for the last jelly bean.

His fingers met a small, sticky mess at the bottom of his pocket. *Oh no! It must have dissolved in my wet clothes!* Wildly, he scraped at it with his fingernails, managing only to get a small amount on the ends of his fingers. Running as fast as he could, he stuck the fingers into his mouth and sucked hard.

He knew he wouldn't make it, because the outline of his hand started to materialize right before his eyes—and the line of trees was still a long, long way away and here he was, right out in the open.

The black rectangle of the swimming pool appeared in the ground a few metres in front of him and Measle began to dodge sideways, with the intention of skirting round it. The last place he wanted to be was anywhere near the Slitherghoul, which he guessed was still down there in the wet darkness. But then his feet stumbled against something that was lying on the grass—something hard and unyielding—and Measle tripped and lost his balance. In the split second before he fell, he glanced down at the obstruction and saw, to his amazement, Officer Offal lying on his back and staring up at him through glassy eyes.

Measle had been running too fast for the fall to be a simple stumble. Instead, his momentum sent him flying through the air, directly into the yawning black rectangle of the pit. He landed at the bottom with a tremendous splash, falling to his hands and knees, his fingers sinking into the mud at the bottom. For a moment, he was too shaken up to take in his surroundings. But then he remembered the Slitherghoul—

Measle froze, his eyes darting wildly around the enclosed area and scanning the surface of the muddy water. There was no sign of the Slitherghoul. But that was hardly any comfort—Officer Offal had seen Measle quite clearly and would be raising the alarm any second now.

There was silence from above. Now that Measle came to think about it, there had been something very odd about the moment when his feet had made contact with the big guard's body. It had felt hard, like a log of wood, and Offal's eyes, while wide open, had looked strangely blind. *Well, whatever that means, I can't risk moving again—not with no jelly beans left—let's just hope nobody else saw me.*

But the outline of Measle's ghostly form *had* been seen. Griswold Gristle had rounded the corner of Merlin Manor and was waiting for his old friend to catch up with him. Panting heavily, Griswold scanned the darkness with his beady black eyes. Across the lawn, and for a brief instant, he saw something that looked like grey smoke, in the rough shape of a small boy. And then the little grey figure dropped down, vanishing from view.

Something sharp and bony bumped hard into Griswold's back and he heard the wheezing of his friend's ancient lungs, pumping like a pair of cracked bellows. Impatiently Griswold turned round and grabbed Judge Cedric's skinny old arms.

'He's there, Cedric!' he squeaked. 'The boy! I sssaw him—he is in the pit!'

'What pit?' panted Judge Cedric. 'There's a pit? Where? Where?'

Griswold didn't bother to answer. Instead, he transferred his grip to Judge Cedric's hand and started to drag the old wrathmonk towards the distant pool.

GRISWOLD BREATHES!

Measle shivered with cold. He huddled in the shallow water, his back pressed tightly into a muddy corner. Soggy paper bags floated on the surface—*but at least that Slitherghoul thing has gone! Now, if only they don't think to look in here—*

He heard the sounds of pounding feet getting nearer and nearer and nearer, and he knew that, whoever was after him, the pit was going to be the first place they would search.

He would be found unless—

There was only one thing left to do. Measle took a deep breath, filling his lungs with as much air as they could hold. Then, pinching his nose between finger and thumb, and closing both eyes tight shut, he ducked the whole top half of his body under the surface of the icy water.

A slight, swirling eddy rippled over Measle's head.

A second later, Griswold and Judge Cedric, both gasping for breath, skidded to a stop at the muddy edge of the pit.

'Oh, *thisss* pit,' huffed Judge Cedric, clutching his side where a sharp pain was stabbing him in the ribs. 'But—but I sssee no boy, Griswold.'

'He's here, I tell you!' hissed Griswold, staring down into the darkness. 'I sssaw him jump—and there is nowhere else he can be! And thisss time, Cedric, we really have him. There can be no essscape from usss now.'

'But where is he?'

Even as Judge Cedric spoke, Griswold knew the answer. A bubble broke on the dark surface of the water—then another—

'He is under water, Cedric!' squeaked Griswold. 'Well, I know how to deal with that!' Hurriedly, he stepped down onto the mud of the shallow end and then slithered down to the water's edge. Once there, he bent down and took a deep, deep breath.

Measle was almost at his last gasp. His lungs were beginning to hurt and he knew that he had only a few more seconds of breath left. He was going to have to surface—or drown.

* * *

Griswold began to blow his stinking wrathmonk breath directly at the surface of the water. At first, nothing seemed to be happening, but the steady falling of the water level, creeping down the mud walls centimetre by centimetre, showed clearly that Griswold Gristle's drying-up spell was working just fine. Exactly where all that water was going was impossible to know, but the effect was as if somebody had pulled a plug out of the bottom of the pit and the water was simply draining away.

Up on the grassy bank, Judge Cedric was hopping excitedly from side to side, clapping his hands and crying, 'Oh, sssplendid, *sssplendid*, Griswold! We shall have him now!'

Measle had no idea what was going on somewhere above his head. The water was too muddy and the night was too dark to see anything, even if Measle had had his eyes open, which he hadn't. But his time was up and, whatever was going on at the surface, Measle was going to find out. His lungs at bursting point, Measle uncurled his body. In one explosive movement, he lifted his head and then his torso out of the water and took an enormous lungful of cool night air—cool night air that was tinged with the scent of dead fish, old mattresses, and the insides of ancient sneakers.

Instantly, the whole upper part of his body, which was clear of the water, dried out. His hair, his face, his leather jacket, the remains of a sodden paper bag that had draped itself over his right shoulder—everything was as dry as if it had just come out of a tumble dryer.

Measle's sudden appearance from under the surface of the muddy water took Griswold a little by surprise. He had been expecting the waters to sink and then reveal Measle's huddled form, but here was the boy, suddenly rearing up out of the depths like a breaching whale.

Griswold snapped his mouth shut, cutting off his horrible breath. It was probably the single luckiest break in Measle's short but eventful life. In the instant before Griswold stopped, his exhalation enchantment had dried off every drop of surface water that was clinging to Measle's upper half and, had Griswold gone *on* breathing, the process would have continued with the rapid dehydration of Measle's body itself. But, instead of continuing with his devastating spell, Griswold chose to gloat. He smiled a wolfish smile and said, 'Ah, there you are, dear boy. Have a nice ssswim, did we? Now, come along out of there—there are ssso many people who want to meet you!'

'My boils!' screamed Judge Cedric from above. 'You promised I could do my boils on him, Griswold!'

'And ssso you shall, Cedric!' said Griswold, beckoning to Measle with a stubby finger.

Measle stood his ground and shook his head. He

282

wasn't going to go anywhere. Especially anywhere that Griswold Gristle wanted him to go.

Griswold frowned. He said, 'Why do you think your top half is dry, Measle? Eh? It's because I was breathing. I was performing my exhalation enchantment on all thisss water, drying it out mossst sssuccessfully, I might add! And then, up you popped, and the ssspell worked on you, too—and it can go *on* working, if I ssso choose! All I need to do is take another breath and ssstart blowing it out again. Let me tell you, the results are *mossst* unpleasant for the victim. Ssso, why don't you do as you're told. Come out of there and join Judge Cedric and myssself up on the grass and perhaps I will allow you a few more moments of life, eh?'

Measle paused for a moment. Griswold took a sudden, swift intake of breath—

'All right,' said Measle, miserably. 'All right. I'm coming.'

He sloshed through the shallow water and then tramped up the muddy slope and onto the grass at the top. When he got there, he took a quick look at the still form of Officer Offal, lying by the side of the pit. Now he could see what he'd missed the first time. Officer Offal's body seemed to be coated with a thin covering of ice. His short red hair was white with frost and an icicle stuck out from the end of his nose like a little sword.

Officer Offal was frozen stiff.

Griswold and Judge Cedric came and stood

close to Measle, both glaring down at him with red, angry eyes. The rain from their two black wrathmonk clouds dribbled down on Measle, making a *tip-tapping* sound as the drops pattered against the dry paper bag that was still draped across his shoulder.

'Now, Griswold?' said Judge Cedric, his long beaky nose twitching with excitement. 'Can I breathe on him now?'

'Why not?' said Griswold, in a fat and oily voice. 'A little unpleasantness before the finality of death! Jussst the ticket, Cedric! But let me move out of the way firssst!'

Griswold stepped away, making sure he was well out of range of Judge Cedric's poisonous breath.

Judge Cedric was determined to savour the moment. He licked his thin, cracked lips and glared down at Measle.

'Any minute now, my boy!' he snarled. 'Any minute now! Spots ... and boils ... and pimples, all pussy and painful and putrid—'

'Oh, do get *on* with it, Cedric!' called Griswold.

Patter, patter, patter went the raindrops against the paper bag on Measle's shoulder. The bag was getting wetter and wetter—and soggier and soggier.

And then a raindrop fell onto something other than just the paper.

It fell onto something that was already *on* the paper.

It fell onto a little glistening glob of snot.

THROUGH MEASLE'S EYES

The drop of rain water that fell onto the glob of glistening snot instantly washed away all trace of the diluted sugar that had, up to that moment, coated the thing's slimy surface.

There was a reason why the Slitherghoul reacted so badly to sweet substances. It was all to do with the character of the wizard that had created it in the first place. Sheepshank was a bitter person, and sweetness is the opposite of bitterness, which was why the Slitherghoul, finding itself floating in a solution of sugar and muddy water, became progressively weaker and weaker. As it weakened, it gave up all its victims. It couldn't die—there was only one thing that could kill it, and sugar wasn't it. But it could be reduced to its original size, and now, empty of all its inhabitants, and coated with a mild solution of sugar and water, which kept it weak and ineffective, the Slitherghoul had reverted to its original form—a yellowish-brownish-greenish globule of snot.

But when the raindrop washed away all traces of sugar that coated its surface, the Slitherghoul became itself again—and the first thing it looked for was Life.

It found it immediately—right next to itself, in fact. Even as Judge Cedric gloated, grinning evilly down at Measle and rubbing his dry old hands together with the sound of sandpaper on wood, the Slitherghoul moved across the paper bag and, extending a tiny tentacle of itself, touched Measle's neck.

By the time Measle realized what was happening, it was too late. The moment the tip of the tiny tentacle touched bare skin, the Slitherghoul slid as fast as lightning off the paper and onto Measle. Once there, it spread out its sticky, jelly body, so that it was thinner than the thinnest paper. It slimed fast up Measle's neck and slid over his right ear, and now Measle could feel a strange sensation as this fine, sticky film rapidly covered his head, then his eyes, then his nose.

Measle opened his mouth to yell out, but the Slitherghoul covered it up before he could even take a breath. Its body spread impossibly thin, it slid down and over the rest of him, absorbing Measle, changing his shape to suit itself, until at last there was no more small boy, just a pile of quivering jelly about the size of a large suitcase.

It was a strange sensation, being inside the Slitherghoul. It wasn't unpleasant: there was no pain, because Measle couldn't feel anything. He couldn't hear anything, either, all he could do was see and think. He could see because his were the only eyes the Slitherghoul had available, and he could think because the Slitherghoul allowed him to.

At first, Measle couldn't think of anything much. He was too horrified by what had happened to him to do anything other than stare at the startled figure of Judge Cedric who—since the Slitherghoul was now a small mound of jelly less than half a metre tall—looked to Measle like a tall tree. The old judge was staring down with a look of blank astonishment at what was lying at his feet, and he made no move to get away when the Slitherghoul, acting on its instincts, made a sudden, slithering lunge in his direction.

No! thought Measle wildly. Even in his dismay and confusion, he knew one thing for sure: he didn't want any wrathmonks in here with him!

The Slitherghoul stopped dead. It stayed quite still for several seconds, then—in a tentative sort of way—it extended a small, stubby tentacle towards Judge Cedric's skinny ankles.

No! shrieked Measle's mind again and,

immediately, the tentacle drew back. Measle concentrated his mind and tried to turn the Slitherghoul away from Judge Cedric—but there was a limit to the control he seemed to have over the creature, because the Slitherghoul didn't move.

Why doesn't that stupid old man get out of the way? thought Measle, and just as if Judge Cedric had heard his thoughts, the old man suddenly came to what little sense he had and stumbled hurriedly backwards.

The Slitherghoul made another, instinctive lunge across the grass and Measle had to use all his mental power to bring it to a halt again. To his relief, Judge Cedric shambled away towards the waiting figure of Griswold Gristle. Griswold's lips moved. Measle couldn't hear what was being said but, from the looks of panic on both the wrathmonks' faces, it was clear what they were thinking. Measle saw Griswold grab Judge Cedric's arm and he watched as both wrathmonks set off, running as fast as a pair of short fat legs, and a pair of old thin ones, would let them. They seemed to be heading towards the line of trees on the far side of the great sweeping lawn . . .

Corky Pretzel was sitting with his broad back leaning against an old oak tree, staring down at the pathetic little figure of Sheepshank. The young chap with the enormous nose was lying on the ground at

Corky's feet, his head pillowed on Corky's rolled up uniform jacket. He was unconscious but he was still shivering with cold. It was hardly surprising. The black robe—made of some sort of coarse wool—was the only thing the fellow was wearing, apart from a length of rough rope knotted round his middle and a pair of old leather sandals on a pair of very dirty feet. Corky thought he looked like a monk from the Middle Ages.

Well, apart from the Gloomstains, that is.

Corky had seen them the moment he laid the man down on the dry leaves of the forest floor. Sheepshank's long stringy black hair had fallen away from his ears, revealing the dark stains that extended all the way from the tips to the lobes.

'So, you're a warlock, are you?' muttered Corky. He got no reply.

Corky had taken off his shirt as well as his uniform jacket and had placed it over Sheepshank's body. Corky didn't know what else to do with the little fellow, who was obviously in a pretty bad way. Every few seconds, Sheepshank's head would roll from side to side and weak moaning sounds would come from his pale lips. His eyelids fluttered and his hands made little pushing movements, rustling among the fallen leaves of the forest floor.

Corky was very confused. So much had happened, so many inexplicable events had taken place, and now here he was, with a very sick young warlock, and no idea who he was, or what to do with him, or how to take care of him. There was no going back towards the house, that was for certain. There were just too many wrathmonks out there for him to handle on his own.

The sound of footsteps, crashing through the undergrowth, took his attention away from Sheepshank. The sounds were coming nearer. Corky could hear the noise of breaking twigs and panting breaths. Cautiously, he stood up and poked his head round the tree trunk.

Twenty metres away were the figures of a pair of rascally wrathmonks he knew only too well. Griswold Gristle and Judge Cedric were stumbling through the wood, running as if all the monsters in the world were after them—and they were running in his direction.

Runaway wrathmonks! This was exactly the sort of situation that Corky was trained to handle.

He pulled his head back, pressed himself against the tree, and waited. A few seconds later, Griswold Gristle and Judge Cedric, gasping for breath, staggered past him, on either side of the oak tree. They didn't see Corky, or the huddled figure at Corky's feet, but they did feel Corky's two massive hands grab them both. One hand seized Griswold's left ear and the other hand seized Judge Cedric's right ear and, before either startled wrathmonk could make a sound, other than utter a horrified gasp of pain, Corky swung both hands towards each other, slamming the two wrathmonk heads together with a *CRACK!* that echoed through the forest.

The Slitherghoul was gliding over the grass towards the line of trees. It moved slowly, because Measle was using all his mental powers to delay it as much as he could. If he had to be inside this horrible creature, he wanted to be the only occupier. But Measle could do nothing about the Slitherghoul's basic instincts, so, following its basic instincts, the creature simply trailed in the footsteps of the last living things it had come across—Griswold Gristle and Judge Cedric Hardscrabble.

It soon found them.

The two wrathmonks were slumped, groggily shaking their aching heads, against the bases of two stout trees. Both had their arms stretched behind their backs, encircling the tree trunks as far as they would go. Round each wrist was a strong nylon strap, and the straps were connected together by yet another length of nylon, so neither wrathmonk was going anywhere, at least not for the time being. The narrow nylon straps looked thin and not very strong, but police forces all over the world use them on their prisoners, because they are impossible to break and the only way to get out of them is to cut them with a sharp knife. Corky Pretzel knew this as well as any policeman and, being a trained Detention Centre guard, always carried a bundle of these straps in a leather pouch on his belt. Tying up two unconscious wrathmonks was a simple job and, once done, Corky knew that there was nothing much to fear from either of them. He had put his shirt on again, wrapping his uniform jacket tightly round Sheepshank's body. Then he'd hefted the little man onto his shoulders and, with one last look at his prisoners, he'd marched off through the woods.

The Slitherghoul slimed its way across the forest floor towards the two bound wrathmonks. It paused in front of Griswold Gristle. The tubby wrathmonk became aware that something very smelly was next to him. Slowly, he raised his aching head—then he screamed loudly.

Inside the Slitherghoul, Measle was doing his best to pull the creature away. But his mind simply wasn't strong enough to overcome the thing's instincts. He managed to force the Slitherghoul to retract its tentacle once, then twice, but, the third time, the tentacle ignored Measle's howling mind and reached out and touched Griswold's terror-filled face. In a smooth movement, it enveloped the wrathmonk. Once Griswold was inside, it started to slither across to the other tree, where Judge Cedric's bony frame was already wriggling and heaving with panic.

The Slitherghoul didn't get very far. Griswold was tied to a tree, which meant that, as long as he was inside the creature, the Slitherghoul was *also* tied to a tree. The tree was a young oak, very strong, with roots that extended deeply into the ground, and no amount of heaving on the part of the Slitherghoul was going to budge it. At last, dimly realizing that, if it ever wanted to move anywhere else, it would have to give up its prey, the Slitherghoul extruded, like a length of toothpaste, a slimy, slippery, and smelly Griswold Gristle from its jelly interior, leaving him coughing and wheezing on the ground by his tree. Then it slithered over to Judge Cedric and attempted exactly the same thing on him.

Measle gave up trying to control it. It was going to do what it wanted to do and there was nothing—other than in the short term—that he could do to stop it. He waited while the Slitherghoul swallowed a whimpering Judge Cedric and then—after a few moments of futile pulling and heaving—pushed the old wrathmonk back out onto the ground again. Then the Slitherghoul sat there, halfway between the two wrathmonks, its jelly sides rippling slowly, as if undecided as to what to do next—which, given the fact that Measle had stopped trying to direct it, was exactly what it was.

Judge Cedric blinked the slime from his eyes. His bowler hat was tilted sideways and his normally bushy white hair hung in gooey clumps on either side of his face.

'Griswold!' he bleated. 'Griswold, dear friend, my head hurts and I appear to be ssstuck! I cannot move my hands, Griswold! Please come and help me, dear friend, before this frightful thing ssswallows me again!'

Griswold gritted his teeth and hissed, 'I too am fassstened to a tree, Cedric! I cannot help you!'

'What shall we do, Griswold?' wailed Judge Cedric. 'What shall we *do*?' He stopped struggling against his bonds because the nylon straps were cutting into his wrists.

'We should breathe on it, Cedric!' hissed Griswold. 'Perhaps, together, we can kill it! Are you ready?'

'Yesss, Griswold!'

'On my count, then. One . . . two . . . three . . . *breathe*, Cedric!'

Both wrathmonks leaned as far forward as their straps would let them and breathed out their stinking wrathmonk breaths over the Slitherghoul—

Nothing happened. No boils appeared on its slimy sides, no hint of dryness dulled its wet exterior, but still the two wrathmonks breathed, until Judge Cedric's face turned a strange shade of purple and Griswold's pigeon chest grew narrower and narrower and narrower. At last, with a final puff, they ran out of air—and the Slitherghoul just sat there, rippling gently, as if nothing whatsoever had happened to it.

If Griswold and Judge Cedric had known of the

futile efforts, over many centuries, of the countless wizards and warlocks who had attempted to destroy the Slitherghoul, they probably wouldn't have bothered to try for themselves. But now, with the evidence of just how useless their exhalation enchantments were against a magical monster like this, they simply huddled against their trees and stared, with wonder and fear and loathing, at the mound of jelly between them. Measle, looking at them from deep inside the Slitherghoul, couldn't help feeling a stab of pleasure at their helplessness.

Then, without warning—and without Measle making any such mental suggestion—the Slitherghoul started to slime its way out of the forest, back towards the dark shape of Merlin Manor in the distance.

GOING FOR HELP!

Nanny Flannel and Tinker had lain low up in the loft of the garage, listening to the various sounds of the hunters and the hunted. There hadn't been any noises for some time now and Nanny Flannel decided that they couldn't just lie here for ever. Anything was better than hiding up in this foul-smelling loft. Measle and Iggy were off on their own somewhere—*please let them be safe. But there's nothing I can do to help them now, unless—unless I go for help! Yes! And the way to do it is sitting there, right beneath me!*

'Come on, Tinker,' she whispered. 'Time to go.'

Tinker crawled close to the old lady, his stubby tail flipping busily from side to side. Nanny Flannel gathered up the little dog in her arms, tucked him into the front of her apron and then, slowly and cautiously, she climbed down the ladder. At the bottom, her feet sank deep into the black sludge and she wrinkled her nose in disgust.

'We'll be cleaning this up *for ever*,' she muttered. The smell was horrible too and, every time she took a step, her feet stirred the black goo, releasing even more of the stink than before.

Nanny Flannel waded across the floor to where the motorcycle and its sidecar stood, still half buried under the sludge. Trying not to breathe, she scooped armfuls of the foul stuff off the machine, until it began to look more like a motorcycle and sidecar and less like an uneven lump in a sea of black gunk. She threw handfuls of the muck out of the sidecar, until there was room for Tinker to sit in it. Then she put Tinker firmly into the sidecar seat and said, 'Stay, Tinker. I know it's not very nice, but stay!'

To Tinker's doggy mind, this black stuff was *exactly* the kind of interesting smelly substance a sensible dog would roll in if he found a little patch of it out on a walk through the woods somewhere. The trouble with it was that there was just so *much* of it. *All a fellow needs is a little tiny patch, not a ruddy great bog of the stuff! Besides, rolling in it is pointless now because I'm pretty much covered from head to paws—and all a fellow really needs is a little dab behind the ears! Oh well, a ride in the sidecar is always fun!*

Nanny Flannel swung her leg over and settled down into the saddle with a thump. She turned the key in the ignition and the green neutral light on the headlamp shone through the film of goo.

'That's a good sign, Tinker,' muttered Nanny Flannel. 'Now, let's hope she starts!'

Nanny Flannel pressed the starter button, and the engine wheezed . . . coughed . . . belched . . . wheezed again, and roared into life.

'Good!' shouted Nanny Flannel over the steady thumping beat of the motor. 'Now, let's get out of here!'

Toby Jugg, Buford Cudgel, and Frognell Flabbit were trudging back from the rose garden, crossing the gravel drive back towards the garage, when they heard the distinctive sound of a twin-engined motorcycle heading in their direction. Buford froze, straining his ears. Then he growled, 'That sssounds like my old bike! Who's riding my old bike, I should like to know!'

'I daresssay we shall sssoon find out, Missster Cudgel,' said Toby. 'It ssseems to be heading in our direction!'

The three wrathmonks waited, their faces gleaming white in the darkness, as the sound of the thumping engine drew nearer.

* * *

Corky Pretzel heard the sounds too. He had skirted the edge of the wood, keeping the distant shape of Merlin Manor always in sight. Now he was halfway across a field that bordered the front drive. Sheepshank's head lolled against Corky's broad chest and the little wizard was muttering to himself. Corky couldn't make out the words but at least the man was showing some more signs of life.

Meanwhile, there was that thumping noise in the distance. Corky thought it sounded just like a big motorbike. A big motorbike could be very useful right now—very useful for both of them.

Corky began to pound across the field towards the long driveway, and Sheepshank's head bounced against his chest with every step he took.

Bounce, bump! Bounce, bump! Bounce, bump!

Dimly, and as if his body was many miles away, Sheepshank's brain began to stir. Sensations flooded through his frame. He was uncomfortable. He was cold. He was damp. His head was banging rhythmically against something smooth and smelly. He seemed to be upside down—or, at least, his head was. He could hear the sound of running footsteps and, close to his ears, panting noises of somebody out of breath. Further off—much further off—was a sound he didn't recognize. It was a horrible sound! A steady, thudding noise, like . . . like the beating of a great heart! An enormous heart, to be heard at such a distance! A heart that could belong only to an awful monster! A dragon, perhaps!

Bounce, thump! Bounce, thump! Bounce, thump!

Sheepshank struggled to move, but he was still too weak. He tried to open his eyes, but some kind of glue seemed to be holding them shut. He tried to speak, but his tongue felt heavy and too big for his mouth. The sounds his ears were hearing were too awful to contemplate. The only sense he felt he could rely on was his brain.

Think, Sheepshank! Remember!

The last thing he could remember was—*what was it? In what action was I engaged? Ah yes! Searching for my little dead spider! I was in my cell, secure from prying eyes, searching for my little dead spider! And now—this? How could I venture from that to this with no conscious thought in between?*

Sheepshank's still sluggish brain struggled to connect the two events. One minute he was in the silence and privacy of his cell, the next—well, what exactly was happening at this precise moment? There was no way of understanding, unless he could see! He must open his eyes! Sheepshank screwed up his eyelids and then strained to pull them apart, and the dried slime that covered one of his eyes split—

Darkness! But just enough light to make out— *what?* Rough grass flying by! A pair of boots— *black* boots—pounding along! And close to his open eye, covering a broad chest, was a tunic of some sort, made of a fine cloth he didn't recognize, against which his head was bouncing at every step.

And that noise! That terrible noise! It was getting closer—

Nanny Flannel and Tinker roared round the corner of the house and almost ran straight into three wrathmonks who were standing stock still in the middle of the circular drive. Nanny Flannel wrenched at the handlebars and the motorbike and sidecar skidded sideways in the gravel, missing Frognell Flabbit by a whisker, before thundering on towards the first bend in the driveway. It all happened so quickly that none of the wrathmonks got even a glimpse of who was on board the bike. All they saw was a blinding beam from the headlamp and, as the machine skidded past, a vague human shape in the saddle, and another, smaller shape in the sidecar, both dimly lit from behind by the red glow of the rear light. Toby Jugg managed to get off a single blast of breath at the retreating machine—and Nanny Flannel felt a sudden, icy chill up and down her spine. She gritted her teeth, leaned forward and twisted the accelerator grip as far as it would go. The engine roared even louder and the motorbike spun its back wheel and raced off down the drive.

Corky Pretzel reached a barbed-wire fence, which ran along the edge of the field. On the other side of the fence was a shallow ditch and, just beyond that, ran the driveway of Merlin Manor. Corky could see a single headlight in the distance and he could hear the roar of the powerful motorbike, and both were getting nearer and nearer.

Corky climbed easily over the wire, with Sheepshank slung over his shoulder like a sack of letters. He stepped across the ditch and stood by the side of the drive, his eyes straining in the darkness. He came to a decision: whoever was coming his way, he would do his best to stop them.

There was a risk, of course, but Corky reasoned that if the motorbike was being driven by wrathmonks— *and who else was there around here?*—it could, at the most, carry only *two* of them—and two was a number Corky could certainly cope with, assuming that their wrathrings were still round their necks, of course.

Corky lowered Sheepshank's limp body gently down onto the grass verge and walked to the middle of the drive and stood, facing in the direction of the approaching motorbike.

Nanny Flannel steered the bike round a long corner and then centred the handlebars, because ahead of her was the long, straight-as-an-arrow stretch of driveway that led all the way to the front gate. The pins holding her hair in its neat bun on the back of her head were blown loose by the wind, and her long grey tresses streamed out, like a plume of smoke, behind her. Next to her in the sidecar—grinning from ear to ear—sat Tinker, his ears flapping in the wind.

Nanny Flannel saw a figure of a man—a big, muscular young man—standing about a hundred metres away, right in the middle of the drive. He seemed to be holding out his arms, as if he wanted her to stop.

Nanny Flannel had no intention of stopping— particularly not for somebody she didn't recognize.

The young man was a complete stranger and this was hardly the moment to be picking up unknown hitchhikers! He'd just have to get out of the way—because she wasn't stopping for anything! Nanny Flannel pressed her left thumb to a button on the handlebar and the two big trumpet-shaped air horns blasted out in a deafening wail that pierced the still night air like the cry of an enraged banshee.

Sheepshank lay quite still in the long grass. The one eye he had managed to open was now closed again and he'd curled himself into a tight ball, in the desperate hope that the approaching monster wouldn't notice him in this darkness. The sound of its advance was terrifying enough but now the monster was screaming in rage and the steady pounding of its great heart was getting louder and louder—and *faster and faster!* Sheepshank whimpered in terror and huddled down against the damp ground.

Let it not spy me! Let it not spy me!

Corky stood his ground, watching the blazing headlight race directly towards him. When it didn't look as if the motorbike was going to stop, Corky began to wave his arms up and down. It didn't help. The blaring of the twin horns went on and the bike was almost on top of him!

Corky wasn't very bright but he wasn't a

complete fool either. When the bike was ten metres away, he stepped quickly to one side—at exactly the same moment that Nanny Flannel (who wasn't a fool either) wrenched the bike's handlebars to the left, away from the strange young man, and away from the ditch, too—and the barbed-wire fence—and away from the small bundle of what looked like dark clothing that lay in the grass at the edge of the drive. Nanny Flannel knew there was no ditch to the left of the roadway, just lumpy, uncut grass, so she knew she was safe to veer hard left. For twenty metres the motorbike bounced across the uneven surface. Then, once she was sure they were past the danger, Nanny Flannel took her thumb off the horn button and steered to the right again and the motorbike roared back onto the driveway and headed fast towards the distant gates.

Sheepshank shivered with relief. The monster had not noticed him! It had passed him by!

Sheepshank had opened his one good eye and had caught a quick glimpse as the terrible creature had flown by. It was definitely a dragon of some sort, with a single blazing eye right in the middle of its head. This strange, one-eyed dragon even had its Dragodon astride its back and Sheepshank had quaked at the sight of the dragon master's long grey hair, streaming in the wind. This Dragodon must be a very great wizard indeed, because the dragon was allowing the dragon master's wolf companion to ride at his side! Sheepshank had quickly closed his eye again; the sight was too frightening to behold. At the same time, Sheepshank couldn't help thinking that, as dragons went, this one had been surprisingly *small*, and the wizard's companion had looked more like a *puppy* than a full-grown wolf. All this was very strange.

Yet, he thought, *for all its smallness, the creature is still a monster to be feared and avoided at all costs*. He could still hear it, the sound of its thudding heart diminishing into the distance. It had stopped screaming at last. Had its Dragodon finally quietened its savage voice? At all events, he was safe for the time being.

Sheepshank allowed his skinny body to relax, uncurling it from the tight ball he'd squeezed himself into. Carefully, he opened one eye again.

'Hello there, matey,' said Corky, who had seen the movement and was now squatting down next to Sheepshank. 'Feeling any better, are we?'

The gates of Merlin Manor loomed ahead of Nanny Flannel. They were wide open and, knowing that directly beyond them lay the main road, Nanny Flannel slowed the motorbike before driving between the stone pillars on either side of the entrance. Once past them, she was about to come to a full stop when she became horribly aware that an enormous *something* was almost on top of her.

Huge, twin headlights blazed into her eyes, almost blinding her, and the blast from a powerful horn almost knocked her out of the saddle. Nanny Flannel grabbed the brake lever and hauled the motorbike to a skidding stop. The big, shiny, single-decker bus, which had been about to turn into the Merlin Manor entrance, slid ponderously to a halt itself, its huge chrome bumper only an inch from the front wheel of the motorbike.

There was a hiss of air brakes, then a second hiss as the door of the bus slid open. Somebody stepped down and hurried to Nanny Flannel's side.

'Miss Flannel! Are you all right?'

The voice was familiar. Nanny Flannel blinked several times, until her eyes lost their temporary blindness. She peered into the darkness at the slight figure that stood beside her, and then she smiled in relief.

'Oh, Lord Octavo!' she cried. 'Oh, you have no idea how happy I am to see you!'

Tinker, his stubby tail a blur, barked once in full agreement.

MEASLE ON THE WARPATH

Toby Jugg, Buford Cudgel, and Frognell Flabbit were still at the front of Merlin Manor, standing right in the middle of the circular driveway, when Measle came slithering up behind them.

They had been bickering amongst themselves about what they should do next. Buford was all for chasing after his motorbike and clobbering the thieving rider with his huge fists. Frognell saw no point in running after something they could never catch. His interest lay more in the desire to get away from this dark and dangerous place and find somewhere warm and comfortable, with lots of beer and a nice new hairbrush. His comb-over was so heavy with dried Slitherghoul slime, it was stubbornly refusing to stay in place and Frognell Flabbit couldn't bear that.

Toby Jugg wanted to stay. He'd got over his initial disappointment at not finding either the Mallockee or the Manafount at Merlin Manor and had worked out the idea that, if he simply waited long enough, then they would be sure to turn up here. And then—well, now that he was a powerful wrathmonk, with a Mallockee and a Manafount under his control there was no limit to what he might do!

So, ever since Nanny Flannel had roared past them on the motorbike, all three wrathmonks had stood under their rain clouds, furiously hissing their demands at each other.

Toby smelt the stink of the Slitherghoul first. He whipped round and saw the awful creature, only a few metres away, sliming fast over the gravel towards them. The Slitherghoul was still quite small, but Toby knew that size made no difference to this thing. It had only been the size of a small dining table when it had swallowed him and Officer Offal.

'*RUN!*' screamed Toby, grabbing Buford's enormous arm in one hand and Frognell's flabby arm in the other. Buford and Frognell paused only long enough to glimpse what was coming up behind them, before all three of them took off at high speed towards the house.

It was extraordinary under the circumstances,

but Measle actually had a vague plan in his head. At first, being inside the Slitherghoul had been such an odd, disconcerting sensation that he'd had a hard time thinking at all. But for some time now, he'd been able to gather his thoughts together and quite interesting thoughts they had been, too. On his way back from the wood, he had passed close by the swimming pool pit. It had occurred to him that perhaps he could urge the Slitherghoul towards the pit and then down into it. Assuming the sweetened water was still there and hadn't yet filtered away through the muddy bottom, logically, once immersed in the stuff, the creature would be forced to give him up, just like it had given up all its other victims. So Measle had used all the power of his mind to try to direct the Slitherghoul towards the gaping hole in the grass—but the Slitherghoul would have none of it. All Measle had managed to do was steer the slimy blob a little closer to the edge, but the creature had sensed what Measle wanted it to do, and instinctively it remembered the unpleasant effect from before. It resisted the order easily, flowing stickily past the pit with several centimetres to spare.

It seemed intent on moving back towards Merlin Manor and Measle was forced to just float within the creature, letting it do whatever it wanted. Quite soon, they were back in the deeper shadows that surrounded the great house. The Slitherghoul slimed its way steadily along the side of the building and then out onto the circular driveway. There, standing in the middle of the gravel, were Toby Jugg, Buford Cudgel, and Frognell Flabbit. Where the rest of the escaped wrathmonks were, Measle hadn't a clue. Besides, wherever they were, they posed no threat to him—not while he was inside this mound of magical jelly! He'd realized at once when Griswold and Judge Cedric had breathed their exhalation enchantments over the Slitherghoul that, encased inside it, he was safe from all of that kind of thing.

In fact, he thought, *I'm pretty much invincible! Which means I can do whatever I like in here!* Then Measle's rational mind took over, reminding him that the control he could exercise over his host was minimal and, if the Slitherghoul didn't want what he wanted, then he had no control over it at all.

Ah, but what if it does *want the same thing I do?*

Right now, it seemed that the Slitherghoul wanted exactly the same thing Measle did. Well, perhaps not exactly; the Slitherghoul wanted to *absorb* the three wrathmonks, Measle wanted to *chase* them. At this stage, that amounted to the same thing.

It was extraordinary how fast the Slitherghoul could move, when all the various parts of its brains were in agreement. Toby, Buford, and Frognell ran as fast as they could and the Slitherghoul slimed rapidly in their wake, not gaining on them, but not losing them either. Measle saw, to his satisfaction, that his initial approach behind them had been the right thing to do, because all three wrathmonks were running fast towards the house, which was exactly the direction he wanted them to run.

Toby was the first to reach the front door. He wrenched at the handle and dived into the hallway beyond. He tried to close the door behind him, but Buford and Frognell—in their panic-stricken attempt to get away from the monster on their tails—managed to jam themselves together in the opening. They were only stuck there for a moment, but it was long enough for the Slitherghoul to close the gap between them. Now there was no time to get the door closed; it was all Buford and Frognell could manage just to get themselves unstuck. They popped free, with only a second or two to spare, and stumbled into the dark hallway, their eyes searching desperately for Toby Jugg.

He was nowhere to be seen.

They turned in time to see the Slitherghoul squeezing itself through the doorway. Frantically, Buford and Frognell dashed around the enormous hall, searching for an exit. Their movements were hampered by the mound of broken wood, plaster, and iron which was piled high right in the middle.

Measle pushed hard at the Slitherghoul's mind, urging it to his bidding, and the Slitherghoul obeyed. It glided rapidly after the two wrathmonks (the thought, *Where is Toby?* flitted through Measle's mind), following the panic-stricken pair as they skirted round the hallway.

Then Buford and Frognell ran into a dead end. With the collapse of the staircase—and then the further collapse of the great pile of furniture—a section of the rubble had slipped sideways, right across their escape route! There was no way they could scramble over this mess of plaster and wood and bricks and upholstery. The only way was back.

Buford and Flabbit turned—and there was the monster, almost upon them!

Buford saw the door first. It was quite small, set into the side of the hall and cleverly concealed, painted to look just like the wall that framed it. Buford reached out and grabbed the handle and pulled it open. It was a heavy door but Buford hardly noticed that. There was a dark rectangle beyond, and no way to tell where it led, but neither Buford nor Frognell had any choice in the matter. Seizing Frognell by the back of his neck and shoving him hard in front of him, Buford plunged through the opening.

The Slitherghoul lunged forward and Measle, using every fibre of his mind, screamed silently at it to *hold back*! For a brief moment, the Slitherghoul paused. It was just long enough for Buford to slam the heavy door shut, shutting himself and Frognell safely (as he thought) behind ten centimetres of ironwood, heavily reinforced with steel bars.

It was exactly what Measle wanted him to do.

Unfortunately for Buford, there was no lock or bolt on the inside of the door and Measle imagined the giant wrathmonk holding tight to the handle and using all his strength to stop it being opened again. In fact, Measle was unable to prevent the Slitherghoul from grabbing the door with an extended jelly tentacle and giving it a long, hard pull. But the Slitherghoul was now too small and too weak—and Buford Cudgel too big and strong —so the door remained firmly closed.

The concealed door in the hall of Merlin Manor led to a very interesting place. Just beyond it was a steep stone staircase. At the bottom was a small room, with walls and floor of thick granite. Being below ground level, there were no windows. Once, long ago, it had been a sort of dungeon, in which wrathmonk bounty hunters held their prisoners until they could get word to the Wizards' Guild to come and take them away. But in modern times, with the invention of the telephone and fast cars, the wrathmonk hunters had little use for the place as a jail and, for some time, Sam Stubbs had used it to store his wine. But the mechanics of the little prison had never been changed. Right beside the door, and painted the same colour as the surrounding walls, making it hard to see at first, was a heavy iron bar, on a pivot. On the other side of the door was an iron slot. Measle waited until the Slitherghoul's small brain decided that pulling at the door was futile. The moment the Slitherghoul relaxed its tentacle grip on the handle, Measle, using all the force of his brain, screamed, *Keep them in there! We can come back for them later! Keep them in there! Use the bar! USE THE BAR!*

The tentacle wavered for a moment, then it reached out, took hold of the iron bar and swung it into place across the door. The bar made a solid sounding *thunk!* as it slammed home, and Measle knew that neither Buford Cudgel nor Frognell Flabbit were going anywhere. Not until somebody came and let them out, at least.

Now all we've got to deal with is Toby, thought Measle. *He's easily the most dangerous one—but there's nothing he can do to me, not inside this thing.*

There was a sudden commotion from somewhere on the other side of the mound of broken furniture as three smashed dining room chairs slid to the floor with a crash. The Slitherghoul instantly turned away from the barred door and sped round the pile, and Measle saw the back of Toby Jugg's head, his mane of greying hair streaming behind him, as he raced for the open front door. Obviously Toby had managed to conceal himself in the heaped-up rubble and had then waited until both hunter and prey were past him. But, in emerging from his hiding place, he'd disturbed the three broken chairs, and they had slid to the floor.

Measle caught a glimpse of Toby's terror-filled face as the burly wrathmonk threw a hasty look over his shoulder and saw the Slitherghoul close behind him. Then Toby was through the front door, his feet pounding over the gravel drive, running as fast as he could towards the distant front gates.

The Measle-Slitherghoul slimed rapidly after him.

SHEEPSHANK TRANSFORMS

Corky Pretzel had dragged Sheepshank into a sitting position, with his back leaning against one of the fence posts. Sheepshank had managed to get his other eye open and he was staring, with utter bewilderment, at his surroundings. Although it was dark, he could clearly see that he was in the countryside. And what strange countryside it was! The fence post he was leaning on held strands of some kind of metal wire, with cunning, sharpened points at regular intervals along their lengths. And the wooden posts that supported these wondrous wires were marvels in themselves, carved square with fabulous precision! And there were other, even more extraordinary, things to see—the young man who was bending over him was adorned with clothes the like of which Sheepshank had never seen! Most peculiar were the shoes—with thick flexible soles, engraved with a wondrous pattern of grooves! A new fashion, no doubt.

There was something encircling the young man's wrist. A band of silvery metal, with a round disc set in the band. There were pointers in the disc, beneath a fine window of glass. It looked a little like the great clock set high in the front wall of the Wizards' Guild building, but it couldn't be a clock, of course, for it was far too small. Cunning pouches were sewn into the man's nether garment, in which one might place various objects—*removing the need for a money purse*, thought Sheepshank. And the young man himself was something of a wonder, too. He looked far fitter and stronger than anybody Sheepshank had ever known. His skin was clear and clean—and that was odd because there wasn't a soul in Sheepshank's circle who didn't have some sort of blemish or boil or spot on their faces. His teeth were straight and white and, what was even more surprising, he seemed to have all of them still in his head! Oddest of all was the look on the young man's face. Nobody had ever looked at Sheepshank with that expression—an expression of friendly and interested concern!

Sheepshank could only stare and wonder.

Corky smiled and said, 'What's your name, matey?'

'Sheepshank, sir,' whispered the little warlock, in a hoarse and shaky voice.

'Sheepshank, eh? Righty-ho. Where did you come from, Mr Sheepshank?'

For the life of him, Sheepshank couldn't remember. It all seemed so very long ago. He tried to search his memories but they were all blank, like plain white sheets of paper with nothing yet written on them. Everything had gone, apart from the clear memory of that moment, searching for his dead spider, then something wet and slimy on his thumb. Then something horrible happened—

But what?

Sheepshank's poor, overwhelmed brain was interrupted in its struggles by a new sound from somewhere off in the distance. This sound was even more terrifying than the awful noise of the passing flight of the small dragon. This sound was a low, steady rumbling roar, which was getting closer and closer.

Corky turned his head and looked away from Sheepshank, down the drive. Sheepshank looked too and saw, to his mounting horror, that there were now *two* dragons approaching them! The small dragon, with the single glowing eye, was in the front, and it was leading a much, much larger dragon. This second monster had *two* glowing eyes and it rumbled and roared as it approached, but it still couldn't drown out the sound of the smaller dragon's beating heart.

Sheepshank reached out and grabbed Corky's sleeve.

'Let them not devour me, master!' he bleated. 'I beg you—if you have a morsel of human kindness—let them not devour me!'

'Nobody's going to devour you, matey,' said Corky, wondering if the little fellow had, perhaps, lost his mind. But he had no time to think about that, there were more pressing questions to be answered. Quite what a bus was doing coming up a private driveway at this time of the morning was anybody's guess, but Corky had a vague thought that it was unlikely to contain any wrathmonks. Buses weren't the kind of vehicles you'd expect to find wrathmonks riding in—but then, who, exactly, had chosen a *bus* to come to visit this place? For a moment, Corky thought they might be a bunch of tourists who had taken a wrong turning, but tourists didn't go sight-seeing at three o'clock in the morning, surely? And another thing—was the bus *chasing* the motorbike, or was the motorbike simply leading it up towards the house?

There was only one way to find out. Once again, Corky Pretzel stepped out into the middle of the drive and held his arms out wide.

It was the bravest thing that Sheepshank had ever seen. The young man didn't have a sword and he wore no armour, yet he was prepared to challenge not just one dragon, but two! He watched as the light from the leading monster swept across

Corky's body, then he shuddered in fear as the twin lights from the eyes of the greater of the two terrible creatures washed over the young man, turning him in an instant as white as snow.

Corky threw one hand up and shielded his eyes from the three blinding headlights. A moment later, both the motorbike and the bus ground to a halt about ten metres from where he stood. A few seconds went by while both vehicles kept their engines running, then there was a hiss as the bus door slid open.

To Sheepshank's ears, the hiss was that of an enraged Great Worm, about to lunge for its prey. Once again, he whimpered with terror, but he couldn't take his eyes off the awful sight.

Lord Octavo hurried past Nanny Flannel and Tinker on the stationary motorbike. Now he too was bathed in the lights of the two vehicles. To Corky, he was just a small black silhouette in a sea of blinding whiteness.

'Officer Pretzel?'

'Yeah—and who are you?' replied Corky, straining to make out who was in front of him.

'It's I, Lord Octavo!'

Corky had never felt such relief until that moment. Apart from the Prime Magus, Lord Octavo was certainly the most important member of the Wizards' Guild and one of the most powerful, too. If Lord Octavo was here, well, everything was going to be all right!

'Oh, very glad you're here, your lordship!' stammered Corky. 'Although I don't rightly know where *here* is, I'm sorry to say—'

'We're at Merlin Manor, Pretzel,' said Lord Octavo, briskly. 'The house of the Prime Magus. Now, Miss Flannel has filled me in with most of what has been going on here—'

'*Who's* filled you in, sir?' said Corky.

'Never mind, Pretzel,' said Lord Octavo. 'Suffice to say, I get the picture—or at least most of it. The big question is—where's the Slitherghoul?'

'I'm afraid I dunno, sir,' said Corky. 'There's been a lot of argy-bargy. It had all the prisoners inside it, would you believe, and me, too—'

Corky broke off because he became aware of a lot of movement coming up behind Lord Octavo. Silhouettes wavered in the beams of the headlights and he called out, 'Who's there?'

'Reinforcements, Pretzel,' said Lord Octavo. He turned and waved in the direction of the bus and, a moment later, the engine was switched off and the headlights died. Nanny Flannel had seen the gesture too, because she leaned forward and turned the motorbike's ignition key. The *thump, thump, thump* of the motor coughed to a halt and the big single headlight dimmed to darkness.

Corky—no longer blinded by the vehicles' headlights—could see that a group of about fifteen assorted wizards and warlocks were clustered in a group behind Lord Octavo.

The old wizard patted Corky on his arm. 'You didn't think I'd come on my own, did you? The moment I discovered that the telephone line to Merlin Manor was out of order, I suspected trouble, so I gathered together a few colleagues and this splendid bus and, well—here we are! I just hope we're not too late. Good gracious—who is that?'

Corky turned round and saw Sheepshank staggering towards him. There was a strange look on the little man's face. It was a mixture of blind terror and fierce determination—and something else, too.

There was madness in Sheepshank's eyes.

There was also an extremely dark and solid-looking rain cloud hovering over Sheepshank's head, and it was releasing a steady, drenching downpour onto his shoulders. The little man was already soaking wet. Sheepshank appeared not to notice this. He simply staggered forward, his eyes now definitely round and fishy, his face even paler than it was before, one bony finger outstretched towards the motorbike and the bus. Sheepshank's hand was shaking wildly and his mouth was working, as if he was trying to say something.

Lord Octavo called out, 'Careful, everybody! That's a wrathmonk! And he has no wrathring round his neck!'

Lord Octavo stepped forward and, in a voice that seemed to crackle with some strange, commanding power, he shouted, 'WRATHMONK!

STOP WHERE YOU ARE! COME NO FURTHER, WRATHMONK!'

Sheepshank stopped walking forward at the sound of Lord Octavo's voice. He stood there, swaying slightly, and getting steadily wetter and wetter. He stared with wonder at the old wizard—and then he bowed low.

'Great magic!' he muttered. 'Great magic indeed! To ssslay not one, but *two* great dragons, with a mere wave of the hand! Thou art truly a massster, my lord!'

'Dragons? What dragons?'

Sheepshank's finger trembled as he pointed over Lord Octavo's shoulder. 'Those Great Worms, my lord! Thou hast sssilenced their roaring voices, their beating hearts! And thou hast dimmed their terrible, glowing eyes! 'Tis a wonder to behold!'

Lord Octavo—and all the wizards and warlocks grouped at his back—turned round and stared at the bus and the motorbike behind them. Then Lord Octavo turned back, a small, puzzled smile on his face.

'Who are you?' asked Lord Octavo, carefully.

'He says his name is Sheepshank, sir,' said Corky,

glaring suspiciously at the little man. Corky was used to dealing with wrathmonks but this was different. For one thing, Sheepshank wasn't wearing a wrathring. For another—well, he didn't like the look of Sheepshank's rain cloud. It was altogether too dark and too heavy and unpleasantly menacing as well. This one was going to take some careful handling. Corky was relieved that Lord Octavo—and a small mob of wizards—were right beside him.

There was a long silence, broken only by the sound of Sheepshank's torrential rain and the steady tick ... tick ... ticking sound of the hot metal of the motorbike engine cooling in the night air.

'Sheepshank?' whispered Lord Octavo, a look of wonder flooding his old face. '*Sheepshank?* It's ... it's not possible!'

Measle had lost Toby Jugg. The man was powerful and athletic and he'd fled though the front door and into the darkness at tremendous speed. For a short distance, the Slitherghoul had followed him, across the gravel driveway, over the grass verge, across the ditch, and then over the barbed wire fence that ringed the field beyond. Toby had taken the fence in one bound, but the Slitherghoul had been forced to flow over the top of it and several of the sharp barbs had caught in its jelly sides, slowing it down enough for Toby to get a good distance ahead. By the time the Slitherghoul had lifted itself away from the fence, Toby was nowhere in sight.

But other attractions *were* in sight and the Slitherghoul's attention was drawn to them. There, in the distance, about three-quarters of the way down the drive, was a group of three bright lights. Dark figures moved through these lights, casting impossibly long shadows across the ground—and the Slitherghoul sensed that these figures were almost certainly human.

Why chase one, when there are many?

Measle's mind tugged at the Slitherghoul's but it was no use. The Slitherghoul started to slide along the edge of the field, towards the distant lights. Halfway there, the lights went out but the dark, shifting figures remained.

The Slitherghoul slimed along a little faster.

Lord Octavo stepped a little closer to Sheepshank, staying just outside the range of the pelting raindrops. Sheepshank smiled uncertainly, exposing his new teeth—two sets of three, on either side of his mouth—and all coming to sharp points, like arrow heads. At the same moment, he seemed to become aware of the fact that he was standing under a cold shower of water and he turned his head and looked up at his hovering rain cloud. He frowned, squinting his eyes against the drops that were falling into them. Then he lowered his gaze and stared back at Lord Octavo, with the beginning of a sly little smile on his face.

'Am I become a Wrathful Monk, my massster?' he asked, his eyes gleaming in the darkness.

'You are indeed, Master Sheepshank,' said Lord Octavo. 'And a powerful one too, as no doubt you have realized. But I suggest you attempt none of your spells at this moment. I am a great Master Wizard—you saw me slay the dragons, did you not?—and here too is a whole host of powerful mages. If you should attempt to harm any one of us, we will all combine against you and, no matter how powerful you are, we shall prevail.'

Sheepshank shook his head, his long stringy hair whipping wetly round his face. 'I shall not, my massster,' he muttered. His voice sounded sincere but, in the shadows, nobody—not even Lord Octavo, who was standing closest to him—saw the gleam of cunning in his fishy eyes.

'For a wrathmonk, you are wise,' said Lord Octavo. He nodded slowly to himself, as if deep in thought. Then said, 'I have a question for you, Master Sheepshank. What year is it?'

'*Year*, my lord?'

'Aye, Master Sheepshank. What year?'

'Why, it is the year twelve hundred and six, my lord.'

There was a collective gasp from the crowd of wizards, and several muttered comments that the fellow must be even madder than the average wrathmonk. Lord Octavo turned to them and said, 'Do you not understand who this is, my friends?'

Nobody spoke. Lord Octavo sighed. 'I do wish somebody would *occasionally* read a book these days,' he muttered. 'So, nobody here knows the story of Sheepshank, the apprentice wizard?'

Again, nobody spoke. This time, the silence had a slightly embarrassed feeling about it.

Lord Octavo sighed again. Then, so quietly that it was almost a whisper, he said, 'Well, gentlemen and ladies, what we have here is a very remarkable person. He has, to all intents and purposes, invented a Time Machine. Master Sheepshank has come to us from the distant past—from the year twelve hundred and six, to be exact about it—and quite what we're going to do with him is anybody's guess.'

A chubby, middle-aged female wizard opened her mouth to speak, but Lord Octavo put a finger to his lips and shook his head firmly. 'Later,' he muttered. 'I will explain later. Now is not the time.'

He felt a tap on his shoulder. Nanny Flannel, with Tinker at her feet, was by his side. She said, 'We have to find Measle, Lord Octavo!'

Lord Octavo nodded. 'Indeed, we do, Miss Flannel.' He turned to his forces and called out, 'I will take care of Master Sheepshank. The rest of you—everybody in pairs! Support each other! Spells only when necessary. And if you come across the Slitherghoul, don't waste them on the creature, because they'll have no effect—'

He was interrupted by a squeaky, excited voice calling out from the shadows of the line of trees that bordered the drive.

'Coo! Is dat you, Lord Octopus? It is I—Missster Ignatius Niggle, sssir!'

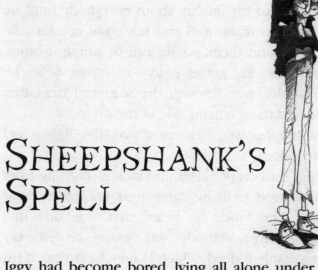

SHEEPSHANK'S SPELL

Iggy had become bored, lying all alone under his rose bush. He'd worked his way through the rest of his jelly beans, which had congealed into a sticky lump at the bottom of his pocket, but which tasted just fine, as far as Iggy was concerned. There were still a few green ones in his top pocket, but as he didn't like them as much as the others he didn't eat them. He'd kept one pointed ear cocked for any sounds, but he'd heard nothing for quite a long time, other than the pattering drops from his tiny rain cloud as they fell onto the leaves of the rose bush.

Deciding to take a risk, Iggy had crawled out from his cover and then worked his way, as silently as he could, through the rose garden. Once he reached the open lawn, he saw the lights near the end of the drive. All wrathmonks are naturally suspicious, and even Iggy (a more trusting one than normal) had his doubts about everybody until he knew them really well and felt quite comfortable being around them. So, instead of simply trotting down the long gravel road and saying hello, he worked his way through the scattered trees that bordered the left-hand side of the drive.

When he was halfway there, the lights had gone out.

Iggy had crept closer and closer, scuttling from tree to tree, until he came near enough to hear voices. The voice he heard first was one that belonged to somebody with whom he felt very comfortable indeed, which is why he dropped his skulking attitude and called out to his old friend.

'Ah, Mr Niggle,' came Lord Octavo's friendly voice. 'We meet again.'

Iggy trotted out of the shadows, grinning from ear to ear. He stopped in front of Lord Octavo and gave him a low bow. 'Jussst in case you was wonderin', Lord Octopus, sssir,' he said, straightening up and beaming into Lord Octavo's wise old eyes, 'jussst in case you was wonderin', I been behavin' myssself, jussst like you told me to! I been *ssstremely* good, Lord Octopus!'

'I have no doubt about it, Mr Niggle,' said Lord Octavo. 'Now, however, we have an very urgent matter to take care of. Do you know where Measle is?'

Before Iggy could reply, Tinker started to bark.

Everybody looked at him. The dog was crouched by Nanny Flannel's feet, glaring furiously at the shadowy figure of Sheepshank who was still standing at the spot where Lord Octavo's voice had rooted him. The hair on Tinker's back stood up in a bristly ridge, his ears were flat to his head, and his tail was tucked firmly between his short legs.

Tinker had caught a whiff of wrathmonk breath. What with having Iggy around all the time, Tinker was used to a wrathmonk's smell and no longer reacted when he sniffed it. But this smell was subtly different.

The scent of *this* breath was old and mouldy, like something dug up from a graveyard. And there was something else, as well, and it was this something else that had made Tinker turn in the direction of its source and begin to bark his defiance.

Evil. Powerful, destructive evil.

I don't know who he is—and I don't want to, neither! thought Tinker, every fibre of his stocky body bunched and ready for action. *He's up to something—something no good! And he's dangerous, too! Anythin' that smells like that has got to be dead dangerous—and dead nasty, too!*

All eyes had swung to Sheepshank. The skinny young man gazed back at everybody from under hooded eyelids. Without warning, he lifted his head, took a deep breath, and blew it out hard.

What happened next was thoroughly unexpected.

Wrathmonks have a single exhalation enchantment and they're all different. Most are hurtful and some are lethal. All are unpleasant.

Sheepshank's breath was none of these.

At first, neither Sheepshank nor any of the other wizards understood what, exactly, was happening. A metre from his pursed lips, Sheepshank's breath stopped as if it had run up against a wall. Then it congealed into a shimmering, silvery fog that spread quickly up, down, left and right, curving back on itself so that in a few seconds it had formed an egg-shaped container that completely enveloped Sheepshank's skinny frame. The fog was transparent, so that Sheepshank was still clearly visible in the middle of the egg. Everybody watched as he reached out a finger and prodded the inner wall of the shimmering shell, and they saw Sheepshank's finger push the transparent skin out into a point, as if it was made of thin rubber. But the fingertip didn't break through, so Sheepshank withdrew his finger and took a couple of steps backwards—and the shell went with him.

Lord Octavo came to a decision. He muttered to himself, 'We really have no time for this, whatever *this* is.' Then, raising his voice, he called, 'Master Sheepshank! Whatever this manifestation means, I fear we shall have to make you fast until such time as you can be examined properly. So, forgive me, but I am taking you prisoner.'

Lord Octavo waved his hands and shouted, *'Circumfretio Infragilistum Bolenda!'* Nanny Flannel, standing nearby, recognized the incantation immediately. It was the same one that Sam Stubbs had used when he'd netted Griswold, Buford, Frognell, and Judge Cedric on the steps of Merlin Manor. Indeed, here came the same net, materializing out of thin air and dropping neatly over and around the silver egg that encased the wrathmonk.

Then something very odd happened.

The moment the net touched the shimmering egg, its strands simply melted away, like ice under a blowtorch. A moment later, it was as if the net had never existed at all. Even its edges which had never even *touched* the egg fizzled away into nothing.

There was an incredulous murmuring from the wizards and Lord Octavo said, 'How very extraordinary.'

Inside his shell, Sheepshank watched with a detached air, as if he'd known exactly what was going to happen. Then he grinned, exposing his pointed sets of teeth.

'Hah!' he yelled, his voice sounding as if it came from a long way away. 'You have no power over me, wizard! For I am Sheepshank, the Wrathful Monk, and my magic is ssstronger by far! No one may touch me now!'

Lord Octavo turned to the cluster of wizards and warlocks and muttered, 'We shall have to put him to sleep. Quickly now, does anybody here have a Stupor Spell?'

An ancient warlock stepped forward. He was almost as old as Lord Octavo, with an abstracted air, a pair of bent wire spectacles on the end of his nose, and a wildly disordered mane of white hair, which didn't cover his ears at all. His Gloomstains were very dark and extended from the tips to the lobes, making his ears look as if they had been dipped in ink. He pointed a finger at Sheepshank and called out, in a quavery old voice, '*Norcoleppo Abstracta Instantium!*'

A sizzling bolt of light streamed out of the old warlock's finger and flashed across the space between himself and Sheepshank. When the bolt of light reached the outer shell of the egg, it ricocheted off it, like a bullet hitting a concrete wall. There was a whistling sound, like a dying firework and then—nothing.

Sheepshank grinned more broadly than ever and his eyes glinted red.

'It would sssseem that I am protected from you all, my masters!' he sneered from inside his shell. 'But be not dissscouraged—perhaps there is another who would try his ssstrength against mine?'

Several wizards and warlocks stepped forward, their hands raised, but Lord Octavo shook his head and said, quietly, 'Don't waste your time, my friends. That is a very powerful force field and I doubt that anything will get through it. All we can hope is that Master Sheepshank won't be able to get anything through it either.'

Iggy sidled close to Lord Octavo and touched his sleeve. 'I could do mine, Lord Octopus,' he said, eagerly. 'You know de one, don't you? It's de only one I got. De opening fings ssspell. P'raps I can open dat old eggy fing, eh?'

Lord Octavo smiled down at Iggy and said, 'An interesting thought, Mr Niggle. One wrathmonk against another. Go ahead.'

Iggy stared hard at Sheepshank and then yelled, '*Unkasssshhhriek gorgogasssshhh plurgholips!*'

A pair of lavender-coloured beams of light streamed from Iggy's eyes, shot across the intervening space and smacked against the rounded wall of the egg. They splashed outwards and then dribbled, in streams of purple water, harmlessly down the sides of the shell.

Lord Octavo patted Iggy kindly on his damp shoulder. 'Never mind, Mr Niggle,' he whispered. 'It was a good idea, though.'

Sheepshank threw back his head and cackled wildly.

'Do you not comprehend?' he shrieked. 'I am invincible! None can harm me! Come—more may try! Cast your magic. I, Sheepshank the Wrathful Monk, am ready!'

Then, out of the shadows of the trees that lined the driveway, slimed the Slitherghoul.

WHEN
SPELLS
COLLIDE

The Slitherghoul headed straight for the shimmering, egg-shaped object, with the small figure of Sheepshank encased inside it.

Measle—without realizing why or how—was making it do it.

The reason the Slitherghoul was speeding towards Sheepshank, and ignoring the cluster of human figures that stood nearby, was because the force field that surrounded Sheepshank shone with an eerie, silver light, which in the surrounding darkness was the most visible thing that stood in the Slitherghoul's path. Since the Slitherghoul was using the only pair of eyes it possessed at the moment—the eyes of Measle Stubbs—it was heading fast in the direction they were staring, and

Measle's eyes were staring with puzzlement at the shimmering egg and wondering what on earth it could be.

Lord Octavo, Nanny Flannel, and Tinker saw the Slitherghoul approaching Sheepshank from behind and, when Tinker turned his attention—and his frenzied barking—away from the wrathmonk and towards the slithering horror, the eyes of all the wizards and warlocks turned in that direction too. Sheepshank, suddenly aware that he was no longer the centre of attention, twisted round to see what was so interesting.

Oddly, it was in fact the first time Sheepshank had ever really seen the Slitherghoul—in its enlarged form, that is. The effect on him was electrifying, particularly since the revolting lump of slimy, dripping jelly seemed to be heading straight for him. In that moment of sudden, panicky fear, Sheepshank lost his head. Oh, he knew how to deal with a bunch of old wizards and warlocks all right, but this was something different. This was something that looked so alien, so horrible, that Sheepshank lost all faith in his shield and decided, on the spur of the moment, to do one of his spells. It flashed through his mind that the old wizard had managed to kill two dragons with one simple wave of his hand—well, here was his opportunity to demonstrate *his* powers on a foul fiend that was approaching fast.

Inside the Slitherghoul, Measle was doing his

best to stop the creature for a few seconds, if only to give the strange man encased in a shimmering, transparent egg a chance to escape. He did manage to slow the Slitherghoul down just a little, adding a few precious moments of freedom to the Slitherghoul's prey.

Why doesn't he move? thought Measle. *Why doesn't he run? Maybe he can't—maybe that egg thing is holding him to one spot!* Measle struggled with the primitive brain of the Slitherghoul, but the creature pushed onwards.

Sheepshank had only a few seconds to pick a spell out of his head. The one he chose was his most devastating and, since he had invented it, only he could perform it! It was his illegal, and massively-destructive, fire-shooting enchantment.

Sheepshank raised his hands and pointed his index fingers directly at the approaching mound of slime. He opened his mouth, took a deep breath, and screamed, '*CALORIBUT!—REGRAMINA!— NUNCIFLAM!—FULMITA!—CARBOREG!— EXPEDICAL!*'

Only Nanny Flannel heard what Lord Octavo then muttered under his breath. She heard it quite distinctly.

'Oh, *no!*'

What happened next was extraordinary and horrible but it happened so quickly that, mercifully, the horror lasted only a few seconds.

A sphere of white-hot flame, about the size of a

tennis ball, appeared at the ends of Sheepshank's extended fingers. It hovered there for half a second and then shot away from the wrathmonk, heading straight as an arrow for the dead centre of the Slitherghoul.

It didn't get very far. It travelled all of a metre before it met the inner surface of Sheepshank's shimmering shield.

When two spells of equal power meet, something bad usually happens. This was no exception. The white-hot sphere smacked against the inner skin—and then simply bounced back off it at the same speed it had left Sheepshank's fingertips. When it met his body—a soft, defenceless little bag of skin and bones—it simply went straight through it and out the other side. A fraction of a second later, the sphere hit the opposite wall of the shield and, once again, bounced away, back towards Sheepshank, making another neat hole through his frail body.

This happened faster than the eye could see. The only thing the horrified spectators could make out was a ball of blindingly white light, flashing so brightly that they had to shield their eyes against the glare. The globe of light seemed to be bouncing, at a staggeringly high velocity, around the inside of the egg.

Next, the shimmering egg collapsed in on itself and the ball of blinding light snapped out, plunging everything into what seemed to the onlookers like inky blackness. Spots of colour danced around in their eyes and they all blinked, trying to get used to the sudden darkness. A panicky voice from the middle of the cluster of wizards called out, 'I can't see a thing! Where's the Slitherghoul?'

Tinker was as temporarily blinded as the rest of them, but he didn't need his eyes—not while he had his nose. The little dog lifted his head and sniffed the night air.

Yup! Definitely—the smelly kid's out there somewhere. Quite close, too. Cor, he's even smellier than ever! Right—let's go and say hello!

Tinker trotted into the shadows, his nose leading the way. Nanny Flannel's eyes adjusted to the darkness in time to catch a glimpse of his stubby white tail heading away into the shadows, directly towards the Slitherghoul—*which she could no longer see*.

'Tinker! No! Come back!'

Then everybody heard it. The sound of somebody out there in the shadows coughing and spluttering and choking.

Tinker found him quickly. The smelly kid was sitting on the grass, surrounded by a wide puddle of slime. He was bent double, his hands clasped tight to his stomach, and he was coughing and spitting in an interesting way—so Tinker trotted up to him and swiped his tongue across Measle's face.

Eeeuooogh! Not a nice taste! Really quite nasty—well, that'll teach me to smell first and lick later . . .

Measle grabbed Tinker and hugged him tightly. Then he got stiffly to his feet.

'Mumps? Is dat you, Mumps?' Iggy shambled out of the darkness and stood peering curiously at Measle.

'Oh, hello, Iggy. Are you all right?'

'*Courssse* I is all right!' sighed Iggy, impatiently. 'I is *talkin'* to you, ain't I? If I *wasn't* all right, den I wouldn't be talking to you, would I? I would be goin' all like, "*AAARGH—OOOGH—EEEGH*", wouldn't I? Or, if I was all like dead, den I wouldn't be going all like *anyfing*, would I? Coz I wouldn't be able to sssay anyfing at all, not if I was all like dead—'

Measle felt a sudden need to sit down again. He swayed, nearly losing his balance. A pair of strong arms took him by the shoulders, steadying him. He looked round and saw the kind, wrinkled old face of Lord Octavo.

'Oh, hello, sir,' he said, faintly.

'Hello, young Measle,' said Lord Octavo. 'We do meet under the oddest circumstances, don't we?'

PICKING UP THE PIECES

Somehow, Nanny Flannel had managed to make tea for everybody in the ruined kitchen. Several of the younger wizards had scoured the rest of Merlin Manor for usable chairs and now the kitchen was crowded with people, all sitting in a wide circle, listening attentively to Lord Octavo, Measle, and Corky Pretzel, who were having a very interesting conversation.

'And where, at this precise moment, are those two wrathmonks you hunted down, Measle?' said Lord Octavo, his eyes twinkling.

'Locked in the cellar, sir. It's Buford Cudgel and Frognell Flabbit.'

'A nasty pair. Splendid. And the other two, Officer Pretzel?'

'In the wood, sir,' said Corky. 'Tied to trees.'

'That's Griswold Gristle and Judge Cedric, sir,' said Measle. It was quite difficult to talk, because Nanny Flannel had a wet face-cloth in one hand and a bar of soap in the other, and she was trying to clean the dried, encrusted Slitherghoul slime off Measle's head.

'Splendider and splendider!' said Lord Octavo. 'And Toby Jugg?'

'I'm afraid he got away, sir,' mumbled Measle, through a faceful of flannel.

'Ah well, never mind. You can't win them all, can you? I daresay we shall catch up with him soon enough. Yes—what is it?'

A young wizard had climbed through the shattered window, approached Lord Octavo, and was whispering in his ear. Lord Octavo's eyebrows rose and an appalled expression flitted across his old face.

'Under *what*?' he asked.

'Under the garage doors, sir,' whispered the young wizard. 'Huge iron things, they are. They're squashed flat, I'm afraid. And I think it's the whole lot of them.'

'Oh dear, what a frightful thing,' said Lord Octavo, not sounding sorry at all. 'And what about Needle and Bland, Measle? What happened to them, eh?'

'They ran away, sir.'

Lord Octavo's face darkened with anger and a

deep frown-line creased his wrinkled forehead. 'Did they now?' he growled. '*Disgraceful* behaviour by two officers of the Wizards' Guild. Well, rest assured, Measle, they will be dealt with.'

Nanny Flannel decided that there was nothing more she could do about getting Measle clean, short of running him a hot bath—which was going to be difficult, since Merlin Manor no longer had a staircase. Clucking disapprovingly to herself like a peevish chicken, she went back to inspecting the ruins of her kitchen.

Free from the face-cloth, Measle said, 'There's one thing I don't understand, Lord Octavo—'

'Only *one* thing, Measle?' said Lord Octavo, smiling.

'I think so, sir. It's . . . what happened to the Slitherghoul? It just sort of melted away, didn't it? I thought it was indestructible?'

Lord Octavo nodded, gravely. 'Well, for eight hundred years it *was* indestructible, Measle.' He looked around at the assembled wizards and then raised his voice a little, so that everybody could hear. 'The Slitherghoul was created by Sheepshank. Whether it was an accident, or whether he did it on purpose, we shall never know, because sadly Sheepshank is no longer with us. As we all saw, that ball-of-fire spell of his—a most lethal and illegal-looking incantation, I must say!—converted him into a heap of ash in a matter of seconds. I don't think the poor fellow felt a thing, it happened so fast. Anyway, as we all know, once a wizard dies, his spells die with him—which was why that force field of Sheepshank's disappeared at the very moment of his death. And that's why the Slitherghoul was destroyed at long last, too. With the death of its creator, it died as well. And, ladies and gentlemen, what is so fascinating about the whole story is this: in the eight hundred years of the creature's miserable life, the only way the Slitherghoul could ever have been destroyed was if Sheepshank himself had died. But Sheepshank was *inside his own indestructible creation*, protected by it and held in suspended animation within its magical body. As long as Sheepshank was there, the Slitherghoul could live for ever.'

Lord Octavo paused, his old eyes scanning the rapt faces of his audience. Then he turned and looked at Measle and smiled.

'Eight hundred years of trying to eradicate the horrible thing and young Measle here—who, by the way, ladies and gentlemen, doesn't have a morsel of magic about him—does it with some sugar lumps and a puddle of sweetened water.'

Measle felt his face go pink. Everybody was looking at him with admiration and Corky Pretzel was gaping at him with his mouth hanging open. Measle decided to off-load some of this awe onto somebody else.

'Well, it was Iggy, really,' he gulped. 'If he hadn't eaten all those jelly beans—'

Iggy jumped out of the chair he'd been sitting in

and bounced crazily round the kitchen, hopping about like a mad kangaroo.

'Hee hee! I did it! It was me! Hee hee! All by myssself I did it! Hee hee! I made dat old Sssquiffypoo be deaded! I am de big hero, Lord Octopus! Me! All by myssself—no help from *anybody*—me, me, *ME*—'

'That's quite enough of that, Iggy!' Nanny Flannel's mop whacked down on the top of Iggy's head and Iggy stopped dancing and yelling immediately and went and sat down again, rubbing his head, a nervous look in his fishy eyes.

'Thank you, Mr Niggle,' murmured Lord Octavo, only just managing to suppress a little bubble of laughter that threatened to erupt from his chest. 'Your . . . um . . . your *contribution* has been noted and is appreciated by all of us.'

All Iggy understood out of that were the words 'thank you'—but that was enough. To be thanked by the great Lord Octopus was more than any small, damp, and pathetic wrathmonk could possibly wish for.

Nanny Flannel put down her mop and picked up a dustpan and brush. Shaking her head at the immensity of the task before her, she started to sweep up some of the debris on the floor. Measle thought, *It's going to take a million years to get this place cleaned up!*

Lord Octavo must have seen the despairing look in Measle's eyes, because he rose stiffly from his chair and using his commanding voice, called out, 'Ladies and gentlemen, we have work to do! This place is a mess! The Prime Magus and his wife—and the Mallockee, too, let's not forget her—will be returning in the next couple of days. We really cannot allow them to see their house in this appalling state. So, to work, everybody. I take it you all have reconstructive spells? Yes? Excellent! Perhaps, Miss Flannel, you could supervise the repairs? We must make sure everything is put back exactly the way it was before. Good—well, let's make a start!'

Everybody got up and Nanny Flannel, after a moment of deliberation, announced, 'The great staircase first, I think. Without that, we can't even get upstairs so let's start there.'

She began to lead the way out of the kitchen, but was stopped almost at once by the mound of rubble that blocked the door out to the passage. A beefy looking wizard with a cheerful red face stepped forward and muttered something under his breath. A couple of hand gestures, and, immediately, the pile of rubble started to reform itself, timbers rising off the floor, brick piling onto brick, plaster smoothing itself across the surface, until the doorway was back the way it was. Nanny Flannel cocked a critical eye at the result and said, 'Very nice, dear. The moulding round the door isn't quite right, but at least we can get through now. All right, everybody—follow me!'

Measle started after the small mob of wizards as they streamed out of the kitchen in Nanny Flannel's wake, but Lord Octavo said, 'No, Measle—I want you to come with me. You too, Mr Niggle. There's something we have to do together—since it was the two of you who started it.'

Lord Octavo winked. Then, beaming broadly, he climbed out through the kitchen window and, with Measle and Iggy at his heels, set off across the lawn.

Toby Jugg crouched in the darkness of the wood, watching with cold, angry eyes the flurry of activity around the great house.

His big, muscular hands held tightly to the necks of Mr Needle and Mr Bland. Neither man made any attempt to resist. They simply stood there, shivering slightly, and waiting to see what awful thing would happen to them next.

What had *already* happened was this: they had been hiding deep in the shadows of the woods, quaking with terror and hoping that nobody would find them ever again. Unfortunately for Needle and Bland, Toby Jugg—who had been steadily making his way round the house, keeping a good distance away from the building while he scouted out the situation—had stumbled across them. Immediately he'd seized them both, turning them upside down and shaking them hard—a bit like you shake a beach towel to get the sand off. Several objects had fallen from the pockets of Mr Needle and Mr Bland but Toby was interested in only one of them. A small brass key. He'd snatched that up, inserted the business end into the latch of his wrathring, and with a single twist, had freed himself from the metal band round his neck. He hurled the wrathring away into the bushes and then grabbed the necks of the unfortunate Needle and Bland. Holding them both painfully tightly, he snarled, 'One peep out of either of you, and you're a pair of dead wizards! I've got a collection of very nasssty ssspells up my sssleeve and my exhalation enchantment is sssomething to sssee—it'll send chills up and down your ssspines, I promise! Ssso, are you going to be good little wizards and do exactly as I tell you or are you going to be ssstupid little wizards who end up *dead* little wizards?'

Mr Needle and Mr Bland—who could recognize a super-powerful wrathmonk when they met one—both expressed fervent promises that they were going to be good and obedient little wizards for as long as Mr Jugg *wanted* them to be good and obedient little wizards.

'Excellent!' hissed Toby, forcing their heads round so that he could stare into their frightened faces. He glared evilly at them with his yellow eyes.

'Yesss,' he hissed, sounding like an angry snake. 'Yesss, I think there's a possibility I could find a use for the pair of you. Ssso, for the foressseable future, you are going to do *exactly* what I tell you to do—and nothing else. Is that underssstood?'

Mr Needle and Mr Bland couldn't move their heads to nod, so they both whispered, in squeaky, frightened voices, 'Y-y-yes, sir.'

With that, Toby Jugg cast one last angry look back at Merlin Manor and, tucking Mr Needle under one massive arm and Mr Bland under the other, marched away into the night.

Measle and Tinker were splashing about in the swimming pool—and Iggy was sitting on a rock watching them—when Sam and Lee and Matilda came home, which was why they weren't on the steps to greet them when they all piled out of the Prime Magus's official car. The first moment Measle knew his parents and sister were home was when a shadow fell across his eyes and, looking up, he saw the tall silhouette of his father, standing by the edge of the pool.

'Oh—hi, Dad!' said Measle, shielding his eyes against the sun. 'Did you have a nice time?'

'Not really,' said Sam. 'It was dead boring, actually.'

'Oh dear. Well, it wasn't boring here.'

'Yes, so I gather. We got a call from the Guild. Lord Octavo told me all about it. It . . . er . . . it sounds like quite an adventure.'

'It . . . er . . . it was,' Measle grinned. Then he said, 'How do you like our swimming pool?'

'Mm. Not bad.'

Measle stopped grinning. He squinted up at Sam, trying to see if his father was joking or not but the bright sunlight behind Sam's head made that impossible, so Measle decided to take him seriously. 'Not bad? *Not bad?*' he squealed, in outrage. '*Look* at it, Dad! It's completely *brilliant*! It's got rocks all around it, so it looks like a real pool in the mountains somewhere! And look at the island in the middle. That's a real palm tree on it! And look at the deep end—look at the waterfall. If you swim through the waterfall, there's a real cave behind it! And if you climb up on those rocks, there's a slide that shoots you out over the waterfall! Not bad? It's *brilliant*, Dad!'

'Mm,' said Sam, trying to hide his smile behind the hand that covered his mouth. 'And you and Iggy did it all, I suppose?'

Iggy jumped up off the rock he'd been sitting on and bounced around, yelling, 'It was me, Missster Ssstubbs, sssir! I did it! All by myssself! I digged it an' I filled it full of water an' I made de mountain fingy—'

'It was Lord Octavo, really, Dad,' said Measle. 'He finished it for us.'

'But the slide and the cave and the waterfall—I imagine those were your ideas, Measle?'

'Er . . . well . . . mine and Iggy's, Dad.'

A second silhouette came and stood close by Sam Stubbs and Measle yelled, 'Hi, Mum! Welcome home! How do you like our pool?'

'It's *fabulous*, darling,' said Lee. 'I love it! And so

does Tilly, don't you, sweetheart?' She lifted Matilda off her hip and held her up for Measle to wave at.

'Hi, Tilly!' shouted Measle.

'Dwiggy booda-gumbum,' replied Matilda, brandishing a chubby fist.

'I see she's not talking yet,' said Measle, treading water.

'Well, we've only been away five days,' said Lee. 'Give her a chance.'

Quite suddenly, the pool around Measle started to get rather hot. In a couple of seconds, it reached the temperature of bath water! Not only that, the colour turned from no-colour-at-all to a pale shade of greenish-yellowish-brown! And not only that—suddenly, there were lots of strange little slimy bits that looked like short white worms floating up on the surface! Not only that—now there was a strong and rather familiar smell.

Measle sighed and said, 'Tilly, that is very nasty, what you just did. And please, don't ever do it again—at least, not while I'm trying to have a swim, all right?'

'Oh dear,' said Lee. Measle could quite clearly hear the catch of laughter in her voice. 'What's Tilly done now?'

'It's not funny, Mum,' muttered Measle, trying to push away some of the white slimy things that were floating nearby.

'No, of *course* it isn't,' gurgled Lee, failing utterly to stifle her laughter. 'But what, exactly—?'

'She's gone and changed the water,' said Measle, deciding to get out of the pool before things got any worse. He swam quickly to the shallow end and then stepped up onto dry land.

'But changed it into what?' said Lee.

'I'm not sure,' muttered Measle, scraping slimy white bits off his chest. 'But I *think* it's chicken noodle soup.'

Why not try another Measle adventure?

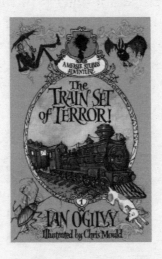

Measle Stubbs is not a boy known for
his good luck. He's thin and weedy
and hasn't had a bath for years—and he
has to live with his horrible old
guardian, Basil Tramplebone.

Just when Measle thinks things can't get any
worse, he's zapped into the world of Basil's toy
train set. There's something lurking in the rafters
and a giant cockroach is on his trail—it's times
like these you need a few friends . . . and a plan!

'Stink is what Ogilvy does best.
This is a book that smells superbly foul.'
Michael Rosen, *Guardian*

'A terrific tale in every sense.'
Amanda Craig, *The Times*

How about another Measle treat?

Poor Measle Stubbs . . . just when things
are looking up for a change, the mysterious
Dragodon and his gang of wicked wrathmonks
cast a spell on Measle's dad and snatch his mum.
So now it's up to Measle and his little dog,
Tinker, to rescue her from the spooky theme
park—The Isle of Smiles.

Being hunted down by horrors in a dark, wet
funfair is anything but fun! But Measle's on
a mission with more ups and downs than any
rollercoaster, and he's determined to save the day.

'badder baddies, more dastardly plots,
wicked spells—and our hero
has his first bath in years!'
Sunday Express

More Measle fun...

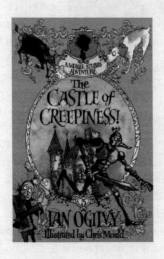

Some double-crossing wizards have locked up
Measle's mum and dad. So now it's just Measle,
his baby sister, and his little dog Tinker—and
they're up against . . . well, just about *everybody*.
And when everybody's after you, you need
somewhere to hide.

Caltrop Castle may look safe enough with its
huge bolted doors to keep the lurking horrors
out. But what if the lurking horrors are already
inside? Poor Measle, even the castle itself is out to
get him . . .

'The writing is perfectly pitched'
Daily Express

Ian Ogilvy is best known as an actor—in particular for his takeover of the role of The Saint from Roger Moore. He has appeared in countless television productions, both here and in the United States, has made a number of films, and starred often on the West End stage. His first children's books were the Measle Stubbs Adventures—and he has written a couple of novels for grown-ups too: *Loose Chippings* and *The Polkerton Giant*, both published by Headline. His play, *A Slight Hangover*, is published by Samuel French. He lives in Southern California with his wife Kitty and two stepsons.

Measle Stubbs is best known as a bit of a hero—in particular for his triumphant role as the charge of the evil wrathmonk, Basil Tramplebone. Now Measle has defeated the slimy Slitherghoul he can relax at home with his family—for a while, at least.